Rogue's Holiday

Praise for Regan Walker's Work

"Ms. Walker has the rare ability to make you forget you are reading a book. The characters become real, the modern world fades away, and all that is left is the intrigue, drama, and romance."

—Straight from the Library

"Walker's detailed historical research enhances the time and place of the story without losing sight of what is essential to a romance: chemistry between the leads and hope for the future."

—Publisher's Weekly

"…an enthralling story."

—RT Book Reviews

"The writing is excellent, the research impeccable, and the love story is epic. You can't ask for more than that."

—The Book Review

"Regan Walker is a master of her craft. Her novels instantly draw you in, keep you reading and leave you with a smile on your face."

—Good Friends, Good Books

"…an example of 'how to' in good story building…a multilayered novel adding depth and yearning."

—InD'Tale Magazine

"Spellbinding and Expertly Crafted"… "The path to true love is never easy, yet Regan Walker leads the reader to an entertaining, realistic and worthy HEA. Walker's characters are complex and well-rounded and, in her hands, real historical figures merge seamlessly with those from her imagination."

—A Reader's Review

"Walker stuns with her gift for storytelling, magically entwining historic fact and fiction to create a thought-provoking, sensual romance, one that will stay with you."

—Chicks, Rogues & Scandals

Acknowledgements

A story always benefits from the contribution of those who have great suggestions and take the time to provide them, so I have several to thank.

Special thanks must go to Maudie na Nakhorn in the UK for her wonderful contributions to my research for the scenes set in Brighton where she lives.

Before I began to write *Rogue's Holiday*, I knew the heroine would have a cat that guarded her well. I asked my readers for suggestions for the cat's name. I received many wonderful ideas. The name "Crispin", the patron saint of shoemakers, was my own thought, but "Demon" was the suggestion of Leigh Hilson, which got me to thinking about how Robbie might perceive the cat who initially likes him not at all. And since he thinks of Crispin as a demon cat, I am grateful to Leigh for her idea. She will get an autographed copy of the book.

As always, I am deeply indebted to my beta readers for their contributions, especially Liette Bougie and Dr. Chari Wessel, whose comments and suggestions are invaluable. Kalinya Parker-Pryce, from the Beau Monde group of Regency writers, also provided invaluable suggestions. My critique group sees the book in monthly submissions and helps me along the way. Along with my editor, Scott Moreland, these folks make my stories better.

The Agents of the Crown series

To Tame the Wind (prequel)
Racing with the Wind
Against the Wind
Wind Raven
A Secret Scottish Christmas
Rogue's Holiday

At the end of this book you can see the complete list of my stories, including the award-winning Donet Trilogy, featuring Jean Donet, comte de Saintonge. In *A Fierce Wind*, book 3 in the trilogy, you meet his young son, Jack, who is all grown up in *Rogue's Holiday*. Robbie, too, you've met before as he was a character in *A Secret Scottish Christmas*.

Characters of Note

Sir Robert Powell

Miss Chastity Reynolds

George IV, King of the United Kingdom of Great Britain and Ireland and King of Hanover

Muriel, Dowager Countess of Claremont

Jean-Jacques Henri Donet, vicomte de Saintonge ("Jack"), Robbie's uncle

Rose Crockett, Chastity's good friend

Crispin, Chastity's cat

Aaron Ings, brother to James Ings, one of the Cato Street conspirators

Agatha, Lady Sanborn, Chastity's great-aunt

Featherstone, Aunt Agatha's butler

Tiller, Robbie's valet

Maria Fitzherbert, Aunt Agatha's neighbor and the Catholic wife of George IV

Sir John Lade and his wife Letty

Sir Bellingham Graham and his wife Harriet

William Arden, 2nd Baron Alvanley, Lord Alvanley

Elizabeth Conyngham, Marchioness Conyngham, George IV's mistress

Mr. Henry Cairo, artisan in time

Love will find a way through paths where wolves fear to prey.
—Lord Byron

Chapter 1

London, 23 February 1820

Robert Powell left the warmth of the Horse and Groom and stepped into the dusty cul-de-sac at the edge of London's sprawl. Darkness hung thick in the cold night air, the nearly full moon its only redemption. Street lamps had yet to arrive on Cato Street. It was as if the world acknowledged nothing of importance ever happened here that would justify such an expense.

A blast of wintry night air caused him to shiver. Slipping his hands into the pockets of his greatcoat, he gripped his pistols, still warm from the tavern. Tonight, they might save his life.

Close by, the silhouettes of two men leaned against a building. Further on, another man raised his head from where he lingered in a recessed doorway. While Robbie could not discern their features, he knew who they were…Bow Street Runners, waiting for the trap to be sprung.

The trap Robbie had planned.

A month back, one chill evening, he had stopped into the White Lion for a pint. There, he witnessed a man named Arthur Thistlewood holding court. To his avid listeners gathered around him, Thistlewood

1

loudly condemned the government for the massacre in Manchester the year before, the debacle the newspapers had dubbed "Peterloo".

Growls of assent from the patrons of the White Lion made Robbie hunch over his drink and attend more closely.

He and his twin brother had been on St Peter's Field that day. The Home Secretary, Lord Sidmouth, had dispatched them to Manchester to spy on the crowd gathered to hear the famous orator Henry Hunt speak about reform. The Terror in France might have ended years ago, but the government still had an unholy fear of riot and mobs, particularly those advocating change.

Robbie could still see Hunt climbing onto the platform as the Manchester Yeomanry charged into the throng, sabers raised, cutting down hundreds of innocent men, women and children.

"We shall have our revenge!" Thistlewood shouted, pounding his fist and splashing his ale. "This time it will be government blood that is spilled and government lives snuffed out!"

The raw anger in the White Lion that night and the call to violence had alarmed Robbie. The next day, he reported to Lord Sidmouth what he had overheard.

"If this is more than idle talk, Powell, these villains must be stopped. 'Tis treason!"

"I have a plan…" Robbie began and laid out the trap he'd conceived.

In the following weeks, Robbie followed Thistlewood and his band of conspirators to the empty stable on Cato Street where they began to stash muskets, bayonets, pistols, knives and swords, along with grenades, plentiful since the end of the war with Napoleon.

With great fanfare, *The Times* announced that the Cabinet dinners, canceled following the death of George III, were to be resumed. The conspirators were pleased. A dinner with all the Cabinet ministers gathered at Lord Harrowby's provided the perfect opportunity for the revenge they sought.

What they didn't know was that the story in *The Times* was a fake, planted by Robbie, an irresistible bait to lure the conspirators to their demise.

Standing watch on Cato Street, Robbie ran his fingers over his false mustache and beard. The damned things had itched him for weeks, but they were necessary to conceal his true identity. Even the slouch hat and the clothes that loosely embraced his body were not the gentleman's attire he typically wore. He had resorted to the disguise after one of the men at the White Lion had engaged him in conversation that first night.

Robbie studied the simple working folks coming and going in their lives of quiet routine. George Caylock at number two, home from his daily work, stood at his window, observing the happenings at the stable across the street. Elizabeth Weston at number one had gone for a short walk with her little boy but now returned to stare at the men entering the stable. Richard Munday at number three left his rooms to indulge in a nightly pint at the Horse and Groom, tipping his hat to Robbie as he returned.

None of them gave him a second glance. He had become a fixture in the tavern and on the street, a "distant relation" of the tavern owner who, for a sovereign, had been happy to cooperate.

Halfway down the street, the door to the stable creaked open. A man with a candle exited to take up vigil. Shielding the flame with one hand, he granted entrance to other conspirators who arrived to slip inside.

So, they gather.

In the candle's flickering light, Robbie recognized Arthur Thistlewood as one of those arriving. He was more the gentleman in appearance than the others, but his purpose just as low.

William Davidson, the educated man of color from Jamaica, stepped outside to stand guard beside the man holding the candle. Davidson carried a carbine but it was not his only weapon. At his belt was a pair of pistols and, at his side, a sword. Even in the dim light the shapes of the weapons were familiar.

The residents of Cato Street continued to come and go as the night grew colder. Silently, Robbie willed them to get off the street. He wanted no innocents in the path of the violence to come.

As the minutes ticked away, the activity on the street died down.

Robbie darted a glance in the direction of Edgware Road. *Where the devil are the Coldstream Guards?* The Portman Street barracks were nearby, so why were they late? He could wait no longer, else he risked the conspirators leaving on their grisly mission.

Robbie lifted his hat, the signal to spring the trap.

A lurking Bow Street officer crept away in the dark.

A few minutes later, Constable George Ruthven strode into the street, the Bow Street patrol behind him in their long topcoats. The constable boldly walked to the stable door and shouted, "Take them!"

A brief scuffle followed. The officers seized Davidson and his companion, grabbing their weapons before they could alert those inside.

Ruthven yanked opened the door and stormed into the stable, the night patrol following on his heels. "We are officers!" he yelled. "Seize their arms!"

Robbie shook his head, regretting their haste. His dismay soon proved well founded. A single shot cracked the night air. Then repeated gunfire rattled the stable.

The light he had glimpsed through the open door went out and the building reverberated with men's shouts.

Some of the conspirators fled out the stable door. The Bow Street Runners who had remained outside seized as many as they could. One tore free and ran toward Robbie, a pistol in one hand, a knife in the other. He fired the pistol at Robbie, but the shot went wide.

Robbie rushed to grab him, knocking the knife away. The man cursed the government as Robbie seized his coat and, lifting his pistol from his pocket, pointed the barrel at the conspirator's head. "The only government official you'll be seeing tonight is the magistrate."

He kept the pistol pressed to the man's temple as he forced him down the street and handed him over to the runners.

Shots and shouts continued to echo in the street. Robbie caught a few more escaping from the stable and delivered them to the runners.

At the zenith of the skirmish, the Coldstream Guards finally arrived, their brass buttons and musket locks reflecting the moon's pale light.

Robbie crossed the street to Captain Fitzclarence. "Where have you been?"

Fitzclarence's voice bespoke his exasperation. "They sent us to the wrong end of John Street. We thought 'twas to fight a fire. We're only here now because of the gunfire."

"'Tis a murderous plot against the government!" shouted Robbie, aghast at the poor communication. "Constable Ruthven and some of the Bow Street officers are inside. Make haste but take care! The place is full of weapons."

"Surround the building!" Captain Fitzclarence ordered his men, who hurried to comply as the captain and his grenadiers rushed into the stable.

Any resistance by those left inside would now be futile. Robbie only hoped the Coldstreamers and Bow Street officers did not shoot each other.

Just then, Ruthven yelled, "Call for a doctor. Everything is under control, but we have a man shot!"

The doctor was summoned.

Satisfied the plan had worked, Robbie consulted with the runners and decided his job was completed. The trap had been sprung and a passel of sorry men, whose only purpose for living had withered to a drastic act of revenge, would pay with their lives. Save for their evil intent, he could almost pity them. Reform was needed and he was confident it would come, but not through violence and murder. There would be no revolution in England as there had been in France.

As he turned to leave, he glimpsed movement nearby. One last conspirator, who must have been hiding, was attempting to slip away. Robbie lifted his pistol and cracked the man on the head as he ran by. The man faltered but did not fall. Robbie grabbed him by the collar. "What's your name?"

"James" was the only reply and that more of a groan.

"You will hang for what you have done," said Robbie, and shuffled him off to the runners clustered at the far end of the street.

The noise of the fracas faded behind him as he turned and walked to Oxford Street to hail a hackney that would take him to the Thames. His father had chosen the Adelphi Terrace south of Somerset House for their residence, expecting to sire a family of shipmasters, which he had.

As the horse's hooves clattered over the street, Robbie's gaze drifted out the window to the passing buildings cast in shadow by the street lamps.

A wave of relief washed over him as he relaxed against the seat. He was done with subterfuge. The job before this had seen him shot on a snowy Scottish street, leaving him with a ragged scar from his left eye to the edge of his hair. He'd let his hair grow over the scar but the memory of his near-death had not dimmed.

And what of tonight? What if the man he'd collared had wielded that pistol and knife with skill? Instead of riding through London, he might be bleeding his life away in a dusty backwater. He breathed out a sigh. Tonight, he vowed, was his last work for the Crown.

Leaning his head back, images of the life he'd abandoned months before flitted though his mind. He had missed his gentleman's pursuits. An excellent cognac and a game of brag at White's. A round of fencing at Angelo's with his uncle. An afternoon of boxing at Jackson's. And women. Ah yes…

After he filed his report on Cato Street, he might just indulge himself in a holiday. And, for that, he would visit Tattersall's to purchase a new horse or maybe a matched pair for a new curricle.

But why wait? Tonight was not too soon to resume his pleasurable pursuits. There might yet be time to enjoy the company of a woman who smelled of spring flowers instead of the backstreets of London.

The carriage pulled up in front of his home and he told the driver, "Wait while I change. We've another stop to make."

Willow House.

He raced up the stairs, smiling all the way. Willow House was an exclusive bordello, the only one in London for which a man needed a recommendation from one of the gentlemen who were numbered among its clientele. Before his brother, Martin, had married, he had vouched for Robbie.

The night was still young.

Chapter 2

Dudley Hall, Northampton, March 1820

"Send Chastity to *Brighton?*"

At the sound of her older sister's voice spouting her name in shrill disbelief, Chastity Reynolds halted in the corridor. *I'm being sent to Brighton?* Surprise and delight raced through her mind.

"The very thought conjures images of disaster," said her eldest sister. Horror shuddered through her sister's voice, bruising Chastity's ego.

The parlor door stood ajar…she crept closer. Her mother paced in front of the crackling fire, while her sister, Penelope, sat perched on the edge of the blue velvet settee, teacup in hand. Her younger sister, Lucy, was nowhere to be seen. "Is there no better option than to send her there? That is where Prinny and his Carlton Set indulge in their wild parties and outrageous entertainments."

In the autumn, Pen would marry a staid, respectable country squire. To Chastity's mind, she was already acting the part. No one believed Prinny, as the king was known to his intimates, was a paragon of virtue but he had always been a great deal of fun.

Chastity's mother stopped pacing and looked askance at Pen. "The prince is now the king, Penelope, and must be respected as such."

"Yes, of course."

"Still, you are right as to the past goings-on at the Royal Pavilion," conceded their mother in a milder tone. "But that doesn't diminish my desire to see Chastity spend the Brighton Season with Aunt Agatha. Your great-aunt might be ancient, but she is a lady of unquestioned character, respected by all." Pausing by the settee, she rested her hand on Pen's shoulder. "Aunt Agatha could do much to shape a young woman like Chastity into a proper lady and see her wed to a gentleman of good fortune. And, while she is away, your youngest sister will be free of Chastity's influence."

"Yes, there is that. But do you truly think this course is wise? Many of the fashionable set flock to Brighton and Chastity is…well, not at all prudent."

Their mother's laugh was vibrant with amusement. "While that is true, I suspect Aunt Agatha can handle her and will derive immense enjoyment from your sister's company."

Chastity's spirits soared. Of course, Aunt Agatha would enjoy her company! How could she not? Her husband, the earl, had been dead more than a year. She had no children and she and Chastity had always been of a similar mind.

From the parlor there came an audible snort. "Aunt Agatha might well consider my sister too great an assignment. Chastity is a hoyden, Mother, and, to my mind, Father indulges her overmuch. He allows her to ride that mare of hers at breakneck speed all over the countryside, leaving her groom behind, I might add."

Chastity smiled remembering her last ride.

"I think it's her name that's the problem," Pen muttered.

"You may have the right of it. 'Chastity' would not have been my choice," said their mother. "But we cannot forget the estate and funds she will soon inherit if she continues to bear that given name."

"'The second daughter in the seventh generation,'" Pen recited.

"Yes, I remember. Still, our Puritan ancestors could not have anticipated—"

Chastity waltzed into the parlor. "The second daughter in the seventh generation. How could I ever forget?"

Pen looked up, startled. "'Tis a great pity our Puritan ancestors could not foresee what a burden the name would be for someone like you," she said, her voice sharp.

"Someone like *me*?"

Their mother subsided into a chair. "Enough, both of you."

Pen gave their mother a knowing look. "Recall that Chastity's first season, which she owed to Aunt Agatha's connections, was an unmitigated disaster."

"Do you really think so?" Chastity asked. "I rather enjoyed it." In truth, Chastity had not much enjoyed it, feeling as she did that she was a lesser debutante compared to the others. And the idle prattling at the many events bored her to death.

"You reject suitors like you're casting off old clothes," said Pen. "The only man you're genuinely fond of is your dancing master."

"Hmmm…" Chastity adopted what she hoped was a dreamy expression. "Had I known Mother would engage such a delightful Frenchman if I stepped on Lord Percival's toes, I would have trodden on them *much* sooner."

Her pleasure in provoking Pen faltered when she saw her mother's pained expression. "That Frenchman is precisely the reason I want you out of Northampton, at least for a time."

"Oh, Mother," Chastity implored, "must I go to Aunt Agatha's? She means well, but she's an elderly widow and she's never had children so she's not at all used to entertaining young people. Please don't send me to Brighton." It wouldn't do for her to appear eager to go. She leaned forward. "Would you not welcome the prospect of seeing me wed here?"

"Not to someone whose only attributes are his good looks, charm and prowess on the dance floor."

"Worry not, Mother," Pen said, her voice tart. *"That* eventuality would only be possible if M'sieur Béranger intended marriage, which I think we all know he does not."

Chastity took hold of the back of a chair and lifted her gaze to the ceiling. "How little you understand me." She had deliberately stepped on Lord Percival's toes to punish him for his wandering hands during a waltz. And M'sieur Béranger was merely a diversion. She had no intention of marrying him or any man in Northampton for that matter. Most of the gentlemen she met were her mother's choices, dreary bores every one. The few who were not were rogues she steered clear of. Marrying one of them one would be the very worst of fates.

Her one venture into love with a man of less than noble character ended badly. Though she had been only seventeen, she had given Roger Westley her heart but then discovered him attempting to kiss her younger sister, Lucy, who was only fifteen. She did not blame Lucy. She blamed the rogue who delighted in conquest, no matter it was Chastity's sister he dallied with. Since that day, she had vowed to stay away from such men.

Besides, there were too many places she wanted to see to marry at twenty. And, since she would gain her inheritance when she turned one and twenty, there was really no need to marry at all. The thought of being her own mistress delighted her. Her own home with no one to say her nay. Of course, now that Pen was to marry, the family would expect Chastity to follow suit—providing her groom was not a certain Frenchman.

Chastity had no such intention. She was more interested in escaping her family's country estate to travel to the seaside resort of Brighton. Her father would not argue with her mother, who reigned over Dudley Hall with a firm hand. He was content to putter in his study reading and designing men's shoes and boots.

His ancestors had secured their fortune supplying cattle skins and bark from the family's oak forests to the local shoemaking industry that had thrived since Cromwell shod his army in Northampton.

Her father, bored with the life of a country gentleman, often found enjoyment in creating the new designs he freely gave to the local cordwainers. That a wealthy country squire occupied himself with such pursuits might appear eccentric to some, but not to Chastity. She adored her father. He was the reason she had developed a fondness for designing ladies' shoes, yet another activity of which her mother and sister disapproved.

Her father loved his wife despite her dominating nature. She was a woman of great beauty, as were Chastity's two sisters. Men who came calling on them scarcely noticed her. A pale blue-eyed blonde in a family of raven-haired beauties, Chastity considered herself the cuckoo in the nest. Even her best friend, Rose, had that same cream-colored skin, ebony hair and dark eyes that captured men's attention.

Added to her pale coloring was Chastity's outspoken nature. In a society where most women did not know enough to form opinions, and those who did rarely stated them in polite company, this was a trait many men frowned upon. She did not consider herself a bluestocking by any means though Rose had told her the word had been whispered about. Chastity's interests were merely uncommon. Embroidery and music were not among her pursuits. When she wasn't designing ladies' footwear, she preferred to read or ride.

As her mother steered the conversation to plans for Pen's wedding, Chastity excused herself. Concealing her excitement at the thought of spending the summer with dear Aunt Agatha in that wonderful place, she strolled toward the doorway. Northampton was a fair-sized market town but it could not compare to Brighton by the sea with its many attractions. And, with the entire *ton* swarming to the shore, Brighton was just the place to observe the latest footwear!

Almost to the front door, she heard her mother say, "What do you think about inviting Rose Crockett to go with her?"

"A marvelous thought," Pen said. "Rose can keep an eye on her. And she doesn't mind Chastity's cat—Chastity *will be* taking the cat with her, won't she?"

"Lord, yes," said their mother. "The cat must go, too."

Angelo's Fencing Academy, 13 Old Bond Street, London

Robbie flourished his foil, hoping he and Jack might have time for another match before heading to Tattersall's for the afternoon. "One last bout?"

His uncle grinned, brushing an auburn forelock from his brow. "Would I forgo a last chance to best you? Though the foil may not be my preferred weapon, *mais non*, I will not decline another match." Jack was the son of Robbie's grandfather, Jean Donet, the comte de Saintonge, and half-brother to Robbie's mother, rendering both Robbie and his uncle half-French and of an age. Now in their early thirties, they had been friends since they were boys.

"You're still on for Tattersall's?" Robbie inquired.

"*Bien sûr*! I am always interested in inspecting good horseflesh." Jack slashed the air with a quick salute and donned his mask, assuming the starting position, his right foot forward and his left arm, bent at the elbow, raised behind his head. "*En garde!*"

Robbie secured his mask and the bout proceeded.

Some minutes later, the blunted point of Robbie's practice foil thumped the front of Jack's padded jacket. "*Touché.* That is four *touchés* now for me."

Jack growled in frustration and pulled his mask off his head. Running a sleeve across his forehead, he wiped away the sweat. "That sneaking *coupé* of yours! I fall for it every time."

Robbie removed his fencing mask, revealing the grin that had been hidden behind the woven wire. "I think perhaps your mind is elsewhere."

Jack nodded. "'Tis that Venus I met at the theater with you last night. I cannot get the dark-haired beauty out of my mind."

"Tsk, tsk. Best to think of your opponent's blade. The sword is not the weapon for a man distracted. Perhaps you should take up something else. The broad-axe, perhaps?"

Jack returned Robbie's grin. "You go too far, Nephew. Knives, as you know, are my weapons of choice." Jack had been taught to wield knives by his father, the comte de Saintonge, a former pirate. Robbie had witnessed Jack throw them with deadly accuracy. It was not Robbie's skill and he admired it.

A shout from the doorway interrupted them. "Powell!" cried Angelo. "A messenger for you. From the Home Secretary's office."

The men who'd been standing around them observing the bout began to whisper among themselves.

Robbie gave Angelo an incredulous look. *Here?* He had submitted his report on the Cato Street Affair a few days before. *What could this mean?*

Angelo gestured toward the door.

"Very well." Perhaps Sidmouth wanted to apprise him of the capture of the miscreants who had escaped. He crossed the room to the waiting messenger who told him the Home Secretary requested his immediate presence.

Returning to Jack, Robbie said, "I must go."

Jack cocked a brow. "Tattersall's in a few hours, *oui?*"

"I'll be there. I'm in the market for a matched pair for my new curricle."

After changing, Robbie took a hackney to Whitehall where he was ushered into Lord Sidmouth's well-appointed office.

The Home Secretary rose from his desk to greet him. The statesman had thinning gray hair and aristocratic features. These rose above his lace-edged cravat and black suit, which pronounced him one of Lord

Liverpool's own. The Prime Minister's Cabinet always dressed in somber fashion. "Have a seat, Powell. I won't keep you long. It is not I who summons you, 'tis the king."

Robbie experienced a ripple of trepidation as he doffed his beaver top hat and settled himself in the chair facing the desk. "I had hoped the conspirators could be arrested without all the gunfire…"

Ignoring his comment, the Home Secretary lifted *The Times* from his desk and tossed it toward Robbie. "I assume you've seen the newspapers. Thistlewood's murder of that runner Smithers has everyone in an uproar."

Robbie had seen reports of the Cato Street incident and his mother had spoken of the murder. Surely that was not his doing, however.

"We're holding Thistlewood in the Tower, along with some of his co-conspirators, awaiting trial for treason."

"You have found the others?"

Sidmouth shrugged. "Most. A few are still at large."

Robbie worried the brim of his hat between his fingers. "Is the king displeased with the handling of the Cato Street Affair?"

A smile tugged at the corners of the Home Secretary's mouth. "Hardly."

Robbie experienced a surge of relief. "So, he is not angered…"

"Not at all. In truth, the king was smiling when he asked me to find you. Knowing your haunts, I had little trouble. Best run along to Carlton House. You are expected."

With an inclination of his head, Robbie turned on his heels and departed, glad he wasn't being called to account for the Bow Street officer's death.

It was not his first visit to Carlton House, the home of the prince regent, now England's king. Even so, the opulent rooms with their gilded and glistening mirrors, chandeliers and velvet upholstered walls never failed to captivate. Truly, it was a grand palace.

"If you will follow me, sir," said an elderly servant attired in dark blue livery trimmed with gold lace.

Passing through several large chambers, the servant came to a halt at the door to the Blue Velvet Room. Robbie stood poised at the entrance, watching the corpulent king, now in his late fifties, sitting behind a magnificent mahogany desk, quill in hand, signing papers.

The room was on the garden side of the principal floor of Carlton House, the first of the reception rooms facing St James' Park and one Robbie had been in before. He cast his gaze around the large room, noting the familiar blue velvet panels on the walls that provided a background for the magnificent art of the Dutch masters. One of the paintings, "The Passage Boat" by Aelbert Cuyp, was a particular favorite of his. What was notably missing from the room the king favored were any paintings of his parents.

The spring days were still cool so Robbie was not surprised to see a fire obediently burning in the fireplace, but the weather would not have mattered. Prinny's rooms were always overwarm.

Owing to the good taste of his French mother, Robbie recognized the white marble chimneypiece as being of French design. The king had loved all things French until the Revolution that had seen that country's monarch executed.

The dominant feature in the room, to Robbie's mind, save the king himself, was the six-tiered crystal chandelier that hung suspended from the ceiling that was painted to look like the sky, complete with cherub. The crystals flickered in the light of the midday sun streaming into the room through the French doors.

When the king failed to look up from the papers in front of him, the servant cleared his throat and announced, "Mr. Robert Powell". Then he bowed and departed.

Prinny looked up. "Come in, Powell, come in! You give me an excuse to leave this pile of papers I am forced to deal with."

Robbie walked forward, wondering if, now that Prinny was king, he might expect a more formal address. He bowed. "Your Majesty."

"I am too much in your debt, Powell, to insist on such niceties. Do sit down." He gestured Robbie toward the gilded chair facing the desk. "I want to hear about the arrest of those men who plotted the demise of my ministers and, I dare say, myself."

Robbie tried to be brief in his recitation of the events of that night on Cato Street. He omitted the fact the Coldstream Guards had been sent to the wrong place and did not describe the chaos that had briefly reigned in the stable. Nor did he mention that some conspirators had managed to escape. Others could supply the king with those details. "All their plotting came to a quick end," he finished. That much was true.

"Well, then, there is nothing left for me but to reward you."

Robbie started. "Sire?"

"Your quick instincts to follow Thistlewood and his band of rebels foiled a plot to assassinate the Cabinet. Think, man, what might have happened had they been successful! It could have been the beginning of a violent revolution, such as happened in France, and the end of the monarchy. I shudder at the thought. Of course, you shall be rewarded! And handsomely."

The king glanced out the windows to the gardens, his mien thoughtful. Returning his regard to Robbie, he said, "I seem to recall that my father made your brother, Martin, a baronet for his service in France."

"He did, Sire."

"I can do better. What say you to becoming a viscount?"

"That is too generous, Sir. In truth, I do not see myself as a peer." Robbie's mother might be the daughter of a French comte, the equivalent of an English earl, but Robbie had no such ambitions. He had been a shipmaster and most recently a spy.

"All right. A baronet it shall be. You shall have the Red Hand of Ulster to wear on your broad chest, Sir Robert Powell." The king rose and offered his hand. "Allow me to shake the hand of the man who may have spared England a revolution in the making."

Robbie got to his feet and reached his hand to the king. "Your servant, as always."

"It seems to me," the king said with a look of devilish amusement, his plump cheeks reddening with delight, "that a respite from your duties is in order, and I have just the place. My Royal Pavilion in Brighton." Before Robbie could reply, the king became enchanted with the idea. "Yes! You shall be my guest and stay in the private rooms, the summer long if you like, with my stables at your disposal. Will that do?"

"Quite," said Robbie. "I am overwhelmed."

The king smiled. "Shall you stay for some champagne or are you off somewhere?"

"I am meeting my uncle at Tattersall's but a glass of champagne shared with my new sovereign would suit me well before I go."

The king stepped to the nearest wall and pulled a cord. A servant immediately appeared at the door.

"Champagne for Sir Robert and myself!"

The servant bowed and left, returning shortly with a tray holding a bottle of the sparkling wine and two glasses. Once the wine had been poured, the king lifted his glass. "To a faithful agent of the Crown."

Robbie accepted the toast and reciprocated. "To a most generous monarch. Long live the king!"

Prinny took a long drink of his wine. "I shall have your medal and the papers brought round to your house. My servants in Brighton will be advised to expect you and see you are properly welcomed. By the bye, what are you about at Tattersall's?"

Happy to be discussing horseflesh, Robbie said, "I have a new curricle and I'm looking for a matched pair."

"Oh, ho! I have just the ticket. Richard Tattersall paid me a call this very morning to advise he has a matched pair of grays he wants me to see. They shall be yours, Powell!"

"But, Sir, if he meant them for you…"

The king held up his hand. "I insist; and you shall have them at my expense."

"That is most generous of you, Sir. I gladly accept." The prince regent had a reputation for being magnanimous with his friends. Apparently he intended to continue in that spirit now that he was king. Robbie was certain any horses selected by Tattersall for the king would be ones he would desire himself.

Prinny went back to his desk and hastily scribbled a note he handed to Robbie. "Give this to Tattersall with my compliments. I think he said their names are Zeus and Apollo." He flicked his fingers through the air. "Something Greek in any event. That should suit a young buck. Now, go and enjoy yourself. I shall soon join you in Brighton!"

Robbie bowed. "It would be an honor, Your Majesty."

The king's eyes held the same sparkle Robbie had observed on prior occasions but he couldn't help wondering if that sparkle would fade now that he officially had the full responsibility for the country. Though he moved with the grace of a much younger man and the curls of his short auburn wig were artfully arranged around his face, Prinny was no longer young. Wondering about the gay life his monarch had led caused Robbie to think of his own. He was tired of playing the spy, but how long could he play the rake?

Chapter 3

Dudley Hall, Northampton

Chastity settled into one of the two winged chairs in the corner of her bedchamber and reached for her tea on the round table between her and Rose. The sunlight pouring in from the paned glass windows cast a glow about Rose's beautiful ebony hair. Chastity tried not to feel envious.

A glance out the windows reminded her that daffodils and crocuses were already blooming in wild profusion. At her feet, Crispin sat licking his black velvet paws.

Idly twisting one of her curls around her finger, Chastity sipped her tea and turned her thoughts to the shoes she would take to Brighton. "The brocade slippers with the green ribbon ties, I think, and the crimson ones to go with my new gown. Too, I must take the green half boots, and—"

Across the table, Rose choked on her tea and whisked her serviette across her mouth. Exasperation filled her gaze. "Really, Chas, what matters our shoes if we are to see Brighton?" In the quizzical way Rose had of wrinkling her perfectly arched dark brows, she asked, "You are certain we are to go?"

"Did I not say so?" Chastity allowed herself a smug smile. "I have been flirting overmuch with my dance instructor of late, which has had the desired effect. Mother is hurrying the preparations to see me gone, and you with me."

Rose leaned back in her chair, smiling. "You are a devious one. But you'll hear no complaint from me. I was ever so grateful when my parents thought a visit to your great-aunt a splendid idea. Country parties and dances are all well and good but the Brighton Season is another matter altogether, one they were eager to see me attend now that I am of marriageable age."

"Do you seek a husband?"

Rose's brows rose. "Of course, don't you?"

Chastity pursed her lips and shook her head. "No. At least not now." She considered the possibility. "Maybe never."

"Truly?"

"As you are aware, I have no need to wed." Although her tone was decisive as always when the topic arose, Chastity's inner thoughts about marriage were less certain. What she really wanted was what every woman dreamed of: the love of a good man, one to whom she could give her heart. Yet she had no high hope for that. Relegated to the shadows of her sisters' beauty and given her outspoken nature, she believed a lasting love was a dream so elusive as to be nonexistent.

"What about your suitors? William Saunders—"

"Pfft! He's merely a childhood friend. Worse, he has grown into a man of awkward manners and foppish ways."

"But he will inherit his father's wealth—"

"I do not desire his wealth." Chastity shot a swift glance at her friend. "And do not, I beg of you, even mention the name of 'he who dangles after me like a lost puppy'. I swear he only seeks my company to be near my younger sister."

Rose's lips twitched. "Very well. If I may not mention Michael Townsend, what of the vicar's son? He is very nice to look at—"

"And desirous of following in his father's footsteps. Truly, Rose. You cannot possibly see *me* married to a vicar."

Rose chuckled. "Well, no, now that you mention it. Nor could I see myself doing so." She took a drink of her tea and set down her cup. "Perhaps if I don't marry, we could be spinsters together."

Chastity smiled. "Oh, you will marry, I've no doubt." For a moment she considered the man to whom she would match her dearest friend. Someone worthy. "I've an idea."

"Oh, dear! You have that look in your eye. What are you thinking?"

"What if I were to help you find a worthy husband? A man who would treasure you?"

"I suppose…"

"Leave it to me," she said, warming to the idea. "Once we are in Brighton, I shall devote myself to finding you a suitable match. Not a country bumpkin or a man consumed with his own merit. No, he must be a gentleman of the best sort, a man of letters with a generous heart and wealth enough you need never worry about the future. What say you?" Chastity was always up for a challenge and to be the instrument of Rose's happiness made the effort one she looked forward to.

"Would we still enjoy ourselves in Brighton?"

"Oh, yes! Aunt Agatha will see to it, I've no doubt." While she had suggested to her mother that Aunt Agatha knew nothing of young women's fancies, her most vivid memories of her great-aunt were of a warm, deeply affectionate woman, who delighted in making merry.

Crispin chose that moment to leap into her lap, part of his large black form spilling onto the chair seat. Her teacup wobbled in its saucer. She placed it on the table and scratched the cat behind his ears. His golden eyes closed as he began to purr. The deep rhythmic sound filled the bedchamber.

"I have never been to Brighton," Rose said wistfully. "What a time we will have!"

Chastity ran her hand over Crispin's soft fur, glistening in a ray of sunlight. "You will like Aunt Agatha. She is a dear. More to the point, if she remains as she was before the earl died, she is a great deal of fun. Mother has no idea, thank God."

Robbie left Carlton House and stepped into the afternoon sun. A quick hail of a hackney and he was on his way, hoping he would not be too late to meet Jack.

He arrived at Tattersall's to find the dirt courtyard where the horse auctions were held crowded with gentlemen from London society. On one side, under a raised roof supported by Doric columns, prospective buyers stood in a line watching a white horse being paraded before them while Richard Tattersall expounded upon the mare's virtues.

Across the yard, standing next to a team of black horses, Robbie glimpsed the tall Sir Bellingham Graham, a noted whip, speaking with Sir John Lade, often a fixture at Tattersall's. Both were members of the Four-Horse Club of expert barouche drivers and wore the yellow-striped blue waistcoats and black-spotted neckerchiefs that were the club's insignia. Sir John always dressed in riding attire, whip included.

Bellingham was of an age with Robbie and a good friend. Lade was older, a contemporary of the king and one of his Carlton House Set. Robbie thought to join the two of them when he saw Jack striding in his direction.

"I say, old thing," said Jack, arriving at his side, "what kept you so long?" Jack was proud of his English half, often spouting English expressions. "Old thing" was his current favorite. However, he invariably sprinkled his speech with French. That and his lace-edged cravat made him appear decidedly French. Robbie found the whole thing highly amusing.

He allowed himself a wry smile. "You won't believe it when I tell you, dear uncle, but, henceforth, you may address me as 'Sir Robert'."

"Sir Robert?" Jack blinked twice. "What have you done to merit such an honor?"

"A favor for the king. And don't ask because I will say no more."

"*Très bien*," Jack said with a smug smile. "Be secretive if you must, but I will have the truth of it eventually."

Robbie lifted his gaze to where Sir Bellingham and Sir John were still engaged in conversation. "What do you suppose those two are talking about with their heads so close together?"

"The word is out," whispered Jack. "Lade is selling off the team to pay some of his gambling debts."

"A sad day when Lade parts with a team of his prized horses," mused Robbie. Sir John Lade was known to have money problems and his notorious wife, Letty, a horsewoman of some repute, did little to discourage her husband's bad habits.

Jack regarded the two whips. "Indeed, and the *on dit* is the Four-Horse Club is having difficulties as well."

Richard Tattersall, leaving the group of prospective buyers, looked toward Robbie and Jack and raised his hand in greeting.

Robbie held up the message from the king and beckoned the horse master to him.

Tattersall strode across the yard. "Good day, gentlemen."

"A good day it is, indeed." Robbie handed him the paper. "For you, from the king."

Tattersall read the scribbled note and looked up, a wide smile on his face. "Congratulations, Sir Robert. Come, I'll show you the grays." He strode ahead of them, saying over his shoulder, "A superb matched pair, already trained and accustomed to London's streets."

Tattersall had one of his assistants lead the pair around the court-yard. Robbie grew excited to think they would be his. "High-steppers," he remarked. "Good bone and a nice slope to the shoulders."

"I like the high-set tails," remarked Jack.

When the assistant brought the horses to a halt, Robbie approached to get a better view of their heads. They had large eyes, well-spaced, and small ears. "I could not ask for a better looking pair."

Tattersall shifted his gaze to the grays he would soon part with, a wistful expression on his face. "You must have done something of great import for the king to give you Zeus and Apollo. 'Tis the best pair I've seen in the past six months." Turning to Robbie, he said, "Sir Bellingham has been admiring them."

"Sir Bellingham will have to content himself with Sir John's team," said Robbie. "I am already quite attached to my Greek grays."

Dudley Hall, Northampton

Chastity gasped as the chest slipped in the footman's hands nearly plunging the precious cargo from the top of the carriage to the gravel in front of her home. She held her breath until the footman regained his hold and safely stowed the chest with the others.

Crispin resettled himself in her arms and her heart slowed to a normal rhythm. "That one is heavy," she told Rose, "but I would not have him drop it. It carries the shoes."

Rose faced her with a surprised look. "You're bringing them all?"

Chastity experienced a twinge of guilt for her indulgence in the footwear she loved but, well, there really was a good explanation. "Most are my own designs and I could not bear to leave them behind. You never know what fancy will strike me to wear a certain pair of slippers. And one needs to be prepared for the weather. Among the new half boots is a pair just right for you. I designed them for rain and mud yet they are lovely. Not those plain brown things or ungainly wooden pattens most women are forced to wear."

Rose's eyes grew round in wonder. "You would gift them to me? Truly? And they are not plain brown leather?"

"No." A sigh escaped her as she thought of them. "They are blue leather with crimson flowers on the shaft, boots to attract a suitor. Very pretty."

Her friend looked down at the blue slippers Chastity had given her with embellished cross straps that matched perfectly her blue pelisse. "These are among my favorites."

"I am glad you like them, but they are ill-suited to rain." Chastity gazed up at the dark clouds hovering above. "The boots will serve better should the weather turn against us. It's spring, after all."

"I suppose…"

The door of the manor opened and Henriette, Chastity's maid, came out carrying Chastity's emerald green pelisse, the same color as her half boots and bonnet of green curled silk. The bright color made for the perfect complement to her round gown of ivory cambric.

"Mistress, would you wear your pelisse?"

"A good thought, Henriette. Here, Rose, take Crispin." She handed the cat to her friend and reached her arms into the sleeves. "Even if it does not rain, the heated bricks will soon cool and the carriage will be cold save for Crispin's warm body and the lap rugs."

The manor door opened and Chastity's parents and sisters came out to say their goodbyes.

"Do try and behave yourself," said Pen.

"I always try," said Chastity with a wink at Rose.

"I shall miss you terribly," said a petulant Lucy, her dark curls falling to her shoulders. "Who shall teach me to ride as you do?"

"No one if we're lucky," said Pen.

Chastity's mother lifted her eyes to the heavens. "Aunt Agatha will be expecting you. I collect from her letter she is eagerly anticipating having you two as guests and introducing you to her friends."

Chastity's father took her by the shoulders and leaned down to kiss her forehead. His hair had been silver as long as she could remember, but his eyes, like hers, were blue. He peered into her face with a forlorn look. "I will miss you, my pet. Do write. I want to know of your entertainments and the books you are reading."

"I will." She kissed his cheek, hoping she and Rose would be too busy enjoying Brighton to have time to read. The coachman opened the carriage door and let down the step and her father handed her in. She took Crispin from Rose's outstretched hands and sat back in her seat. Rose climbed in beside her.

Chastity set Crispin on the seat between them and leaned out the open window to wave to her family.

The coachman cracked the whip and the carriage lunged forward.

With a sigh of relief, she rested her head on the tufted velvet. "I thought we would never leave. Just think, Rose. Tonight we shall stay in London!"

Two weeks after Robbie met with the king a small item appeared in *The London Gazette*:

> *His Majesty George IV has bestowed a baronetcy on Robert Pierre Powell for service to the Crown.*

His mother, knowing of his new address, must have been watching for the notice to appear. *"Oui, c'est vrai!"* she exclaimed at breakfast that morning, pointing to the page in the *Gazette*. Her black hair was neatly coiffed beneath her small cap, the few strands of gray adding to her dignity but taking nothing from her beauty. She looked up from the page, addressing Robbie's father. "Now all of London will know we have yet another son who has been favored with a baronetcy."

"I didn't seek it," said Robbie, shooting a glance at Jack across the table.

Simon Powell ran a hand through his golden hair, for several years now generously laced with silver, and stared at Robbie. "I never ask you and your brothers what you do for the Crown, but given the timing, I have my suspicions. Allow me to congratulate you on a job well done."

Robbie did not want to tell them exactly what he had done but he couldn't fail to acknowledge the compliment. "Thank you, Father."

With a mischievous grin, Jack said, "I believe I shall continue to address him as 'Nephew'." Turning to Robbie's mother, his half-sister, Jack said, "Did Robbie tell you we are off to Brighton?"

"You're coming with me?" Robbie asked, surprised for they had yet to discuss it.

Jack shrugged. *"Bien entendu!* I would not be left behind! I have the summer before the harvest in Saintonge to indulge my fancies."

Robbie's mother glanced between Robbie and Jack, a frown forming on her lovely face. "Try not to get into trouble in Brighton, you two. Use your time to find worthy brides. As a man of means with a title, Jack, you will be a catch no matter you share my French origin. And you, Robbie, as a new baronet from a prominent shipping family, will be well received by the parents of the young women spending the summer there even if you are in trade."

Robbie was the only one of Simon Powell's four sons who still lived at home due to his unmarried state and his frequent travels for the Crown. His twin brother had taken a wife the year before, prompting Robbie to consider the leg-shackled state. When a man had achieved all his goals, what was there left to do except sire an heir? Yet no woman had captured his attention, at least not for more than a few weeks.

The Powells were related to nobility on both sides of the family tree, which, together with their wealth, gained them invitations to every ball in London. The patronesses of Almack's Assembly Rooms might adore the Powell men, but the young debutantes appeared to Robbie like frightened does. They could never hold their own among the remarkable women in the Powell family.

"Mother," Robbie gently chided, "I go to Brighton to enjoy myself. As the king told me, I deserve a holiday."

"One you have already begun if your failure to appear at the shipping office is any indication," said his father, looking over his newspaper. "Recall that one of our six ships is yours."

"I have not forgotten," said Robbie, "and I am weary of the Crown's business. Claiming my home on the sea again appeals but there might be other options." Robbie had been restless for some while. The adventure of spying for the Crown had held his attention for the last few years, but with Cato Street, he had come to the end of it.

"So, what will you do now?" inquired his father.

Robbie stared ahead but, seeing nothing, replied. "I have no idea." Dropping his gaze to his coffee, he said, "I might return to the family business. Then again, how would you feel about one of your sons being destined for something on land?" One of the reasons Robbie had become an expert navigator was his fondness for charts and maps, which had fascinated him since he was a boy. He'd made good use of his skill in his work as a spy. Perhaps he could turn that into some worthy endeavor.

His father smiled. "I suppose one of my sons could be an outlier. Your twin and his wife design ships in London and Scotland, only going to sea to travel between them."

Robbie let out a sigh. "I will think on my future while I'm away. It is possible I will return to my ship when Jack returns to his vineyards. But I make no promises."

"For the present," put in Jack, "we take our *vacances, non?*"

"So you shall," said Simon Powell, "but let us know how you fare. Your father, Jack—my wife's father, I remind you—and your mother in Guernsey will be anxious for news."

"Tell them we are to be the guests of the king," put in Robbie. "They can find no fault in that."

His mother raised a dark brow. "Unless they recall his reputation." She had never been overly fond of Prinny.

That afternoon, as Robbie and Jack were leaving for White's, a messenger arrived with a letter addressed in flowing script to *Sir Robert Powell*. Sealed in red wax was the Claremont coat of arms.

A message from The Grand Countess.

Robbie broke the seal and read the terse message: *Please call upon me at your earliest convenience.*

It was signed *Muriel Claremont.*

Muriel, Dowager Countess of Claremont, had been in Scotland with Robbie and his brothers last Christmas. During that time, he had grown rather fond of the older woman, hence the sobriquet "The Grand Countess". He enjoyed her keen wit. She had kept them regaled with her quips and retorts when the snow forced them inside.

What could she want?

The next morning, Robbie reined in Zeus and Apollo in front of Claremont House. Four-storied and surrounded by gardens, the grand estate was the countess' home in London.

Robbie handed the reins to the groom, warning him of the spirited pair, and took the short flight of stairs leading to the front door.

At the drop of the brass knocker, the door opened to reveal Cruthers, the countess' always impeccably attired butler. "Good day, sir," he intoned with a face devoid of emotion.

"Sir Robert Powell to see the countess."

Robbie detected a flicker of surprise in the servant's eyes, which quickly vanished. While Cruthers knew him from other visits, the butler might not be aware of Robbie's new form of address. Cruthers bade him enter and took his hat. "Lady Claremont is receiving in the parlor, sir."

Robbie left the entry hall with its crystal chandelier and gilded staircase and followed the butler to the sitting room where the elegant older woman sat on one of two ivory sofas flanking a white marble fireplace that harbored a warming fire. The scent of flowers drew his gaze to a large bouquet of pink roses sitting on a table next to the far window.

The countess beckoned him near. A woman of classic taste, she wore a dark gray gown set off by the ivory sofa. Around her neck hung her usual adornments, a long string of pearls and a quizzing glass on a gold chain. She was never without them.

"Do come in," she said. And then to Cruthers, "Some brandy for Sir Robert and sherry for me, if you will."

The butler bowed, walked to the sideboard and poured the requested drinks.

Once Robbie had his brandy in hand, Muriel raised her glass of sherry. "A toast to you for your daring and courage that has saved the Cabinet and perhaps the king as well."

"How did—"

"You forget, Sir Robert, the king and I are old acquaintances. He simply told me. Quite proud of you he was, too."

Robbie dropped his gaze to his amber drink, a fine cognac. "It's not generally known I was involved."

When he looked up, there was a twinkle in her gray eyes. "Yes, yes, I am aware. You have no cause to worry that I will say anything. I asked you here to congratulate you on your service to the king. And to beg a favor."

"Anything."

"The king tells me you are bound for Brighton. A holiday at the Royal Pavilion, as I understand it."

Robbie nodded, wondering what she had in mind.

"My very good friend, Agatha, Lady Sanborn, lives in Brighton on the Old Steyne near the Pavilion. She informs me she is to have a guest for the summer season." The countess paused, and then added, "Her grand-niece, Chastity, is a lively girl in need of watching."

"Chastity?" Images of a pious young girl warred in his mind with a hoyden who "needed watching".

Between sips of sherry, the countess said, "Miss Chastity Reynolds of Northampton, to be precise. Lady Sanborn tells me Chastity is an accomplished horsewoman even at her young age."

Robbie's brows drew together, puzzled. An accomplished horse-woman at such a young age? "What is it you want *me* to do?" Muriel dabbled in matchmaking with some notable successes. But surely a child was not among her projects.

"I want you to keep an eye on the girl, to make sure she does not find trouble or come to any harm. She cannot very well ride hell-for-leather across Brighton by herself. Perhaps you might escort her to a play or a ride along the shore. A handsome fellow like you would hold her girlish attentions."

"Is there no nursemaid or governess?" Robbie had no desire to assume either role.

"No. She comes alone, although I understand she may be bringing a friend, a girl of a similar age. But Chastity is the one that must be looked after." With a twinkle in her eye, she added, "Think of her as your ward for the Brighton Season."

When he didn't reply, the countess gazed up at him with a hopeful look in her soft gray eyes. "Won't you do this for me?"

Robbie did not wish to be saddled with a rebellious child, but his family adored Muriel, who was a grand dame in London society. Moreover, he liked The Grand Countess. Perhaps he could indulge her. After all, how much of his time could a young girl take? A ride in his curricle, a walk along the seafront…he could manage those. "Yes, dear Countess, I will do it for you."

"Splendid." Muriel returned him a satisfied smile. "Now, how about another brandy?"

Chapter 4

Grillon's Hotel, Albemarle Street, London

"I'll return in a moment," said Chastity as she rose from the table where she and Rose dined in their shared room.

Rose looked up, her fork paused in midair. "Are you going out…alone? You're not dressed for town."

Chastity considered her plain brown gown that she had changed into thinking she would remain in their room. "No one will see me save the desk clerk to whom I will direct my inquiry." The carriage ride to London had been plagued with muddy roads and much rain, and the drafty lobby had left her chilled. The fire kindled for them had begun to warm her but a glass of sherry would go far to complete the process.

"Do you wish me to accompany you?" Rose cast a look of longing at what remained of her braised veal.

"Nay, finish your meal," Chastity said, crossing the room to the door.

"Hurry back," urged Rose. "I peeked under the silver dome that hides the sweetmeats. A most delectable selection."

"They will go well with what I have in mind." As she reached for the door handle, Crispin, who had been curled up before the fire, raised his head and opened his golden eyes briefly considering her before returning to his nap. The bumpy carriage ride to London had not been to his liking either.

Chastity closed the door behind her and entered the corridor devoid of heat. Drawing her shawl tightly around her, she hurried downstairs to the lobby, dismayed to find no one at the front desk.

A single footman stood just inside the hotel's entrance. She hastened toward him. As she did, she collided with a hard body, the impact forcing the air from her lungs. Stunned, she backed away, trying not to fall. With her eyes downcast, she placed her hand over her racing heart.

The first thing she noticed as she looked up from the tiled floor was a pair of black Hessian boots polished to a high gloss with a silver-white braid circling the top, ending in shimmering tassels. Boots that could only have been the creation of George Hoby, the first bootmaker in London, who had acquired a few of her father's designs.

From the boots, her gaze traveled up long, muscular thighs encased in tight buckskin breeches. Hands fisted on narrow hips and an impatient sigh suggested he thought she was in the wrong.

Impudent man! Oaf! He had run into her!

Her scrutiny continued up to the black coat he wore over a cinnamon suede waistcoat. His cravat was simply tied yet stylish.

"Well, Miss, have you had your fill of me?" he said in an amused tone.

Chastity met hazel eyes rimmed with green and pierced with shards of gold. A chiseled face with a strong jaw was framed by wavy dark brown hair and trim side-whiskers. Altogether an attractive man if she didn't consider his smirk.

She could not abide men who thought themselves desired by all females, which he clearly did.

"What?" she said, her voice dripping sarcasm. "Is there to be no apology, no begging my forgiveness for nearly knocking a lady off her feet?"

"A lady?" His gaze boldly traveled the length of her. "If you be a lady, you are a very pretty lady, indeed."

She glared at him, dismissing his compliment as insincere, one he likely gave to all women to whom he liberally doled out his charm. She would not be diverted by such undeserved flattery. "Pretty or plain makes no difference, sir. A gentleman who causes distress to a lady will make amends."

"Not to put too fine a point on it, Miss, but whatever were you thinking darting across the lobby without a care of where you were going?"

So, there was to be no apology. Worse, a scold. "I knew very well where I was going, sir. It was you who apparently did not."

"Very well," he inclined his head, "if you insist. Allow me to make amends."

Without warning, he took her by the waist and forcibly drew her to his chest, pressing his lips to hers in a burning, invasive kiss that left her breathless and her lips throbbing.

When he finally released her, she backed away, stunned, and covered her pulsing lips with her fingertips. Never had she been kissed in such a manner. And in front of a footman!

Before she could say a word, the arrogant rogue turned on his heels, crossed the lobby and disappeared through the door to the coffee house. The scent of cigar smoke wafted to her nostrils, making her grateful she had no business there.

Pressing her lips together, she fisted her hands and glared daggers at the door, imagining it was his back.

A moment passed as she made an effort to restore her calm demeanor. She ignored the footman, who stood like a statue next to the door.

At the front desk, she was pleased to see the clerk returning to his post.

She had meant to ask for two glasses of sherry but her encounter with the cad made her choice clear. "Sherry, if you please, a full bottle, delivered to my room."

She would need more than one glass to forget the man's arrogant kiss.

Robbie reclaimed his seat next to Jack in the coffee house. "You missed a tasty bit of fluff dashing through the lobby. A lady's maid, I should think, and strikingly beautiful."

Jack set down the newspaper he'd been reading and raised one auburn brow. "Oh?"

Robbie couldn't resist a chuckle. "I confess I was not looking when I ran into her. However, the collision was not at all unpleasant." He recalled the warm softness that had met his hard body, her disquieting examination of his person and the glaring blue eyes that had confronted him after he gave her a sample of his excellent kissing skills. "Not much of a sense of humor, though, and a sharp tongue."

"You exchanged words?"

"We did. Nothing as polite as an introduction. Didn't even swoon when I kissed her."

"You dared kiss a strange woman?"

"It wouldn't be the first time," he said with a shrug. "Alas, I have no idea who the delightful creature is."

Jack's brows drew together. "Why is it you have all the fun? While you were enjoying yourself with the maid, I had to fend off Sir Bellingham's inquiries about your new pair of grays." Jack shifted his gaze to the very man sitting with Sir John Lade on the other side of the room. "He was most curious."

"What did you tell him?"

"Only that they were a gift and you were delighted."

"He could hardly doubt that," said Robbie.

"By the bye, he tells me that he and Sir John are coming to Brighton for the Season along with Sir John's wife, Letty."

Robbie grinned. "Oh, ho. That should make for some interesting rides. She's an amazing horsewoman."

"And some interesting evenings," said Jack. "You know how the Lades love to indulge."

"Aye, they are true friends of our new king, who will also be coming to Brighton at some point, or so he told me when he gifted me the grays."

"Do we leave tomorrow?" Jack was eager to reach Brighton and had kept Robbie entertained with stories he'd heard of Prinny's evenings at the Royal Pavilion.

"We do. Immediately after breakfast. We shall depart from the White Horse Cellar in Piccadilly. I've sent my valet ahead to Brighton with our baggage. He has agreed to serve us both while we are there."

"Most generous of him. Tiller ties a perfect cravat."

"I tie my own cravats," Robbie corrected him. He glanced at the newspaper Jack had set on the table. Splashed across one column was a story about the Cato Street conspirators.

"They are preparing for trial with a special commission," said Jack. "Have you been following the story?"

"All of London is following the story," said Robbie. He did not wish Jack to know of the reason for his keen interest in the matter.

Jack fixed him with an assessing gaze. "I have never known you to be overly interested in His Majesty's justice being meted out."

"You have to admit this case is different."

Jack accepted more coffee from the waiter. "Well, *oui*, if only because of the ambitious nature of their plan. But according to one piece I read, the government was on to them early in the game. The king and his Cabinet were never really in danger."

"Hard to say. It could have so easily gone wrong. As it was, one officer was killed in making the arrests."

Jack picked up the newspaper and focused his attention on the story. "This article says they are still searching for some of the conspirators who have yet to be captured."

The hairs on the back of Robbie's neck stood on end and his coffee suddenly tasted bitter in his mouth. He'd believed all the conspirators had been taken into custody. Hoping Jack could not see beneath his feigned indifference, he said, "I'm sure the runners will find them. After all, 'twas one of their own they lost to that man Thistlewood and his followers."

"Insufferable oaf!" Chastity muttered as she slammed the door to her chamber. "Arrogant rogue!" Her blood boiled with indignation.

"Who has you in such a state?" Rose inquired from where she sat nibbling on a tart.

"A rude, conceited man who trampled me, but lacked even a smidgeon of good breeding to apologize." She would not dare to mention the very improper kiss. The kiss that still had her lips throbbing.

"My mother warned me against the London bucks. It seems you have met one."

Chastity huffed out her frustration and dropped into a chair. "Except we didn't actually meet. He did not bother to introduce himself though, judging by his fashionable attire, he passes for a gentleman." A picture of his long legs encased in buckskin breeches came to her mind. "Nice boots."

"Only you would notice his boots. Was the oaf handsome?"

"Passably so," she admitted, remembering his stunning hazel eyes and attractive face. "But what is that to a gentleman's manners?"

The sherry arrived. Chastity was glad to see a full bottle on the footman's tray.

"Shall I pour, Miss?" he asked.

"Indeed, yes," said Chastity. "A generous portion, if you please."

The footman poured two glasses and departed.

Chastity soothed her ruffled feathers with a drink of the honeyed liquid and a tart from the pudding tray. Her peace slightly restored, she leaned back in her chair, contemplating. If fortune were with her, the man was not a guest in the hotel and she would never see him again.

Crispin jumped into her lap and she stroked his ebony fur.

A few minutes passed. "I have a thought…"

Rose looked up from the candied nuts. "Oh?"

Trying to forget the troublesome encounter in the lobby, Chastity said, "Tomorrow morning before we leave for Brighton, I want to stop at Wood's, that fashionable shoe store we passed today. The window had several pairs of brightly-colored slippers and I'd like to get a closer look." Seeing Rose's frown, she added, "Worry not. We'll still arrive in Brighton in time for tea with Aunt Agatha."

"All right, but what about your father's coachman? Will he allow such a stop?"

"Old Bronson? I've been winding him around my little finger since I was a child. He won't mind the stop as long as he can keep an eye on the shop door."

Aaron Ings sat in the coffee house of Grillon's Hotel, listening to the conversation at the next table. He'd followed the bastard Powell there hoping he might hear of his plans. He'd heard more than enough. So, it was to be Brighton and they would depart from the White Horse Cellar tomorrow. That left him this night to recruit the men he needed to see his revenge upon the spy who would rob him of his brother.

He wasted no time in returning to the riverside tavern he had visited a few days earlier. The Prospect of Whitby, fondly called "The Prospect" by its customers, sat on the banks of the Thames close to its unsavory clientele, including sailors from the countless foreign vessels in port. It was the ideal place for Aaron to hire men looking for coin but with few scruples about how it was earned.

A noose hung outside the tavern in memory of the notorious "Hanging Judge" Jeffreys who showed little mercy to river criminals. Aaron didn't need the reminder that his own brother James would soon face the noose for his plotting with Arthur Thistlewood. Ironically, it was here Aaron's revenge would begin.

A bell over the door sounded his presence as he entered and stepped onto the flagstone floor. The stench of unwashed bodies and stale ale greeted him as a few men turned in his direction. But Aaron had dressed for the part, leaving his fine clothes and finer boots behind in his lodgings. He'd come dressed as a river pirate, one like the men he sought to hire. Men who would help him see the task done to do away with Robert Powell, the government spy.

The approach to the Royal Pavilion in Brighton always left Robbie awestruck. With the addition of an onion-shaped dome, tent-like roofs and numerous pinnacles and minarets, Prinny's architect, John Nash, had transformed the original mansion into a Mogul's dream. An extravagant Indian palace set down on England's south coast where the prince regent, now king, could forget the staid palace in London and entertain his eclectic bevy of friends.

Beside him, Jack broke the silence. *"C'est magnifique, n'est-ce pas?"*

"That and more. I once attended an event at the Pavilion but have never stayed there. This should be a holiday to remember."

"Ah, *oui*, I am counting on it," Jack said with a smile.

His uncle might like to act as one of His Majesty's subjects but his French accent, dress and mannerisms made clear he was half-French, more so than Robbie who had been raised in London.

At the end of the long curving road, Robbie pulled his curricle to a stop beneath the domed porte-cochère. He handed the reins to Jack and climbed down to offer his new card to a liveried footman who summoned a groom.

"We've been expecting you, Sir Robert," said the footman. "Your luggage and that of Monsieur Donet have been placed in your chambers. You and your friend are to be the king's honored guests. His Majesty said to tell you he hopes to arrive within the week."

A groom came to relieve Jack of the reins and lead Zeus and Apollo toward the king's stables. The Rotunda, as the stables were called, was as magnificent as the Pavilion itself. "They will be well tended, Sir Robert," said the groom. "And the king's stables are available to you should you wish to ride."

"Thank you," said Robbie before following the liveried servant into the Pavilion.

"Refreshments will be served in the Red Drawing Room and from there you will be shown to your chambers."

As they passed through the Long Gallery, Jack gazed up at the painted glass ceiling from which hung huge bright Chinese lanterns.

"Do the lanterns with their red tassels speak to you of China?" Robbie asked.

"Indeed, they do. And the walls, painted with bamboo trees against that pink background make it appear like a grove of bamboo. If I had not seen Versailles, I would be overly impressed."

"You still might be. You have yet to see the dragon hanging above the Banqueting Room."

In the Red Drawing Room, Robbie and Jack quenched their thirsts and then followed the footman to their bedchambers, which they were pleased to learn were located across from the king's chamber. "We'll not lack for comfort here," observed Robbie.

He left Jack at the door to his chamber and proceeded on to his own room. The first thing he noticed was the canopied four-poster bed adorned in bright blue silk, the same color as the eyes of the maid he had kissed in London.

His valet, standing in the corner, had been busy. Robbie's chest was placed against the wall and his clothing for dinner laid out on the bed. "Good man, Tiller," said Robbie to the wizened old seaman, who had once sailed with Robbie's father. When Tiller was no longer able to climb the rigging and Robbie began taking on assignments for the Crown, he offered Tiller the position as valet.

"Aye, Cap'n," Tiller said, stepping forward. "'Twas my pleasure." The valet's gaze traveled around the well-appointed room. "Seems ye and yer uncle have found favor with the king. I've been all agog since I arrived."

"His Majesty has been generous," said Robbie.

Jack entered Robbie's chamber and thanked the valet. "My clothes for the evening were set out in perfect order, Tiller."

In response, the old sailor beamed a toothy smile. He had told Robbie on numerous occasions that he enjoyed his new role. And why not? He received full pay even when Robbie was on assignments for the Crown and didn't take him along. And he found amusing Robbie's many disguises. But of all his attributes, Robbie valued most Tiller's loyalty to him and the Powell family.

Jack rubbed his hands together, a sign Robbie recognized as impatience. "Say, as long as we have a bit of time, I'd like to take a stroll around the grounds and see the stables you were telling me about."

"While you are doing that," said Robbie, "I have an errand to accomplish. I must call on Lady Claremont's friend." Robbie wasn't looking forward to his visit to The Girl Who Needed Watching but since he had promised The Grand Countess, he'd best meet her.

Jack took his leave and, with a sigh, Robbie faced his valet. "I must change into a gentleman's attire for my next stop."

"Aye, aye, Cap'n."

As Tiller pulled the needed items from Robbie's chest, he thought to ask, "Have you been provided accommodations?"

"Aye, Cap'n. They gave me a snug cozy chamber just next door. If ye be needing me, ye have only to call."

Once Robbie had changed into appropriate clothing for a meeting with Lady Sanborn, he advised Tiller his time was his own until evening.

The valet dipped his head. "Thank ye."

Robbie glanced in the mirror, assured he was respectable enough for a countess.

Chastity pulled back the sheer curtain from the tall arched window to glimpse the wide swath of green lying in the center of the dirt road that was the Old Steyne. An immense fountain formed an oasis in the middle of the park in front of her aunt's house. They had arrived only minutes before and Rose, wanting to see her chamber, had gone upstairs with the maid. Chastity had lingered behind, wanting to hear more about Brighton from her great-aunt before she was forced to undertake so mundane a task as changing for dinner.

Aunt Agatha lived at number 54 in what, at one time, had been the Duke of Marlborough's house. When her husband, the Earl of Sanborn, died, she leased the large, two-story mansion to be close to all that Brighton offered. A well-furnished house to begin with, according to her great-aunt, in the last year she had redecorated it in brilliant colors. The parlor in which Chastity stood featured two red velvet sofas, a red and blue Axminster carpet and a gilded fireplace over which hung a painting of the late earl as a young man. His powdered wig, white satin waistcoat and blue velvet frock coat trimmed in gold braid spoke of an earlier era.

On the other side of the room, a vase of red tulips graced a round pedestal table. Oddly, Chastity was more at home here than at her own house in Northampton. There, she experienced the constant comparison with her beautiful mother and sisters; here she was free to be herself.

From behind her, Aunt Agatha said, "You have grown into a lovely young lady, Chastity. I must face the fact you are no longer a child but a woman full grown."

Chastity turned to smile at her great-aunt, convinced the compliment was overstated. "Lovely" was not a word she would have used to describe herself, but she adored Aunt Agatha, so it was with a smile she said, "Thank you."

The older woman had changed since they were last together. The glimmer of mirth in her brown eyes had not been there shortly after the earl's passing when her eyes had been full of sadness. Then she had worn a widow's somber clothing. Now she wore a deep marine blue silk gown, a bronze shawl and a turban of bronze and blue silk adorned with an aquamarine jewel and a yellow feather. Even her graying brown hair did not affect the impression Chastity had of an actress in a whimsical play. Her slippers, which Chastity had noticed as soon as she'd entered the house, were a unique design of marine blue silk with appliqués of yellow and bronze flowers.

"You're not sad to be a widow, are you, Aunt?"

"Oh, no, child. My mourning days are behind me. I lead a full life in Brighton. I think of the earl as having gone ahead of me to Heaven. I will see him again one day. Meanwhile, as Lady Sanborn, I am having great fun. I'm invited to all the soirées. I have my rose garden to tend and a wonderful collection of books to read, which you are welcome to enjoy, and I sometimes invite neighborhood children into my parlor in the afternoons to hear a story. As well, I have many friends with whom I take tea. My next-door neighbor is one of them. Maria Fitzherbert and I have become particular friends."

"Mrs. Fitzherbert, the king's Catholic wife?"

"Well, yes," Aunt Agatha said, rather sheepishly, "although no one in Brighton pays any mind to her faith. She and the king parted nearly ten years ago, which I collect he must deeply regret, particularly after he was forced to wed that German princess he so dislikes. Maria Fitzherbert is still greatly respected here." Her great-aunt sighed. "I can't think his many mistresses make up for the loss of the devoted and loving wife of his youth. Maria is a very special woman. I consider it fortunate to call her my friend."

A beautiful young widow, virtuous by all accounts, who had charmed and then dared to marry the Anglican prince, had to be interesting. To defy the opinions of a whole nation for love and then to be forced by Parliament and royal decree to part. It was as romantic and tragic as a play by Shakespeare. It thrilled Chastity to think of the fearless young woman, who chose love against all odds. "Will Rose and I get to meet her?"

"Undoubtedly. We dine together often."

Chastity turned back to the window. The wide thoroughfare in front of her great-aunt's house that constituted the Steyne kept up a steady parade of men trotting by on their horses and fashionable women walking together while children played around them. Flowers bloomed in every front yard rendering the sunny spring day delightful. After all the rain, it was a welcome change.

A short distance away was the Royal Pavilion and, in the other direction, the shore they had passed on their carriage ride into Brighton. The cool breeze wafting in through the open window smelled of the sea. Chastity breathed in the salty air, so different than the country air in Northampton that spoke of farms, animals and tanneries.

She turned at Aunt Agatha's words. "The earl and I spent our honeymoon here in Brighton. When Sanborn died two years ago, I thought it appropriate I should return to where we had been so happy."

"I think it's a fine place to live," said Chastity.

The sound of steps caused her to look toward the open door. Featherstone, her great-aunt's butler, appeared on the threshold, his wide girth filling the doorway. Red hair and side-whiskers prominently framed his ruddy-cheeked face.

Aunt Agatha raised her head, casting her gaze in his direction. "Yes?"

"A gentleman caller, my lady." The butler approached and handed his mistress a card. "Sir Robert Powell from London."

For a moment, Aunt Agatha's face took on a puzzled look, but then her thin lips curved upward in a smile. "Oh, yes. The gentleman Muriel Claremont said was on holiday in Brighton." She looked at the card and then fixed her eyes on Chastity. "You must meet him, my dear." To the butler, she said, "Do show him in."

Featherstone bowed and left, returning shortly with a tall man. To Chastity's utter shock, he was the man who had nearly knocked her over in the lobby of Grillon's Hotel and stolen a most improper kiss. Today, he looked positively civilized being attired as a gentleman in dark blue tail coat, gray pantaloons, mustard-colored waistcoat and neatly tied white cravat. His black shoes were nothing out of the ordinary but at least they were well polished.

The cad. She could feel a frown forming on her face. *What is he doing here?*

His face sported a wry smile as his eyes met hers. Striding into the room, he bowed before her great-aunt. "Sir Robert Powell, my lady. At your service."

Sir Robert Powell. Egad, the cad is a knight.

Aunt Agatha offered her hand. "You are the very thing we need to add to our company, Sir Robert. My dear friend, Lady Claremont, speaks well of you and your family."

He shifted his gaze to Chastity. She glared back, dismissing his manners as feigned for the benefit of her great-aunt. Perhaps he could call them forth as need dictated, like the paper flowers pulled from the sleeve of a stage conjurer.

Aunt Agatha glanced at him and then at Chastity. "Do you two know each other?"

"We have never met," Chastity said shortly. "He ran into me in London." Which, all things considered, was true.

"It was a very brief encounter," he said with amusement dancing in his eyes. "Alas, I regret we were not introduced on that occasion."

"Well, then, Chastity, may I present Sir Robert Powell?" At the mention of her name, a flicker of surprise appeared in his hazel eyes. People often reacted that way as her name was of Puritan origin; old-fashioned and not much used among the gentry. But for the legacy attached to it, she would have begged her parents to change it.

She forced a smile. "Sir Robert."

He bowed slightly only to wrinkle his brow. "*You're* Chastity? But I thought—"

"Miss Reynolds is my great-niece, Sir Robert. Did you have some other impression?"

"I did. Lady Claremont mentioned that your great-niece was visiting you and asked me to call upon her, but she led me to expect a much younger woman, a girl really."

"Upon my word!" exclaimed Aunt Agatha. "How ever did Muriel get that idea? No, no, Sir Robert. Chastity is nearly one and twenty. The perfect age." For what, Chastity's great-aunt did not say, leaving her to wonder. "Of course, I still think of her as a girl." Aunt Agatha flicked her aged and bejeweled hand in the air. "As one gets older, everyone seems very young." Gesturing to one of the sofas, she said, "Won't you join us for a drink?"

"Thank you, I'd be delighted."

As soon as Chastity settled onto the sofa next to her great-aunt, Sir Robert took a seat opposite them, crossing his long legs in front of him. Here was a man at ease, like a panther lounging in the sun.

A footman entered, likely dispatched by the efficient Featherstone, to pour sherry for Chastity and Aunt Agatha and a brandy for Sir Robert.

At that moment, Rose swept into the room, coming to a halt when she saw they were entertaining company.

"Miss Crockett," said Aunt Agatha. "Come, meet our guest, Sir Robert Powell, who has just come from London." To the man Chastity now thought of as The Rogue, Aunt Agatha said, "Miss Crockett is my great-niece's good friend and has traveled with her from Northampton."

Sir Robert got to his feet and greeted Rose in gentlemanly fashion. Chastity was tempted to utter, "Tsk."

Rose blushed the color of her carmine gown and offered her hand.

Taking it, he said with a smile, "It is a pleasure to make your acquaintance."

Rose's blush deepened and she cast her gaze downward.

Oh, for goodness' sake. Was there no end to the man's sham charm?

Chastity narrowed her eyes on her friend who lowered her lashes in coy fashion. *Oh, for the love of God.* Surely Rose was not taken in by the man's good looks and suddenly acquired manners.

Rose gracefully subsided onto the sofa next to Sir Robert and accepted a glass of sherry from the footman while surreptitiously stealing glances at the man beside her. She had no idea of the character of the man she was admiring.

"How long will you be in Brighton, Sir Robert?" asked Aunt Agatha.

He shot Chastity a glance. "I'm not certain. Several weeks, I should imagine." Then, with another look at Chastity and a smile she thought overconfident, he added, "Perhaps the entire summer."

Conceited oaf!

From the corner of her eye, Chastity glimpsed Crispin strolling into the parlor, his tail flicking from side to side, which told her he was agitated. Seeing Chastity, he came and sat at her feet, his golden eyes fixed on The Rogue.

"Your cat?" he asked, leaning toward her as he studied Crispin.

Crispin rose on all fours, arched his back and hissed. *Oh, very good, Crispin.* "Why, yes, he is," she said politely.

"Now I wonder what made him do that," said Aunt Agatha. "He's been ever so sweet since the young ladies arrived."

Chapter 5

Robbie warily eyed the huge black cat, hoping it wouldn't suddenly lunge for his throat. In an effort to make conversation, he calmly asked, "Has he a name?"

"Crispin," said the intriguing blonde. Somehow, she managed to be beautiful even with her blue eyes narrowed on him. "Named after the patron saint of shoemakers." Her words were clipped as if she only grudgingly supplied the information. Ah, well, he *had* run her down in the hotel lobby and kissed her, sins for which he would doubtless be made to pay.

"Interesting choice of names," he muttered, wondering how the cat had come to be named for a saint. Robbie was far more inclined to name him Demon for the image he portrayed. The cat stood guard at his mistress' feet, his bright gold eyes glaring at Robbie out of midnight black fur.

He had not been unhappy to discover the fair damsel he had collided with at Grillon's was The Girl Who Needed Watching. But he chaffed at the thought of what it signified. Lady Claremont would not have mistaken Chastity's age. She was too wily a woman for that. Yet there was no use becoming annoyed. He should have known the matchmaker countess was never off duty. Lady Sanborn, on the other hand, was a picture of aged innocence. Could she be in on the plan to match him with Chastity Reynolds or had that been the idea of The Grand Countess alone?

He wasn't opposed to marriage in the abstract but he would choose his own bride, one graced with spirit, intelligence and beauty. One not unlike Miss Reynolds, in point of fact. But, of course, he required a woman who actually liked him. Still, it wouldn't be a difficult assignment to escort her around Brighton, that is, if she would consent. And Jack might like to meet her friend. His uncle had always preferred women with dark hair and eyes. Robbie generally favored blondes. Well, except for that one redhead, but she'd gone and married his twin.

"My friend, Muriel, told me you are here at the king's invitation," said the great-aunt. The teasing glimmer in her eyes made him think she might be aware of Lady Claremont's scheming. But then spies were ever suspicious.

"I am," he said. "His Majesty has been very generous."

Lady Sanborn sagely nodded. "Prinny is at his best when he is giving things away."

"How wonderful you are staying at the Pavilion!" enthused Miss Crockett, her voice rising with her excitement.

He gave the ebony-haired beauty a warm smile. "My uncle, the vicomte de Saintonge, and I were invited to stay there for the summer, if we like."

He glanced at Miss Reynolds, who returned him a look of utter disdain.

Her companion, Miss Crockett, however, turned her face to him in delight. "How marvelous! I so want to see the Pavilion."

"If the king comes to Brighton while you are here," interjected Lady Sanborn, "I expect you shall. Prinny often invites me to his dinners. If you can endure the heated rooms and long evenings, I am certain he would not object to adding two attractive young ladies to his table."

"My uncle and I might escort you there ourselves," Robbie offered, trying to make up to Miss Reynolds for his initial familiarity. That would please Muriel, too. Prinny would doubtless allow them partners for one of his evenings at the Pavilion. However, one glance at Miss Reynolds told him she was not receptive to the idea.

Rose glided into Chastity's bedchamber after the evening concluded with stars in her eyes. A deep sigh preceded an exuberant description of The Rogue.

"You can't be serious!" Chastity blurted. When Rose averted her eyes, Chastity inwardly grimaced. She had not been mistaken about her friend's budding tendre for the man. "You don't even *know* him, Rose."

Her friend sat on the edge of the bed. "And why should I not admire such a man? He's ever so attractive and charming. And those shoulders." Another sigh followed. "Besides, he was sent here by a countess, a friend of your great-aunt's, who obviously trusts him to act the gentleman."

"'Act' is a most accurate word," muttered Chastity as she took up her place in one of the chairs flanking the fireplace where Rose joined her. "He is the man who nearly knocked me to the floor of the hotel lobby in London without, I remind you, a hint of an apology."

Rose's brows rose. "He is *that* man?"

"The very same, which might explain Crispin's reaction to him." She stared into the fire burning on the grate, the memory of his demanding kiss vivid in her mind. She could still feel his lips on hers and was shamed by her reaction, giving in to the power of his kiss. A log collapsed sending sparks up the chimney and startling her out of her reverie. "Why would a friend of my great-aunt send him to call upon me?"

"Yes, that is curious. And how could she think you a young girl?" Rose shrugged and returned Chastity a steady gaze. "Still, if he and his uncle can gain us entrance to the Pavilion or an invitation to dine with the king, I would put up with most any bad habits he might possess."

"I daresay he has some you would not like," said Chastity, mentally listing what those might be as she got to her feet and went to stir the fire. The Rogue's handsome visage appeared in the flames, like Lucifer rising out of his element. "Womanizing, wagering and drinking until deep in his cups doubtless are the least of his lesser attributes."

"That sounds like a description of Prinny," said Rose with a chuckle. "And, as I recall, you were inclined to like him."

Chastity reclaimed her seat on one of the chairs in front of the fire. "I suppose I am, for he is, by all accounts, a jolly host to his friends."

"You didn't like the staid country gentlemen of Northampton," Rose reminded her. "At least Sir Robert isn't one of those."

"Indeed. More dangerous, perhaps, yet he and his uncle might be useful in showing us more of Brighton." *If I can tolerate his smirks.* "That is why I accepted his invitation for us to join them for a ride tomorrow."

Rose smiled, a wistful expression on her face. "I am so pleased you did."

Owing to his promise to The Grand Countess, Robbie had offered a ride around Brighton to the woman he now thought of as The Keeper of the Demon Cat. Jack would want to meet Miss Crockett, of course, so he invited his uncle along. It was unfortunate that the fetching creature Robbie had encountered in London had taken a dislike to him.

Over breakfast, they discussed the ladies. "I must compliment you, Nephew. You wasted no time in finding us two lovelies, as you describe them, though I expect, from what you have told me, Miss Reynolds is not overly fond of you."

"In that you are correct," Robbie said with a frown. It occurred to him that Miss Reynolds might be a country hoyden in search of a man of good fortune, excluding him, of course. Nevertheless, he had promised Lady Claremont to see to the lady's welfare, and he would. Perhaps he could find her a suitable husband. Surely The Grand Countess would be pleased with that.

"What of Miss Crockett?" By the look on Jack's face, he eagerly anticipated meeting her.

"Unlike her friend, Miss Crockett is all that is sweet, a country miss to be sure, but one with a biddable temperament. She, too, comes from Northampton, but from her proper speech and manners, I expect she had a governess."

"Tell me she has dark hair and you'll set my heart pounding."

Robbie chuckled. "She does."

"Then I shall leave the virago to you."

The morning had begun with a drizzle but by ten o'clock, though a chill remained in the air, the sun was making an effort to shine as they reined their horses in front of Lady Sanborn's house. They'd brought two more of the king's horses for the ladies.

In the entry hall, Robbie bid good day to Miss Reynolds and introduced Jack to Lady Sanborn and Miss Crockett. Thankfully, the Demon Cat was nowhere in sight.

Soon after, the ladies gathered up the skirts of their riding habits, took their short whips in hand and followed Robbie and Jack outside.

Robbie had to admit The Keeper of the Demon Cat made a beautiful picture in her crimson riding habit with her blonde curls dangling from her jaunty hat set at an angle on her head. As she had gathered her skirts to walk down the stairs, he had glimpsed the beginning of a slim calf above a stylish half boot.

With a sly smile, he said, "I selected a spirited mare for you, Miss Reynolds, assuming that would be your choice."

Chastity met his impudent gaze, annoyed he should think to know her so well. Pursing her lips, she turned her attention to the roan mare waiting for her. She might not have liked that he had been the one choosing the horse, but she had to smile as she looked into the mare's intelligent brown eyes. The Rogue, who had knocked on Aunt Agatha's door attired as a gentleman, had guessed correctly.

His uncle, the vicomte de Saintonge, led Rose to another mare. "Allow me to assist," he said before giving her a hand up into the sidesaddle. The Florentia blue riding suit Rose had chosen this morning set off her coloring to perfection and, though they could not be observed in their full glory, the blue half boots Chastity had given her were lovely.

Chastity had been pleased to discover the uncle was not an older man as his noble title and relationship to Sir Robert suggested. Rather, he was a very handsome man of an age with his nephew but with perfect manners. His auburn hair fell in soft waves to his nape, a complement to his finely carved features and cinnamon-colored eyes. His accented voice had the same effect on her as a glass of sherry after a trying day.

"May I help you into your saddle?" Sir Robert asked.

Shifting her gaze to him, she said, "If you will, thank you." It was impossible for a lady to mount on her own or she would have done so.

He made a quick check of the girth and straps before coming to stand before her.

Thinking he would hold out his cupped hands for her to step into, she put her short whip in her left hand and reached for the pommel, whereupon he placed his hands on her waist and lifted her into the sidesaddle in one quick move. "Sir!" she protested, resisting the temptation to swat him with her whip. Again, he had done with her as he willed with no deference to her being a lady.

"I thought it the most efficient way to seat you," he said. "Do you object?"

She settled herself into the saddle, hooking her knee around the pommel. "Too late for that," she acknowledged, impressed, notwithstanding her pique, at his strength in lifting her without effort. She was no tiny thing, after all, taller than many women. Still, it was not the done thing to touch an unfamiliar lady so. By his manner, she judged he was quite indifferent to her protest. Amused, more like, given his teasing manner.

He looked the picture of a well-dressed London buck, his neckcloth perfectly tied in an understated manner and his beaver hat perched upon his dark brown hair. But he was no dandy. The fit of his coat suggested he spent considerable time at Mr. Jackson's boxing club. But then, what else did a man of leisure do in London, she asked herself, besides participating in sporting events, horse racing and cards? *Oh, yes, and women.*

From the front door, Aunt Agatha stood watching them. Her gown, the color of the daffodils in her garden, spoke of her cheery mood. Chastity had noticed her levity at breakfast when she bubbled over with joy at some new plants she was installing on the side of the house. Had she witnessed the impropriety of Sir Robert's lifting her great-niece into the saddle? Perhaps not as she'd said nothing of it. Instead, she waved them off. "Enjoy yourselves!"

The four of them rode abreast as they followed the path Sir Robert chose. It led them first in front of the Royal Pavilion where they paused to admire the otherworldly domes and turrets rising from the surrounding vegetation as if out of a dream.

The sheer magnificence of the king's Brighton home brought to mind Coleridge's *Kubla Khan*. Under her breath, Chastity began to recite,

In Xanadu did Kubla Khan
A stately pleasure-dome decree:
Where Alph, the sacred river, ran
Through caverns measureless to man
Down to a sunless sea.

"The king's Pavilion does seem as if it were lifted out of the Far East," said Sir Robert. "Outside, it speaks of India but much of the interior decoration is in the Chinese style with fantastic dragons, lotus blossoms and walls painted to make you believe you are in a bamboo forest."

Chastity looked at him askance, thinking he must be jesting, but his expression told her he was serious. "Aunt Agatha tells such stories of it, I did wonder. She calls it 'Prinny's fantasy'."

"And so it is," put in the vicomte.

"Do you like what you see, Miss Reynolds?" asked Sir Robert.

She allowed a smile to form on her face as she gazed at the other-worldly Pavilion. "I like that it's not ordinary but speaks of dreams and exotic places."

Sir Robert regarded her for a moment before turning his attention again to the Pavilion. "You are a romantic, Miss Reynolds."

"Not I, sir. I'm as practical as salt." In truth, Chastity did harbor romantic notions though she would not admit that to him.

He gave her a disbelieving look and then gazed again at the Pavilion. "I expect Prinny's Brighton home provided the escape he needed from his father's palace of piety and pride. George III never understood his son."

"Do you think his father drove him away?" she asked, genuinely curious.

"Most certainly. Perhaps more than anyone else, Prinny's father was responsible for his son becoming The Grand Corinthian. His mother, too, did not favor him, even though he was heir to the throne."

Chastity pondered this for a moment feeling more sympathy for the stylish young prince who did not fit with his dour family and had sought acceptance in other places. "My great-aunt tells me Prinny is revered in Brighton. Did you know that he is expected to visit soon?"

The Rogue smiled. "I did, yes."

His smile had the smug air of one who hid a secret he had no intention of sharing. "Come, let us continue our ride."

They turned up the Steyne.

"Lady Sanborn says the whole town is making ready for the king," said Rose.

"As I would expect," said Sir Robert, a smile playing at the corner of his mouth. "Prinny is the fire that lights the hearth of the town, the one whose presence makes the Brighton Season what it is. Where he goes, the *ton* follows."

Chastity was certain Rose thought The Rogue's smile was directed at her for she gave him a look of adoration. "Sir Robert, will you give us a tour of the king's Pavilion?"

"I am sure that can be arranged," he said, darting a glance at Chastity.

Rose beamed at him.

Chastity fought the temptation to roll her eyes. Over pastries and coffee that morning, Rose had spoken of Sir Robert in glowing terms. But the arrogant rogue was not the suitor Chastity had in mind for her friend. Better the continental uncle than the rakish nephew.

As they paused to take in the magnificence of the Pavilion, the vicomte spoke in his rich melodic voice. "The Pavilion makes me think of that collection of Arabian stories I once read, *The Thousand and One Nights*...an intriguing set of tales."

"I shall have to read them," remarked Chastity, which drew a smile from the vicomte, revealing a dimple in one cheek. An auburn curl fell across his forehead making him appear younger than he was. The uncle fascinated her. Clearly he was French in dress and manner, yet his English was flawless. "You make me eager to see the inside of the Pavilion. The stables are said to be extravagant, too."

"They must be seen to be believed," he said. "They are home to more than sixty horses. Why, the domed building itself dwarfs the Pavilion."

Given the vicomte's accent, Chastity had to know what place he called home. "Do you make your home in France?"

"My home is on the Isle of Guernsey," he said, "which, I expect you know, is a dependency of the British Crown. French is spoken there as well as English. My father, the comte, has a chateau and vineyards in the west of France in what was the province of Saintonge before the revolution. My family travels frequently between France and England. My mother is English, you see. Like Robbie's family, we are in shipping."

"Shipping?" Chastity asked, surprised. "Do you mean the importing trade?"

"Robbie's father and mine are both shipmasters," said the vicomte. His lips curved up in a smile as his gaze rested on Sir Robert. "They are merchants now but once privateers."

Chastity had difficulty thinking of The Rogue as "Robbie", though his smile conjured images of a small boy always into mischief. She could well believe his father was a privateer. While she was aware of the role of privateers in the war with France, she would never have thought Sir Robert had ships. "*You* have ships?"

"More like a shipping empire," his uncle interjected.

Sir Robert raised a brow. "Do you find that surprising, Miss Reynolds?"

"Well, yes." She had thought him an indulged, well-moneyed London buck. She could imagine family wealth amassed through ill-gotten gains, but it had never occurred to her that he might be a man of industry engaged in something as serious as a shipping enterprise. There was certainly nothing of the sea captain about him. "Have you sailed?"

His eyes fixed on the reins in his gloved hands, he said, "Once or twice."

"My nephew, Miss Reynolds," put in the vicomte, "is a talented navigator, a man of coveted skill on the sea."

Sir Robert blushed, that is, if a rogue can blush. "The ships belong to Powell and Sons Shipping, the family business."

"How many brothers have you?" she asked.

"Two older and a twin, five minutes younger."

"And Robbie never lets Nash forget it," said the vicomte, laughing.

"How about you, Miss Reynolds," the uncle asked her. "Tell us of your family."

"I have two sisters, one older and one younger. My father is a country squire and an eccentric designer of men's shoes and boots."

"Chastity designs ladies' shoes as her hobby," said Rose. She extended her half boot. "A sample of her talent."

"An unusual pursuit for a lady," said Sir Robert, appearing to admire the blue half boot though it occurred to Chastity he could well be admiring Rose's ankle instead.

"I think it's a splendid talent!" exclaimed the vicomte. "And you, Miss Crockett? Do you have any unusual talents?"

"No, not really," Rose said, apologetically.

"That's not true," Chastity protested. "Rose has a voice like an angel and can play the pianoforte rather well."

"You will have to play for us," replied the vicomte. "My mother plays the cello and my father the violin, so we are a musical family. Robbie's, too."

"Do either of you have musical talent?" asked Chastity, trying to imagine The Rogue with a musical instrument.

He and his uncle shared a look. "Not that I know of," said the vicomte. Chastity had the feeling each of them was thinking of some other skill they had chosen not to reveal.

From the Pavilion, they turned the horses south, heading toward the shore. When they reached the Marine Parade, they rode along the seafront. A brisk breeze from the sea made Chastity glad she had worn her warm merino riding habit, the deep red color the same as the red flowers on her brown half boots.

During the ride along the seashore, she managed to exchange pleasantries with The Rogue while Rose chatted merrily with the vicomte who Sir Robert had called "Jack". An odd name for a French vicomte.

As they turned toward the Steyne, Chastity fell silent, thinking of Sir Robert and her new image of him. He carried himself with confidence, his manner with the horses was assured, and now she learned he was a navigator of ships, the industry that had made Great Britain the sovereign of the seas.

She was faintly embarrassed that she had lumped him in with the notorious bucks of London, about whom she had been warned. It was all due to how they'd met, of course. Thinking about how rude he had been and the kiss he had claimed, she recalled what a disorderly lot sailors were. He could well be a rogue of the first order notwithstanding his family business. Hadn't Prinny been just such a one and he ruled a kingdom? Thus, she would remain on her guard. After all, Crispin had taken a dim view of the man and she trusted the cat's instincts.

Robbie and Jack bid the ladies good day and began their short ride back to the Pavilion, the two extra horses in tow. As he rode, Robbie thought about The Keeper of the Demon Cat who had made clear her dislike of him. Perhaps he should not have taken the liberty he had, but her sweet lips had called to him and the reward had been almost worth her present ire.

The two young women from Northampton were certainly attractive, each in her own way, and very different from the London women he had known. Miss Reynolds intrigued him, as Lady Claremont no doubt knew she would. His own expectations for a country miss were not consistent with the traits Miss Reynolds possessed. He would have expected a young woman from the country of marriageable age to be overawed, to simper and flirt, especially if the man were well moneyed. Miss Reynolds did neither. She obviously admired Jack, but then most women did, and titles often impressed women from untitled families.

But Miss Reynolds gave no hint of being superficial or impressed by his own family's shipping enterprise.

A sudden thought sprang into his head. "Snow White and Rose Red," he murmured aloud.

"What's that?" asked Jack.

"Miss Reynolds and Miss Crockett. It's as if they emerged from a fairy tale I was reading to one of my young nephews just before we left London."

"Do tell, old chap."

Robbie reached into his memory for details. The boy had curled up on his lap fascinated with the story. "As I recall, it's a tale about two sisters, one fair and one dark, whose kindness gets them entangled with an ungrateful dwarf. In fact," he said, remembering, "that's the name of the tale, *The Ungrateful Dwarf*."

"Do not leave me in a state of suspense. What happened?"

"Well, the sisters give shelter to a bear during the winter and are surprised to find him gone in the spring."

"They didn't know much about bears," said Jack. "What happened then?"

"Afterwards, the sisters encountered this nasty dwarf who they helped out of several scrapes. One day, they discover the dwarf with a great treasure of gold and he turned on them in a rage. Just then, the bear reappeared to save the sisters. As it turned out, the bear was actually a prince who had been cursed by the dwarf who had stolen the prince's treasure. Freed from the curse, the prince married Snow White and Rose Red married his brother."

"I see," said Jack, "Now, we have only to figure out which of us is to be the bear and who, precisely, is the evil dwarf."

"'Tis only a children's story," said Robbie, wondering why he had thought of it. "I'm sure it was the ladies' strikingly different appearance that brought the story to mind, that and Miss Crockett's given name."

"By the bye," said Jack. "I do not believe the fair one is the shrew you made her out to be. For me, she had only smiles."

"Don't be too sure of yourself. You have yet to meet her demon cat."

Jack laughed. "Oh, yes, the cat you warned me about."

It was as Robbie turned into the path leading to the Pavilion's stables that he had the queerest feeling he was being watched. A silly notion when he considered the other riders passing him and Jack. But a spy's instincts had not failed him in his many missions for the Crown. So, while he did not mention his discomfort to Jack, neither did he dismiss it.

Chapter 6

"Good fortune, my dears!" Aunt Agatha pronounced from her seat at the head of the dining table as Chastity and Rose joined her for breakfast a few days later. Her great-aunt had donned an orange morning gown with puffed sleeves and stripes of bright yellow ribbon from the high waist to the hem. It was a surprising choice of colors for a lady her age but they suited her lively personality.

Chastity instantly thought of slippers she would design that would complement the dress. Taking her seat, she asked, "What is this good fortune?"

"Maria Fitzherbert has invited us to tea tomorrow afternoon!"

"Lovely!" exclaimed Chastity. "I so look forward to meeting her." Placing a slice of pound cake on her plate, she watched the footman pour steaming chocolate into her cup, the morning drink favored by her great-aunt.

"How was your seaside stroll?" asked Aunt Agatha, rising to look out the window. "Windy, I expect, as the branches of the trees are blowing around."

Rose set down her coffee. "Our walk was most refreshing, Lady Sanborn."

"Brisk, if the truth be told," said Chastity. She had been glad for the fire burning in the hearth that gave warmth to the room. "You are right about the wind, Aunt. The wind off the Channel was downright cold. And if one is to walk along the shore, one must traverse over rocks. Definitely a cause for half boots and not slippers," she said, shooting a glance at Rose who had worn what Chastity considered an insubstantial pair of shoes for such an outing.

Aunt Agatha returned to her seat. "Ah, yes, the shingles are a nuisance. As for 'brisk', it will grow warmer as the day goes on, though the shingles will remain. If you enjoy the seafront, one thing you simply must try is sea bathing. The dippers, who assist you to the water, operate all year as cold seawater is considered beneficial."

Chastity shivered, still chilled from her walk with Rose. Taking up her chocolate, she took a hearty drink of the warm liquid. "The idea of sea bathing appeals but perhaps not in frigid water."

Aunt Agatha reached over and patted Chastity's hand. "I always like to wait for a warm day myself before seeking out the bathing machines. By then, everyone will be flocking to the water, of course."

"Bathing machine?" asked Rose.

"Those small chambers that are wheeled into the water so that a lady may take the seawaters in privacy. 'Tis quite invigorating."

The idea of swimming, perhaps without clothes, sounded delightfully wicked to Chastity. "I think I would like to try that."

"Then you shall," said her great-aunt. "We *all* shall," she enthused. "In the meantime, until the weather warms, there will be shopping and other things to occupy us."

"I would love to go to a shop that sells silk cloth," Chastity said. "I've a mind to purchase some for slippers."

"Slippers?" asked Aunt Agatha.

"Chastity designs shoes," said Rose. "Beautiful slippers and half boots. You should ask her to show you the ones she brought with her that are her own designs."

"How is it I never knew this?"

Chastity recalled just when she began to design shoes in earnest. "I don't think I was doing as much of it when I last saw you, not as I am now."

"I should be most interested to see them," said Aunt Agatha with a smile. "Let me see, what else might you two look forward to? Well, *soirées*, which reminds me, I am planning a reception to introduce you to my friends."

Chastity exchanged a knowing look with Rose, suspecting they both pictured a gathering of white-haired men and women speaking of the days gone by, but she would not discourage her great-aunt's kindness. "When might that be, Aunt?"

"I am thinking 'twill be a week from Saturday. That will allow time for word to spread that I have young, attractive guests."

Chastity helped herself to another piece of cake, thinking of the evening gowns she and Rose had packed. She had only to decide what shoes she would wear.

As the morning wore on, the weather turned dismal. Chastity spent the middle of the day inside, her sketchpad in her lap, designing slippers for her aunt. Rose, sitting beside her, read a novel. Her great-aunt, whose chair, like theirs, faced the warming fire, devoted herself to needlework. As Chastity looked closer, she glimpsed embroidery featuring an intricate sunflower in bright yellow. It gave her an idea for the shoes she would design.

"Aunt," said Chastity, "since we're to take tea with Mrs. Fitzherbert tomorrow afternoon, might you tell us more about your friend?"

Aunt Agatha looked up from her needlework. "I'll be interested in your opinion once you've met her. I find Maria as poised as any noblewoman, perhaps more so. She conducts herself with all propriety, even teases me for my extravagant ways. I suppose I should add she is still lovely even at two and sixty though she has become a bit plump. But then the same could be said of me," she added with a twinkle in her eye. "There are men in Brighton who seek her company but, for the most part, she remains a solitary figure, still faithful to her unfaithful husband."

"But they are not together," put in Rose.

"No," said Aunt Agatha sadly. "After nearly ten years as man and wife, he cast her off to marry that German princess who was foisted upon him."

"That hasn't gone well," said Chastity.

"Indeed," said her great-aunt. "And once Princess Charlotte was born, Prinny, who had come to hate his German wife, left her to pursue Maria once more."

"And she took him in?" Chastity asked, aghast.

Aunt Agatha nodded.

Chastity screwed up her face in a grimace. "How could she deign to take back that... that man?"

Rose inhaled sharply. "Chas, you speak of the king..."

"You must understand," explained Aunt Agatha, "in the Catholic Church's eyes, they were still married. Maria is a woman of faith. She only returned to the prince after consulting with Rome and was advised that she was the prince's true wife."

"So she went back to him," said Rose under her breath. "Imagine!"

Chastity stared into the fire trying to imagine what it must have been like for Maria Fitzherbert, not to share the name of the man she loved, not to be acknowledged as his wife.

"I think they were happy for the next years they were together," said Aunt Agatha. "But nine years ago, she broke it off."

"Why?" asked Rose, her brows wrinkling.

Aunt Agatha shook her head. "Because of his philandering. It was quite outrageous, you know."

"The poor woman," said Rose.

"Another victim of a rogue," added Chastity, remembering her own painful experience.

"Maria prefers the quiet life," said her great-aunt. "Like you, she was a squire's daughter, a country lady. Though she does not say, I think she still loves the king." Concentrating on her embroidery, Aunt Agatha said, "She often wears that diamond-studded locket the prince gave her, the one containing his picture. He was a very handsome youth." She raised her head, staring into the distance as if seeing the young prince. "Tall with magnificent blue eyes, light red hair, clear skin and rosy cheeks." She looked back at her stitchery. "Oh, yes, quite handsome. And charming."

"Rogues are invariably handsome," put in Chastity, an image of Sir Robert coming into her mind unbidden. "And charming." She determined right then not to allow herself to be charmed by him. She did not wish to end up brokenhearted like Maria Fitzherbert.

Aunt Agatha glanced up from her needlework. "The worst of it is that even though he married her before a priest and spent nearly twenty years of his life with her, he allowed the world to think she was no more than his mistress."

"Why?" asked Rose.

"Because of her commoner status and her Catholic faith, of course." Seeing Chastity's frown, she added, "He wanted the Crown, you see."

"A rogue, indeed," pronounced Chastity, stiffening her resolve to resist the allure of Sir Robert, for she remembered his kiss. Any woman would.

Robbie was aware the instant the king arrived at the Pavilion. Servants straightened at their posts, tugging their waistcoats into place. Fires were stoked to a blaze. And the servants attending the king's suite of rooms hurried in for a last check.

Robbie had persuaded Jack to join him in the Long Gallery where they now stood awaiting the king's appearance. Soon, Prinny strode into the Gallery, his long legs quickly eating up the carpet. Covering his hair was the same curled auburn wig Robbie had seen him wear in London. On the left breast of his coat the large diamond star of the Order of the Garter flashed in the light of the lanterns above him. Behind him, his entourage of servants hurried along in an attempt to keep up.

As he was about to pass Robbie and Jack, he came to a sudden halt. "Sir Robert! How do you find my Pavilion since your last visit?"

"Magnificent, Your Majesty," he said bowing. "As is the pair of grays you generously bestowed upon me." With a glance in Jack's direction, Robbie said, "May I present my uncle, Jean-Jacques Henri Donet, vicomte de Saintonge?"

Prinny regarded Jack with a curious expression. "A French vicomte has come to visit us?"

Jack bowed. "With your gracious permission, Sire."

The king's face broke out in a wide grin. "We are glad the French monarchy has regained its titles, young man. You are welcome to join your nephew at the many entertainments to which he will be invited."

The king took a deep breath and exhaled. "I am weary of London and alive, once again, now that I breathe Brighton's air."

Without another word, he marched off toward his apartments, his entourage acknowledging Robbie and Jack with brief nods before scurrying off to join the king.

"He cuts quite a figure," remarked Jack. "A royal presence even if he had not donned his splendid attire."

"I have always thought so," said Robbie. "And he appears to be in a happy mood. Meanwhile, let us see to our breakfast. Tiller told me it's being served in the South Galleries."

The room set for breakfast was smaller than others in the Pavilion, but the walls were painted a vivid azure blue and overlaid with strips of paper made to look like bamboo. A footman led them to a small table where Robbie pulled out a chair whose legs and back were also made to look like bamboo.

"Would you like coffee and a newspaper, sir?" the footman asked them.

"Most assuredly," said Robbie.

The coffee arrived shortly along with *The London Times*. Jack lifted the paper and began to read.

Robbie contented himself with his coffee as he'd had only the one cup Tiller had brought to his chamber. "Is it possible to get eggs and ham?" he asked the footman when he again approached.

"Oh, yes, sir. The Pavilion's kitchens can prepare most anything."

Jack looked over the edge of the paper. "I'll have the same, *merci*." When the waiter walked away, Jack said, "You'll be pleased to hear they have captured all of those criminals who thought to attack your Cabinet."

"Oh?" Robbie said with feigned indifference as he experienced a flood of relief. "When will the trial be?"

"It says here that the trial begins this week in Session House of the Old Bailey." Jack set down the paper and lifted his coffee to his lips. "Twill soon be over."

Robbie would only completely relax when the conspirators had met their inevitable ends. Only then would he know a measure of satisfaction that his last assignment was truly over.

Chastity followed Aunt Agatha and Rose to their next-door neighbor's house, her great-aunt explaining that the house in which Mrs. Fitzherbert lived had been a gift to her from her husband when he was the Prince of Wales. It boasted a long veranda overlooking a well-tended front garden. Beyond the garden lay the Steyne and the park in its midst.

The butler opened the door and immediately recognized Aunt Agatha, smiling widely at her. "Lady Sanborn, do come in. Mrs. Fitzherbert is awaiting you and your guests in the parlor."

"I know the way," said Chastity's great-aunt, raising her hand. With

Chastity and Rose in tow, she glided toward a sunny room with tall paned windows facing the Steyne.

The smell of freshly-baked pastry greeted them as they entered. "Oh, you are serving my favorite!" exclaimed Aunt Agatha.

Mrs. Fitzherbert rose from a green upholstered chair near the windows. A shaft of sunlight made her silvered golden-blonde hair glisten. Chastity thought her dark brown eyes were quite lovely. "I have not forgotten you are partial to apricot tarts, Agatha. You and Lord Alvanley," she added with a warm smile.

As she approached them, her gaze shifted from Chastity to Rose. "Introduce me to your young friends."

"May I present my great-niece, Miss Chastity Reynolds," said Aunt Agatha.

Chastity briefly curtseyed.

"And her friend, Miss Rose Crockett."

Rose, too, made her curtsey.

Mrs. Fitzherbert gave them a warm smile. "Brighton has not seen two lovelier young women since we were girls, Agatha."

"I don't doubt you were lovely, Maria, but I cannot say the same for myself."

"Modest as always." Maria Fitzherbert gestured toward the gold sofa facing two chairs upholstered in the same green brocade as the chair in which she'd been sitting. "Come, sit. I shall pour."

Once each had a cup of tea and a slice of tart on the table between them, Mrs. Fitzherbert said, "Has your great-aunt told you that we have become good friends?"

"Oh, yes," said Chastity. "Rose and I were eager to meet you, Mrs. Fitzherbert."

"You may call me 'Mrs. Fitz'. My closest friends do, well, except for my particular friends who call me by my given name."

Mrs. Fitz asked them about what they'd seen of Brighton and, hearing they had done little yet, proceeded to describe the summer activities they could expect in the seaside town, promising to show them her favorite shops in Castle Square. "It's the Bond Street of Brighton. A part of it extends onto North Street, which has dozens of shops."

Chastity would have described Mrs. Fitz as a handsome woman with a calm assurance of one who is content within herself. Stately, if a bit plump, her skin was still smooth and fair. And there was a regal air about her, even in the simple gown of blue cambric she wore. Chastity could well imagine her as a queen, more so than the woman who, in the eyes of the populace, claimed that title. Perhaps in Brighton, however, Mrs. Fitz was treated like a queen. Aunt Agatha had hinted as much.

"Would you like another cup of tea?" she asked Chastity and Rose.

"Yes, please," said Rose.

Chastity nodded.

Their hostess reached for the silver teapot but was interrupted by Aunt Agatha. "Do let me pour, Maria."

"If you like," she said, resuming her seat. Then, returning her attention to Chastity and Rose, she said, "There will be young men for you to meet here in Brighton. They come for the races in July and before that the gambling and theater. The town has many entertainments to offer."

"Maria is very good at cards," said Chastity's aunt. "She will know the best places for a lady to play."

Chastity did enjoy the game of whist and would look forward to an evening of cards.

"There are several good ones," said Mrs. Fitz. "But perhaps young ladies such as you might be more interested in the balls. One is held at The Old Ship Inn each Monday. Agatha can act the chaperone and introduce you to some of the young men. And there are private balls, as well."

"I love to dance," said Chastity, wondering if Sir Robert would attend any of the balls when he had the Royal Pavilion to enjoy. Silently, she chided herself for thinking of him. Her mission, after all, was to find a match for her friend, not fend off The Rogue.

Aunt Agatha refreshed their tea and helped herself to another slice of tart. "We plan to indulge in sea bathing, too, Maria."

"Knowing your proclivities, Agatha, I am not surprised, however, I shall leave the bathing machines to you and your young charges. I don't care if the water is good for one's health. I prefer my own bath, heated to just the right temperature."

Chastity liked a hot bath, too, but where else could she indulge in sea bathing?

"My friend likes to do her own market shopping," said Aunt Agatha. Her eyes shone with pride. "Though I suspect your cook wishes you did not, Maria."

"That is because Mrs. Ayers thinks I buy too much. I love to watch the ships returning in the morning and listening to the fishermen's wives with their fresh catches. It seems only right I should buy their fish." To Chastity she said, "The fish market is a lively place. Mackerel will soon be in season. And there is always fresh sole and turbot."

"I should like to visit the fish market," remarked Chastity. "Rose and I saw the ships returning this morning on our walk."

"Chastity discovered the shingles make for difficult treading," put in Aunt Agatha.

"I do agree," said Mrs. Fitz, "but if one is to traverse the beach, they cannot be avoided."

"Shall we take my great-niece and her friend shopping on the mor-row?" Aunt Agatha inquired.

"If the weather is fine, why not?" replied Mrs. Fitz. "They might like to see Hannington's department store." To Chastity and Rose, she said, "Agatha is a splendid shopper as her many...ah, costumes have no doubt told you."

"Now don't go speaking ill of my brightly-colored gowns," scolded Chastity's great-aunt in a friendly tone. "They bring me great joy."

"Oh, very well," said Mrs. Fitz. "We shall shop for garish hats, bright silks and shimmering gewgaws!"

Aunt Agatha laughed. "Indeed, we shall!"

Chastity enjoyed the repartee between the two women. It was clear they enjoyed each other's company. They laughed and teased and cajoled until Chastity found it quite impossible not to laugh with them. She discerned that Mrs. Fitz's spirit was unaffected by her many trials at the king's hands, making Chastity admire her greatly. Serene and secure, no wonder all of Brighton held her in high esteem. She'd been wronged by a rogue and survived with no bitterness on her tongue.

"They remind me of us," Chastity later said to Rose when they were alone. "Mrs. Fitz is my great-aunt's anchor as you are mine."

"I have always thought so," said Rose. "You don't mind, do you?"

"Not in the least. I expect we will be enjoying adventures together when we are their age. I'll still be visiting you when you are married and your children grown."

"And I will serve you an apricot tart!" Rose said, laughing.

The next morning at breakfast, before their shopping trip with Mrs. Fitz, Aunt Agatha waited until the footman set the teapot on the table and left, and then said, "I did not want to speak of it in front of Maria yesterday, but we have been invited to dine with the king at the Pavilion tonight."

Chastity shared a look of excitement with Rose. "That is marvelous. Just think, Rose, we'll see the Pavilion in all its splendor." Her great-aunt had told her of its grand décor and the evening entertainments. But to experience them in person would be the highlight of her trip.

"To think we shall dine with the king," said Rose wistfully. "I shall have to write my parents."

"I wonder who the king's other guests will be," said Chastity.

"There is always a surprise," her Aunt Agatha chimed in.

The first thing Robbie noticed as he and Jack strolled through the

Banqueting Room Gallery on their way to the dinner to begin promptly at six o'clock was the heat of the rooms. The temperature suggested every fireplace in the Pavilion had been stoked to a hot blaze. They had been out all day, first riding, then enjoying the local taverns and finally scouting the best places for cards. Having experienced the cool air from the sea, the air in the Pavilion was oppressive and warmer than he'd remembered.

"I had forgotten how warm the king likes his rooms," he said to Jack.

"A few hours of this and we will be melting," came Jack's reply. "Versailles is often cold with all the glass and high ceilings. *Dieu merci*, 'tis nothing like this."

They had not yet reached the entrance to the Banqueting Room when a liveried footman approached Robbie with a folded letter on a small silver tray. "Sir Robert?"

"Yes," said Robbie.

"This was delivered less than an hour ago," said the footman, holding the tray out for him. "I've been watching for you."

Robbie thanked him and lifted the note, stepping to one side to read it.

You horrid spy! You brood with hellish delight on the sacrifice ye intend to make of those poor creatures you took out of Cato Street on the pretense of punishing them for what you yourself instigated. But know this, on an approaching day when you least expect it, ye will suffer. You will pay!

The note was unsigned. A lump arose in Robbie's throat and his hand holding the note went rigid.

"What is it, Robbie?"

He must have gone quite pale for Jack's tone was suddenly serious. Robbie wadded up the note and threw it into the nearest fireplace. "Nothing important. In any event, it can wait. Let us proceed."

They walked through the large opening before them and into the Banqueting Room. For a moment, Robbie was distracted by the grandeur around them.

People milled about the long table set for twenty guests. From a shallow dome above the center of the room painted with palm fronds, there hung a magnificent crystal chandelier suspended from the claws of the silvered dragon.

Jack gazed up at the ceiling. *"Mon Dieu!* It is as you say! *Fantastique."*

Above the dangling crystals of the extravagant chandelier were six smaller dragons exhaling light through lotus glass shades of gas lamps. Robbie had seen it before but, still, the workmanship never ceased to amaze him.

"'Tis dazzling," Jack murmured. "However, the room smells like a bordello. Too much scent, even for a Frenchman."

Robbie nodded his agreement but his mind was elsewhere. *How have they found me? And if all the conspirators were captured who could have authored the note?*

The same footman who had delivered the missive approached. "Sir Robert and Monsieur le vicomte, may I show you to your seats?"

Robbie wanted to ask him if he recognized who had brought the note but did not wish to draw attention to his interest in the matter. Instead, he nodded and, with Jack beside him, followed the footman farther into the room, past wall panels featuring scenes of the royal court of ancient China.

Against the tall windows covering the left side of the large room, servers stood at side tables pouring red wine into decanters. The sun had not yet set and light poured into the room adding to the heat from the fireplaces and gas lanterns, making the room's temperature nearly unbearable.

Down the middle of the main table marched golden candelabra and baskets spilling over with grapes and other fruits.

"Your seats," the footman said, gesturing to two chairs, one on either side of a lady. As she turned to look up at him, Robbie recognized Lady Lade, wife of Sir John Lade. Though she was seated, he recalled her being a very tall woman at six feet, who her friends fondly referred to as "the Amazon".

"Good evening, my lady," he said. "May I introduce you to my uncle, the vicomte de Saintonge, or, as he would prefer, M'sieur Donet?"

Jack bowed over her offered hand. *"Enchanté."*

Letty returned him a wide grin of approval. "A Frenchman, how *merveilleux*. Are you as much of a devil as your nephew? And do you ride?"

"Oui to both, my lady," Jack said in a tone of feigned innocence, belied by the sly grin that accompanied it.

"Then the evening promises to be quite memorable," she said, returning his grin. "Wait until I tell Sir John. He's just over there." She gestured across the table. "Too far for him to hear in this crowd."

The conversations that filled the Banqueting Room had risen to a cacophony and, agreeing he could not be heard, Robbie waved to Sir John.

As Robbie took his seat on her right, Letty said, "What's this I hear of you being made a baronet?" When he did not reply, she said, "You devil! You've done something very brave, haven't you?"

"I cannot imagine what," Robbie said with a shrug. He intended to reveal nothing.

"Damn you, Powell!" She slapped his sleeve with her fan. "I must know what noble deed it was, else I'll have little to tell the Brighton gossips."

He returned her a smirk. "Just as I feared."

At that moment, the band that had been quietly sitting in one corner began playing *God Save the King*. Everyone got to their feet and turned to welcome the king who strode into the room in his glorious finery, his current mistress, Elizabeth, Marchioness Conyngham, at his side. That her husband was not in attendance was likely noted by no one, save possibly Robbie.

The king stopped at the head of the table and raised a hand to motion them back to their seats. The music stopped.

Once he had seen the marchioness to her place beside him, the king said, "Welcome, my friends! I trust you will enjoy the splendid menu this evening. I approved it myself. After we dine, there will be rooms for cards with plenty of refreshments. And, of course, there will be music."

Easing his great girth into the chair a footman held out for him, the king accepted a glass of iced champagne. Immediately, the first course of green turtle soup was served.

Robbie was relieved to hear the band begin to play something more conducive to the dinner hour.

Conversations resumed. Robbie turned from Letty, who was getting acquainted with Jack, and introduced himself to the woman on his right, who had slipped into her chair as the band stopped playing. The attractive woman turned out to be Dorothea, Countess Lieven. Many tales were told of the intelligent and politically savvy wife of the Russian Ambassador to Great Britain—and of her affairs—but he had not met her before now. He judged her to be about his age, perhaps a bit younger and nearly his height.

"Sir Robert, you are a friend of His Majesty?"

"I like to think so, Madam."

The footmen served steamed turbot in butter sauce, a mild fish Robbie quite liked. Along with the iced champagne, wine was served.

His gaze shifted to the king's mistress whose high-pitched trilling laughter caught his attention.

Countess Lieven huffed. "Alas, that woman has not an idea in her head, not a word to say for herself. Nothing but a hand to accept pearls and diamonds, and an enormous balcony to wear them on."

Robbie sputtered, nearly choking on his wine. Sweeping a napkin over his mouth, he whispered, "You must warn me, Countess, when you are to make so witty a remark."

The countess tilted her head and smiled coyly at him, allowing a dark auburn curl to fall to her forehead. For the astute female he knew her to be, the gesture surprised him. But the interest in her gray eyes and the suggestive sweep of her long fingers over the mounds of her breasts rising above her gown could not be mistaken. It was an open invitation to come to her bed.

Many of the king's guests would be surprised to learn that when it came to *affaires de coeur* Robbie had rules to which he assiduously adhered. Unlike the king, for example, Robbie did not share the bed of married women, even if invited. Widows, on the other hand, were fair game and almost always willing. And there were never husbands to make cuckolds.

The next course was venison served with carrots and roast potatoes. Pondering the vegetables, Robbie turned to respond to something Letty was saying and was distracted by a movement of blue-green froth on the other side of the table some way down. *Miss Reynolds*. He had no idea she would be attending the dinner but, given Lady Sanborn's friendship with the king, he should have considered it a possibility.

The fair-haired hoyden presented a captivating picture in a gown of some wispy sea-green material that reminded him of a lagoon he'd encountered on a voyage to the South Seas. The room was certainly warm enough to bring back a memory of those hot tropical days. He imagined her there on a white sand beach, the breeze blowing her pale gold hair behind her, only in his imaginings, she wore nothing at all.

He lifted his wine and took a sip, watching her as she chatted gaily with the two men sitting on either side of her, unaware, as Robbie was, of their character. He had to wonder what had been the thinking of the one who arranged the seating. The two were rakes of the first order. He suddenly felt protective of her and, though he was certain she believed she could take care of herself, he decided a rescue was in order. The Countess of Claremont would surely expect it.

At last, the dessert was served, accompanied by more wine. Robbie watched his lemon ice melt in the heat of the room, anxious for the dinner to end. When it did, he rose from his chair and bid Countess Lieven and Lady Lade a good evening. The two ladies departed together. The countess gave Robbie a lingering look over her shoulder.

He took a step away from the table as Jack came to his side.

"I expected you would be leaving with that striking woman with whom you've been conversing."

"The countess?" Robbie watched her tall, retreating figure. "No, I think not. What do you say to a game of whist, Uncle?"

Jack's brow furrowed. "I thought your game was brag."

"Most often it is, but 'tis not a lady's game and I thought to invite Miss Reynolds and Miss Crockett to join us."

"Snow White and Rose Red?" Jack asked with an amused expression. "That might be entertaining."

"Exactly my thought."

"Give me a glass of the king's potent brandy, Nephew, and you're on. But you will first have to pry the two of them loose from those men who have been monopolizing them all evening."

"You noticed?"

"I did happen to glance in Miss Crockett's direction once or twice, a lovely figure in that rose gown."

Robbie looked over Jack's shoulder where the two men were escorting the young women toward the door. A concerned Lady Sanborn followed. "This will not be a problem, Uncle. Stay close and watch a master at work."

Jack chuckled. "Lead on, old thing."

Robbie crossed the room to the small group making their way to the exit. He first greeted Lady Sanborn, which had the effect of bringing them all to a stop. "Good evening, Countess."

"Ah, Sir Robert, how nice to see you!"

Relieved more like, thought Robbie.

"You know my great-niece, Miss Reynolds, and her friend, Miss Crockett."

Robbie tipped his head to the ladies.

"But do you know Mr. Flowers and Mr. Groves?"

"For many years," he replied. "We were at Eton together." The two men winced ever so slightly. Jimmy Flowers and Matty Groves had been fixtures at Eton, bullies of the meanest sort. Robbie still remembered the day he'd pulled the swaggering Flowers off of Nash, Robbie's twin.

He introduced Jack to the two men and then said, "I am certain you won't mind if my uncle and I claim that game of whist the ladies promised us."

Miss Reynolds furrowed her brows but remained silent. Miss Crockett bestowed a benevolent smile on Robbie.

"Oh," said Lady Sanborn, "I am sure they would not." She turned to the two men, who looked as if they'd just lost fish off their lines. "We wish you a good evening, gentlemen." Then to her charges, "Come ladies, let us join Sir Robert and Monsieur Donet in the card room."

Miss Reynolds took Jack's arm, shooting Robbie a self-satisfied smile. Content to abide by her choice, at least for now, Robbie offered his arm to Miss Crockett. "What say you, oh winsome beauty? Shall we sally forth together?"

Miss Crockett beamed up at him and set her hand on his sleeve. "Lead on, Sir Knight. I care not that we promised no game of whist. I intend to enjoy partnering with you."

He couldn't be sure but he thought he detected a "humph" from The Keeper of the Demon Cat. At that moment, she reminded him very much of The Grand Countess.

Chapter 7

Chastity surreptitiously glanced to her right and met the piercing gaze of her nemesis, his hazel eyes sparkling in the light of the single candle that lit their table. "I do believe it's your play, Miss Reynolds."

Quickly she looked to her hand, concentrating on her next move, hoping he had not detected her stare. "A moment please." Whist was her favorite game and, with her acquired skill and partnered with the vicomte, she intended to win. It mattered not that The Rogue was dealer and had just turned up the trump card, the six of hearts. Hearts was her least favorite suit. It only reminded her how fleeting love was and how dangerous it could be to one's wellbeing to get involved with a rogue.

She had not forgotten his laughter in response to the brazen flirtations of the woman sitting beside him at the king's table. When she'd asked Mr. Flowers who the woman was, he said, "Oh that's Countess Lieven, the wife of the Russian Ambassador to Great Britain. I don't see her husband here tonight."

The wife! Why should she be surprised that a rogue like Sir Robert would encourage the attentions of a married woman? After all, his friend the king did the same. And why did Countess Lieven have to be one of those beautiful women with very dark hair, in this case auburn, and skin like the purest ivory?

Chastity hadn't minded when Sir Robert turned away the two men who'd entertained her and Rose at dinner. They were not the brightest of fellows and neither was good enough for her friend, Rose, but at least the two had been lavish with their attention. And Sir Robert did lie when he said she and Rose had promised him and the vicomte a game of whist. That he had lied as an excuse to take them away from the two men annoyed her but she was unsurprised. It was just the thing a rogue who wanted his way would do. She had met his penetrating gaze often enough to know he was a man who did as he pleased. Surely, the fact he would impose a kiss on a total stranger was evidence enough!

Chastity laid down the six of clubs and the play moved to Rose, who would have to play the same suit if she could.

Rose stared at her cards, deep in concentration.

Two rooms had been set up for whist, backgammon, chess, vingt-et-un and loo. In a third room the king's guests were treated to music. Chastity could hear the sounds echoing throughout the Pavilion.

The foursome played whist under the watchful eye of Aunt Agatha who sat in a nearby chair drinking tea with one of her woman friends.

Finally, Rose laid down the jack of clubs.

Across the table, Chastity gave her partner a hopeful glance. But he must have had nothing in the suit of clubs ranking higher, for he laid down the two of clubs and returned Chastity a sympathetic look.

Sir Robert inserted the trump card back into his hand and set down the five of clubs.

With a smile of delight aimed at her partner, Rose gathered the cards, taking the trick.

The game continued with each set of players taking tricks. Despite the best effort of Chastity and the vicomte, Sir Robert and Rose managed to gather the most tricks and were the first to compile the winning score of five points. She was thankful that at least Sir Robert did not gloat.

When the game ended, the vicomte gathered the cards into a neat stack. "Shall we adjourn to the Music Room?"

"I would enjoy that," said Rose with enthusiasm.

As they stood, Sir Robert offered Chastity his arm. Unless she wished to look the veriest shrew, she had no choice but to take it. Beneath her fingers, the muscles of his arm flexed. It annoyed her that she should notice. Or that, notwithstanding the heavy perfume in the Pavilion, she could detect his masculine scent of bergamot with a hint of orange. As he guided her toward the Music Room, her every sense was attuned to him.

They were about to pass her great-aunt when he paused. "Lady Sanborn, with your permission, we are escorting the ladies to a better vantage point to hear the music."

"That sounds like a splendid idea," said Aunt Agatha. "I will join you shortly."

Chastity was amazed at the scale of the Music Room. She imagined it a concert hall in a Chinese emperor's palace. As they entered, the band began playing Handel. Halfway down the large room on the left, she glimpsed the king sitting with his mistress, Lady Conyngham, a gilded couple in their middle years. Lady Conyngham had to be in her fifth decade. Chastity might have expected the king to have a young mistress but, seeing them together, she recalled Aunt Agatha saying that Prinny favored older women.

Across from the king, on the other side of the parquet floor, guests sat in long rows of chairs listening to the music. Behind them were four tall pagodas that had to be fifteen feet tall. The many-tiered towers featured stories of diminishing size as they rose in the air, an ornamented projecting roof on each one.

Above the parquet floor, hanging from the elaborately decorated recessed domed ceiling, were nine huge bowl-shaped chandeliers made to look like giant lotus flowers.

Chastity opened her fan. The room was very warm, a circumstance, she told herself, having nothing to do with the man beside her. Nevertheless, she was glad she'd taken Aunt Agatha's advice and worn her lightest, sheerest gown, a blue-green confection perfect for such an occasion.

Sir Robert guided them to three chairs, urging them to sit. "Place your reticule on the vacant chair," he told Chastity, "so your great-aunt will have a place when she joins us." Chastity set her reticule on the open chair, grudgingly admiring the kindness in his purpose for chairs were in short supply.

"What about you and your uncle?" asked Rose.

"Jack and I will stand behind you," said Sir Robert. Which is what they did, making it difficult for Chastity to think his behavior anything but that of a gentleman.

"That is very gracious of you both," said Rose, turning to smile up at the two men.

Chastity worried that her friend was forming too great an attachment to Sir Robert. His uncle, however, would make a fine suitor. Handsome, well-mannered and rich. And she'd not observed him with any married women. Perfect for Rose.

As Chastity considered Sir Robert's gallant gesture, she softened toward him. But that only lasted until Countess Lieven, sitting a short distance away, drew their attention with the dramatic opening of her fan. Over the top of the gilded fan she fluttered in front of her face, the countess winked at Sir Robert, making Chastity wonder if he had made an assignation to come to the countess' bed later that night.

Vowing not to think about his nighttime pursuits, Chastity forced herself to focus on the beautiful music of Handel. After all, what did she care of his lady partners? Instead, she became enthralled with the large painted scenes of Chinese costumes in red and gold arrayed about the room and held up by flying dragons. It was something she would expect to see in the palace of a Chinese lord.

Sir Robert leaned in to whisper, "I do love the music, don't you?"

His lips touched her ear, causing her to shiver. Then came his warm breath against her delicate skin. As he withdrew, she turned to see him smile. Surely he had meant to do it.

"I do," she said, turning back, trying to still her racing heart. He had deliberately teased her with his sensuous lips, the scoundrel. Dismissing his bold gesture, she sat back and returned her attention to the music.

Not long after, Aunt Agatha claimed the chair reserved for her.

At twelve o'clock, the music stopped and sandwiches, wine and water were handed around. Muted conversations filled the great room.

Sir Robert and his uncle nibbled on sandwiches but, by then, the heat had risen to such an extent that Chastity asked only for water.

"The king always keeps the Pavilion's rooms overwarm," said Aunt Agatha. "It makes one thirsty, but one can hardly tell the king to snuff the fires."

Shortly after, the king got to his feet, bowed and wished his guests a good night as he escorted Lady Conyngham from the room.

"May we see you ladies to your home?" Sir Robert asked.

"That would be most kind of you," replied Aunt Agatha. "We are not so far as to justify a carriage unless it is raining."

Chastity was delighted when Monsieur Donet offered her great-aunt one of his arms and Rose the other. She had hoped her friend could get to know the vicomte better. Of course, when Sir Robert offered his arm to her, she could not refuse it.

Despite her intention not to enjoy his company, Chastity soon found she was laughing at some witty remark Sir Robert made.

"So you can laugh," he said. "I should have thought you preferred to scowl."

"It might surprise you to know that I laugh often, Sir Robert, just not with you."

Chastity couldn't be certain in the dim light of the street, but she thought his jaw tightened. If so, he quickly recovered. "Before the summer is over, I should hope to see more of your mirth, Miss Reynolds."

"We shall see." A smile spread across her face as she realized his walking her home delayed him from Countess Lieven's bed. Perhaps the woman would be asleep by the time he arrived, her door locked.

"Well, what do you know...?" Robbie muttered, reading the invitation that arrived days later as he and Jack returned from their morning ride.

"What?" asked Jack from where he stood in front of Robbie's mirror admiring his cravat.

"We are invited to a reception at Lady Sanborn's. She has added a note promising to introduce us to some of the most eligible young ladies of her acquaintance in Brighton."

"I shall look forward to that," Jack said, facing Robbie. "Does this mean I shall finally meet the demon cat?"

"I daresay you will."

Tiller came through the door to help Robbie change. "Do ye dress for town, Cap'n?"

"I think so," said Robbie. "We've a few taverns to visit, a game of brag, and Sir John Lade, who we encountered on our ride, wants to show us a horse."

Tiller busied himself setting out Robbie's clothes. "Once I see to ye, Cap'n, I'll attend the vicomte."

"I do appreciate your service, *mon ami*," said Jack.

"'Tis nothing, M'sieur. As ye're companion to my master, 'tis my pleasure." The old salt puffed out his chest with pride. "'Sides, when we're at sea, I have more to do than seeing to just two gentlemen. And that don't even go into the Cap'n's many costumes."

"Costumes?" asked Jack with a puzzled look. Then to Robbie, "Is there something you're not telling me, Nephew?"

Robbie shot Tiller a look that said, "Say no more" and began to dress. "A gentleman has a need for many kinds of attire, does he not, Tiller?"

"Aye, Cap'n," Tiller said, dropping his gaze. "He surely does."

As Robbie pulled on his polished Hessians, he remembered the note he'd received the night he'd dined with the king. There had been no others since but, whenever he and Jack went into town, he could feel eyes on his back. Someone was monitoring his movements. He'd made sure he was carrying one of his smaller pistols at all times, and Jack always had a knife or two hidden on his person, though none of that would save Robbie from a bullet in the back.

Excited to be out with her great-aunt and Mrs. Fitz on this late spring morning, Chastity stepped down from the carriage and let her gaze travel the length of North Street. There was only the slightest wind. "Why, there must be fifty shops!"

"The last count was sixty, I think," said Aunt Agatha, "and even I have not been to all of them. We creatures of habit tend to frequent our favorites."

"What shops would you like to see first?" asked Mrs. Fitz. "We've plenty of time before Agatha and I take you to our favorite spot for tea."

Rose glanced at Chastity. "I know what you're going to say."

Chastity had just finished the design for Aunt Agatha's slippers that morning. "A fabric shop that sells silk, the kind that makes elegant slippers, would be my choice."

"I always like to see silk," said Rose. "And I need a new pair of gloves."

Mrs. Fitz smiled. "We can easily attend to both of those requests. Thomas Nightingale is an excellent glover and Mrs. Bull, the silk mercer, has lovely fabric. But if you want a gown, I recommend Mrs. Sanders."

"My great-niece designs shoes, Maria," Aunt Agatha informed her friend.

"Shoes?" Mrs. Fitz's brows rose in question.

"She does," Aunt Agatha said, answering for her, "lovely ones. See those she is wearing today?" Aunt Agatha looked down at Chastity's red half boots peeking out beneath her morning gown of cream muslin edged in crimson. They matched her dark red spencer jacket.

"Those are remarkable," said Mrs. Fitz. "I had not noticed before."

"Mine, too, were designed by Chastity," said Rose, lifting her skirt to show her blue half boots.

"A most unusual pastime for a lady," remarked Mrs. Fitz. Then she smiled. "I approve."

"Do you wish to take the silk fabric to the shoemaker's, Chastity?" asked her great-aunt. "Thomas Lulham makes fine boots and shoes and his shop is just here on North Street."

"Yes, please," replied Chastity.

In no time at all, they had visited the silk mercer and Chastity had the fabric she needed for Aunt Agatha's slippers. The respect with which Mrs. Fitz had been welcomed by the shopkeeper spoke much of her worth in the eyes of Brighton's merchants. The king might have forgotten his Catholic wife but Brighton had not.

Their next stop was the shoemaker, where Chastity persuaded Rose to distract Aunt Agatha and Mrs. Fitz long enough for Chastity to pull out her drawing and tell the shoemaker what she desired.

"Of course, I can make the slippers for you, Miss. Check back with me in a week and you will have them."

Delighted with the shoemaker's enthusiastic response, Chastity left Rose and the two older women to pay for their orders while she drifted to the bay window to watch the comings and goings on the street. Many people were taking advantage of the good weather. As the summer grew closer, more Londoners arrived each day, making the streets more crowded.

She was just about to turn away when, across the street, the door of the Blacksmiths' Arms tavern opened and two gentlemen stepped out. She recognized Sir Robert and his uncle at once. They spoke for a brief while, as if trying to decide what to do next and then turned down the street. Before they had gone but a few steps, a woman came scurrying out of the tavern, her dark hair flying behind her, and threw her arms around Sir Robert's neck and kissed him.

Though he was startled at first, he embraced her fondly before letting her go.

Chastity inhaled sharply, covering her mouth with her fingers.

Rogue that he was, he just laughed as the girl ran back inside. Chastity supposed he had no end of women pursuing him. He was, after all, a handsome figure of a man. That he should accept the kiss of the tavern wench in the middle of North Street in the full light of day, however, surprised even Chastity. She turned away, condemning her thoughts of Sir Robert Powell to the outer reaches of her mind. His errant ways did not concern her and it was certain he cared nothing for her opinion.

Robbie had already turned his attention from the girl to their next stop, when Jack asked, "Whatever did you do to earn that kiss?"

"What? Oh, 'twas nothing. I merely left her more coin than she expected. I was trying to make up for that bothersome lout in the corner who was giving her a rough time."

Jack stuffed his hands in his coat pockets against the wind. "You always seem to notice more than I do, *mon ami.*"

His work for the Crown had rendered the smallest detail of great importance, sometimes the difference between life and death. "She could do little to please him, though she certainly tried. I was sorry for her sake."

"The kindness you did her might have gained you a hearty thanks, not that kiss. That kiss, Nephew, was an invitation to return."

"Don't be silly," Robbie said, striding ahead. "We must hurry if we're to play a round of brag before we meet Sir John." He did not mention to Jack that they were being followed. He'd noticed the solitary figure in the brown greatcoat leaning against the tavern counter. Robbie could discern few distinguishing features since the man had pulled his hat down on his head. It was a meager disguise but Robbie's instincts had been roused.

When they left the tavern, so did the man, who was now dogging their steps.

Robbie led Jack down a side street and entered Woolbridge's cigar shop only to leave by the back door moments later, managing to lose their shadow.

"What was that excursion about?" asked Jack, perplexed. "I thought to buy a few cigars but your quick exit made that impossible. And weren't we hurrying to a game of brag?"

Robbie kept walking but he knew he had to give Jack an explanation. Perhaps it was time for the truth. "We were being followed. I can't explain now, but I will later."

"*Très bien*, I shall hold you to it."

Robbie worried that whoever the man was, he had gained a knowledge of Robbie's favorite haunts and his daily pattern. He would alter those to determine if the man was acting alone.

After a quick round of brag and a luncheon of cod pie and ale, Robbie hurried them on to meet Sir John Lade at the Brighton racecourse. He found Lade standing at the edge of the course that would soon play host to races patronized by the king, drawing out the whole town.

With Sir John was a tall lady wearing an enormous plumed hat. He recognized her as Sir John's wife, Letty. They were talking with Sir Bellingham, who was equally tall, and another gentleman of a powerful build he knew to be that belonging to Lord Alvanley. Except for the Lades, who were older, the other two were of an age with Robbie and

Jack.

Behind the small group stood a beautiful chestnut mare. As they drew closer, he said to Jack, "I'll introduce you to the ones you have yet to meet."

"Ho! If it isn't the newly knighted lion," said Lord Alvanley with his slight lisp.

"So it is," said Sir John. "And right on time."

"How nice to see you again," said Letty, smiling at Jack.

Robbie made the remaining introductions. When Lord Alvanley learned that Jack was a vicomte with vineyards in Saintonge, he broke into fluid French. *"Bienvenue à Brighton, Monsieur Donet. Saintonge produit l'un des meilleurs cognac de France! Vous devez vous joindre à nous pour une soirée de plaisir."*

Since Robbie well understood French, he had heard Alvanley's compliment concerning the cognac of Saintonge. Though the province where the Donet vineyards were located had been renamed the *Charente-Maritime* during the Revolution, the family title, now restored, remained the same.

Jack returned Alvanley a broad smile. *"Il me fera plaisir de me joindre à vous,"* Jack said, accepting the invitation to join Alvanley for an evening out.

Sir John ran his hand across the mare's withers. "Now, how about this fine mare, Powell? Are you interested?"

"If he isn't," put in Jack, "I am. She's a beauty and I need a riding horse for the frequent times I am in England."

Much was said in praise of the fiery red mare named Electra after King Agamemnon's daughter. Sir John never owned a horse that did not win accolades. Robbie had two riding horses in London, so he suggested that Jack should have this one.

A price was agreed upon and Jack had his horse. "I'll bring her around to the king's stables," offered Sir John.

Lady Lade suddenly spoke up. "Might we have a ride together tomorrow with you? John and I would enjoy that."

Robbie glanced at Jack and then at the others.

"Go on," said Sir Bellingham, "you won't often get a chance to match yourself against riders as accomplished as the Lades."

Robbie looked at Sir Alvanley expectantly.

He held up his hands. "Not me! A good walk is enough exercise."

Robbie said, "Very well, Letty, you're on." Recalling that Miss Reynolds was supposedly an experienced rider who, according to The Grand Countess, was known for riding hell-for-leather, he added, "I might bring a lady friend, if that is acceptable. I expect Miss Reynolds would love to meet you."

"Of course!" exclaimed Letty. "I should be delighted to have another woman with us who likes to ride."

Surprisingly, Jack did not rush to the opportunity. Instead, he said, "Might I borrow your new curricle, Robbie, to take Miss Crockett for a ride about Brighton while you are with the Lades?"

"But of course!" To the Lades and Alvanley, Robbie said, "My uncle, the vicomte, has a fondness for Miss Reynolds' companion." Whether Jack cared for Miss Crockett or Robbie's curricle and fine pair of grays, he could not say but, this way, Jack could have his wish and Robbie could keep his promise to The Grand Countess to watch over Chastity. At least that's what he told himself.

As Robbie and Jack walked back to the Pavilion, Robbie kept a watch for any who might be following them but saw no one who drew his attention.

"All right, Nephew. Time to confess. Who's been following us and *pourquoi*?"

Robbie took a deep breath and let it out, his mind seeing again that night on Cato Street. "You have asked what I did to earn the baronetcy. It was the Cato Street Affair."

"That was *you*?"

"The plan to trap the conspirators was mine but, for the most part, their capture was the handiwork of the Bow Street Runners."

"And the one who is following you now?"

Robbie shrugged. "I don't know who he—or they—are but there was that note. Someone knows who I am and has followed me here."

"The message that turned you white as a ghost in the Pavilion?"

Robbie nodded. "It was nasty and threatening. Even before then, I had the sense I was being followed, but after…well, since that message, I have glimpsed a man, possibly two, trailing me as I did this morning. I don't want you to be involved in this, Jack."

"You have no choice. *J'insiste*, Nephew." Jack raised his chin. "We will face this together. With your skill at pistols and mine at knives, we are equipped to defeat them."

Robbie glanced at his uncle and friend, thankful they had grown close. "It comforts me to know we are in this together though I regret the risk you take."

Jack held up a hand. "A risk I am happy to take. But wait…I thought the conspirators had all been captured."

"According to the reports, yes. But my relief was short-lived. It seems even the wicked have friends."

"Indeed they do," said Jack.

Robbie frowned. "The question is, how many?"

Chastity returned from a delightful tea at The Old Ship Inn with Rose, Aunt Agatha and Mrs. Fitz to find Featherstone, her aunt's portly ginger-haired butler, holding out a silver tray. "For you, Mistress."

She handed her bonnet and pelisse to a footman and lifted the note from the tray, noting her name in elegant script. "Thank you."

As she began to climb the stairs, Rose joined her.

"Be down in time for dinner!" Aunt Agatha cried up at them.

"Who is the message from?" asked Rose.

"Wait until we are alone and I shall tell you." Chastity carried the sealed note into her chamber and sat on the bed. The long day of shopping had tired her.

She opened the red wax seal and scanned the signature first. "It's from Sir Robert Powell, The Rogue."

"I'm certain he did not sign it 'The Rogue'," teased Rose.

"No, he need not have done." Remarkably, the man's handwriting was clearly that of a gentleman, one taught penmanship from a young age.

Rose drew up a chair next to Chastity. Her friend's brown eyes sparkled with anticipation. "Well, what does he want?"

Reading the message, Chastity said, "He invites me to go riding tomorrow with some of his friends. He mentions Sir John Lade and his wife, Letty." She looked up from the paper in her lap. "Oh, Rose, just imagine! The famous Letty Lade. Why, she rides better than most men!"

"And curses up a storm if the newspapers be true. Will you go?"

"Indeed I will. I'm sure Aunt Agatha will not object."

Rose pulled a face. "But how very wrong of you to have the hand-some Sir Robert all to yourself!"

Chastity could not very well tell her friend one of the reasons she would accept Sir Robert's invitation was to remove his person from Rose's presence. Her friend was too enamored of him. But there was also her desire to meet Letty Lade. "We will not be alone, Rose. Lady Lade will be accompanied by her husband. I so want to meet her. Why, the woman is famous or, more accurately, infamous. Did you know she was once the mistress of the highwayman 'Sixteen String Jack'? And later the mistress of the Duke of York?" Thinking of it, she added, "Perhaps I shan't mention that last bit to Aunt Agatha."

"Likely, she already knows, Chas. She seems to know everyone."

Chastity glanced down at the note. "There is a postscript. He says his uncle would like to take you for a drive in Sir Robert's curricle."

Chastity met her friend's eager gaze. "I think it's a good idea, Rose. You'll have more the measure of the vicomte once you've spent time alone with him. And do not forget, he is nobility of the old order and has vineyards and a chateau in France."

Rose inclined her head, a grin forming on her face. "He does, doesn't he? A curricle is all the rage and with the handsome vicomte, I shall be much admired." Rose looked down at her fingers twisting in her lap. "Though Father would never approve of a suitor who lives in France."

"Then you can tell your father that Monsieur Donet is from Guernsey, a Crown dependency. For that is where the vicomte makes his home, is it not?"

"I'd forgotten," said Rose, her face brightening. "Still, Chas, I might prefer Sir Robert were I to have a choice."

"Sir Robert, despite his apparent wealth, is not a suitor of whom your father would approve. Your parents will want a man whose reputation is above reproach, a man who would ever be faithful. After all, what has he been doing these past years but living a wastrel's life?" Even as she asked the question, Chastity considered the possibility she might be wrong. But then she thought of the tavern wench and his bold flirtation with the married Countess Lieven. "There will be others, Rose. The Brighton Season is only beginning. And we have Aunt Agatha's reception to look forward to.'

Rose smiled, her dark eyes glistening with anticipation. "We do, don't we?"

Robbie arrived at Lady Sanborn's house on the Steyne at the expected hour of nine o'clock and tied the two horses to a fence post before proceeding to the door where he knocked twice.

The door opened but, before the footman could invite him inside, the demon cat came flying out. Robbie thought he meant to attack, but the beast raced past him. A large dog, passing by and seeing the cat, leapt onto the fence, barking ferociously. The cat hissed but obviously not trusting the fence, scaled the tall tree in the front yard.

Through the front door came Miss Reynolds, looking quite beautiful in her butter yellow riding habit. Ignoring him, she cried to the cat, "Crispin, oh Crispin, do come down at once!"

"Apparently, he does not wish to confront the dog," said Robbie. "Allow me to remove the menace," he added with a grin.

A frown furrowed her forehead as if she were reluctant to accept his help. Letting out a sigh, she said, "That would be most helpful, Sir Robert."

Robbie strode to the fence and, waving his hat at the annoying canine, shooed him away. That accomplished, he joined the lady beneath the tree, staring up at the cat. "He does not appear to be in any hurry to descend."

"I can see that," she said, tossing him a look of incredulity. "Crispin is very frightened of large dogs. Small ones he can intimidate rather well, but the big ones remain unimpressed."

Robbie still had penance to do for running her down in Grillon's lobby, so he decided to be magnanimous even if it might gain him scratches aplenty. "Here, hold my hat and I'll fetch him down."

"You?" she said, taking his hat. "Crispin loathes you."

"Nevertheless, I shall manage." Grabbing the trunk, he swung onto a lower branch. Having climbed the rigging on his family's ships for years, he was well equipped for such a rescue. Once his face was level to the cat's, he looked into the animal's golden eyes. "Now Crispin, it is time we made friends. Allow me to assist you to the ground."

The cat glared at him but, perhaps realizing this was his only path to salvation, did not hiss at Robbie when he pried the cat's paws from the branch to which he'd been clinging. Free of the tree, the cat clung to Robbie's chest. With one arm holding the cat, he slowly descended to where he could hand the feline to his mistress. "Here, your familiar, er...your cat, returned to you."

"Highly amusing, I'm sure," she said, reaching for the cat. "Still, I am much in your debt. Do come in while I retrieve my hat and riding crop." As she walked toward the house, she scolded her cat. "Naughty Crispin!"

Inside, he greeted Lady Sanborn and Miss Crockett, who had been watching from the open doorway.

"A magnificent rescue, Sir Robert," said Lady Sanborn.

"You were wonderful!" exclaimed Miss Reynolds' friend.

The accolades made his face heat. He did not take well to the hero's role, preferring anonymity. Perhaps that is why the role of spy had suited him.

Answering Miss Crockett's unspoken question, he said, "My uncle will be along shortly to collect you."

"I look forward to our ride," she said. "I've never ridden in a curricle before."

Miss Reynolds descended the stairs, having retrieved her hat and riding crop. He noticed her half boots were an unusual combination of red and yellow leather and wondered if they were her own creation. He thought it clever of her that she should design shoes. A singular woman to be sure. A woman who could *do* something. And one he was finding increasingly interesting.

He bid Lady Sanborn good day and followed Miss Reynolds out the door. "I brought you the same mare you rode before, as you and she did well together."

"We did," she said. "I like her very much."

As before, he placed his hands on her waist and lifted her into the sidesaddle.

"I don't suppose it would do any good to protest the manner in which you assist me into the saddle."

He grinned. "None at all, Miss Reynolds." Robbie had much experience with women and he was well aware that if he gave Chastity Reynolds an inch, she would take a mile. More than a mile. He had no intention of granting her an inch.

The Lades were mounted and waiting when they reached the race-course.

"Allow me to introduce you to Miss Chastity Reynolds," he said.

Sir John dipped his head. "Charmed."

Letty, being Letty, would have to remark on Miss Reynolds' given name. "Chastity? What a moniker! A damned anvil to carry around, what? Did you not think to adopt another?"

"Many times," said Miss Reynolds, unoffended. "My inheritance requires I bear it. Vengeance from my Puritan ancestors, I believe, my lady."

Letty laughed. "If you know my beginnings, they are quite opposite yours and so I insist you dispense with 'my lady' and call me 'Letty'."

Chastity smiled, her blue eyes shining beneath her saucy hat. "And you must call me Chas, as do my particular friends."

"Splendid," said Sir John. "Now, whither shall we ride? A fast ride down the racecourse or along Brighton's shore at a more leisurely pace?"

"Let's race first," said Letty. She might be entering her sixth decade, but Robbie had always thought Letty Lade was not one to be held back by the passage of time.

One look at Chastity told Robbie she was eager to run, too. "A race it shall be."

Sir John nodded. "Very well."

The four of them took off at a run, the ladies outpacing Robbie and Sir John. Based on all he had been told about Chastity Reynolds, he should not have been surprised at how she galloped away a smile on her face. His gaze fixed on the ribbons from her hat flowing down her back to her narrow waist as it flared into gently rounded hips and a perfect derrière.

The two women took the bend in a blur, laughing as they did, like two Furies bent on punishing mere mortal men with stings of conscience. Did such women cause men like him to reflect upon their lives? That was certainly the effect Chastity Reynolds was having on him.

He did not count his life as a spy as the kind of stuff that made for a legacy. He was proud of his service to the Crown, but legacies arose from families where love abided and where children resided in great numbers, like his own. He wanted that kind of legacy.

Thank God it is not too late.

The women plunged down the track with Robbie and Sir John in their wakes. At the end, Letty pulled reins and Chastity Reynolds drew alongside her. They slowed their horses to a trot and Robbie and Sir John followed at the same pace.

"I see your wife has lost none of her spirit for the horse," Robbie observed.

"No, though these days she much prefers her high perch phaeton. Thankfully, seeing her commanding the reins scandalizes society less today than it once did."

"You and Letty have been well matched," Robbie remarked, thinking of the controversy that had always swirled around the couple for his gambling and her outrageous past.

"I tell you true, Powell, women with spirit like Letty keep a man warm at night. I have no regrets."

"Doubtless you speak the truth," Robbie said, thinking of Chastity Reynolds. The woman had spirit in spades. As he pulled up alongside her, he noted her brow beaded with sweat, her complexion glowing in the morning sun.

She sat her horse with excellent form. Her blonde curls had fallen free of her hat and he pictured them lying across a pillow. She would warm any man's bed.

Leaving the racecourse, they rode along the shore for some time, the wide Marine Parade affording them a grand view of the beach and the blue sea beyond. Where they had room, they cantered but most of the time they walked the horses to avoid crowding the people who were on either side of the Parade.

"I hear Prinny means to have his yacht, the *Royal George*, brought to Brighton," said Sir John. "I expect we'll all be invited aboard."

"Have you ever sailed on the king's yacht?" Miss Reynolds asked Letty.

"Yes. Last year, John and I sailed on the *Royal George*. It has been Prinny's yacht for several years."

"Since you are here as the king's guest, Powell, you'll doubtless be one of the king's guests," said Sir John.

Robbie could see the idea of being on the royal yacht enchanted Miss Reynolds. Her eyes were alight with excitement. Though he suspected the yacht might remain anchored offshore, he would enjoy a sail on the *Royal George*. All of the royal yachts were fully rigged, square sail ships. "If I'm invited, would you like to be my guest?"

"I would, indeed," she replied.

An hour later, he returned her to Lady Sanborn's house. A footman held the horses while he escorted her to the door. The red-haired butler welcomed them back, taking Miss Reynolds' hat, gloves and riding crop.

The demon cat sauntered into the entry hall and rubbed his furry body against Robbie's boots, purring loudly. Laughter bubbled up in his chest at the change.

"It seems Crispin has decided to accept you," said Miss Reynolds.

Robbie raised a brow. "And what of his mistress?"

"I'm still considering the possibility," she said. But he was pleased to see her lovely mouth curve up in the merest hint of a smile.

"You are fortunate I am a patient man, Miss Reynolds."

She scowled at him, reminding him of her once hissing cat. He chuckled to himself, tempted to take her into his arms and kiss that scowl from her face. Remembering how she had responded to his first kiss, he was certain he could do it.

With a bow, he bid her good day and returned to where he'd left the horses. As he did, his attention was drawn to two men watching the house from the small park in the middle of the Steyne. They were partially hidden by the vegetation, so he could not discern their features, nor could he tell if one was the same man who had followed him and Jack the day before. They could be visitors to Brighton curious to observe the goings-on at the house of the Catholic woman next door who had dared to marry the heir to the British throne. Or, they could be traitors to the Crown intent on vengeance.

He experienced a sudden dread when he realized if they were among those who had been following him, he had led them to Lady Sanborn's home—and to Chastity Reyrolds.

Chapter 8

Chastity had just made her choice of the gown she would wear to her great-aunt's reception when Rose burst into her bedchamber, an anxious expression clouding her face. "What gown are you wearing?" she asked in a tone that conveyed panic.

Chastity gestured to the gown the maid had laid across the bed. "The claret silk and my slippers to match. The color gives my pale skin and hair some life. At least I shan't fade into the walls."

"You silly goose! You could never fade into the walls. 'Tis only you who thinks so."

Chastity glanced at the deep wine-colored gown she intended to wear, its silk folds shimmering in the candlelight. "I do love this color."

"It will look glorious on you. But what am I to wear?" Rose sank onto the edge of Chastity's bed. "I'm torn between my jonquil silk and the ivory satin with the pink petticoat I wore at the Winter Assembly."

Chastity thought for a moment. "I recall the gowns. I think you might save your new jonquil silk for another event we are sure to attend and wear the satin tonight. Both are lovely on you. But the satin with the pale pink petticoat has a low bodice that hints of your splendid attributes. You will have all the men in a twitter. And first impressions *are* important."

"Very well," Rose sighed, "I shall wear the ivory satin."

"You can borrow my pink silk shawl to drape over your arms, if you like."

"Oh, thank you! The shawl will be perfect. Besides, it will give me something to do with my nervous hands."

"Worry not. I intend to keep a sharp eye out for any gentleman who might be worthy of you. Speaking of which, did you enjoy your ride with M'sieur Donet?"

Rose smiled and looked down at her folded hands. "More than a little. He is ever so accomplished. He told me of his vineyards in France and his father's ships. Can you imagine he will inherit a chateau? His skill with the reins soon had us racing down the road. I had to hold my bonnet on at one point or see it fly away."

"But what about the man himself?" Chastity asked, subsiding into a chair facing her friend. Crispin took that opportunity to rub against her legs, meowing his desire to be scratched behind his ear. She was happy to oblige him.

"Oh. He is very kind and most considerate with the gallant manners of a gentleman. I enjoyed his descriptions of the vineyards and the harvest time. How I would love to see that. And his conversation was laced with French, which I found very romantic."

"As I would expect of him." Chastity had been hoping Rose would become attracted to the vicomte. With the summer before them perhaps, in time, love would bloom. Though Chastity would hate to see her friend leave England, if it meant Rose's happiness, she would support her.

Rose inquired, "What of your ride with Sir John and his wife Letty?"

"I have never met a woman like her. She's as bold as a man. I must own that quite delighted me." Remembering some of Letty's expressions, she added, "Her speech is a bit off-color, but that did not bother me overmuch."

"And the ride?"

"Letty—she insisted I call her by her given name—is truly an accomplished rider. I had to work to keep up with her even given her years. Our gallop down the racetrack left me breathless. I can only imagine what she was like when she was our age."

"Controversial if the tales be true."

Chastity didn't mind the thought of being the subject of controversy if it gave her an exciting life. Her mother already considered her difficult. Could "controversial" be far behind? She imagined living in her own small estate, designing ladies' shoes. Perhaps she would become an eccentric and add outrageous hats to her appearance. Aunt Agatha, at least, would approve.

Rose left for her own room and Aunt Agatha's maid came to help Chastity dress and style her hair, simply as she liked it.

When the maid finished, she said, "I'll just see to Miss Crockett. Lady Sanborn will soon be asking for you."

Chastity thanked the maid, grateful she didn't seem to mind having two young women to attend. Left alone in her bedchamber, she took a seat at her dressing table to consider her reflection in the mirror. The young woman who stared back at her was almost ghostlike with her pale blue eyes, fair hair and skin like cold alabaster. She fretted that her eyes lacked the warmth of her sisters' rich brown and Rose's dark eyes.

She tweaked her cheeks to bring a blush to them, glad she had chosen the claret gown.

She glanced down at Crispin whose golden eyes stared up at her. "Crispin, I must remind myself tonight isn't for me. It's for Rose. I intend to devote myself to finding my shy friend a suitor worthy of her."

Rose returned to interrupt Chastity's conversation with her cat. She looked much like Chastity would have envisioned her sisters. Her dark eyes sparkled with excitement as she twirled around. "So, what do you think?"

"You look beautiful," she told her friend sincerely. With her dark hair piled on the crown of her head and curls left dangling to her nape and the gown displaying her lovely attributes, she would garner the attention of many men. "But don't waste your splendid appearance on me. Come, let us go."

As they descended the stairs, the first guests were just arriving and paying their respects to Aunt Agatha in the entry hall.

"Good evening, Lord Alvanley," said her aunt. "Ah, here are my summer guests now. Meet my great-niece, Miss Reynolds, and her friend, Miss Crockett."

The tall Alvanley with the prominent chest made an elegant bow over their hands and glanced up, smiling broadly. "Delightful creatures!"

So, this was the nobleman whose wit was celebrated by all of London, the man Mrs. Fitz had said loved apricot tarts.

Inclining his head, he said, "Summer in Brighton looms more intriguing by the moment, Lady Sanborn."

Rose blushed as Lord Alvanley wished them a good evening and passed into the parlor. Following on his heels came the Lades, Sir Bellingham and his wife, Harriet, and Mrs. Fitz, who Chastity warmly greeted as if she were her own aunt.

Richly attired, the woman who had wed Prinny so long ago had a calm, unruffled demeanor. "Good eve, my dears. Don't you both look lovely!"

"As do you," said Chastity. She meant it sincerely. Some women didn't age well, but Mrs. Fitz was not one of those. Her face reflected an inner light, a graciousness few possessed.

A dozen more guests entered behind Mrs. Fitz, greeting Aunt Agatha, Chastity and Rose. After that, the guests came in smaller numbers. As each arrived, Featherstone ushered them into the parlor where footmen waited with trays of sparkling wine, canapés and savories.

The last to arrive were The Rogue and his uncle. While her aunt was speaking to another guest, Rose chatted with the vicomte, giving Chastity a chance to surreptitiously peruse Sir Robert.

He had come dressed as the finest of gentlemen, a superfine black coat well fitted to his broad shoulders set off by a brilliant white shirt and ivory satin waistcoat with a black silk cravat. His long legs were encased in tight-fitting cream-colored pantaloons, leaving no doubt as to his manly attributes, which, she surmised, had been his intention. His ebony shoes, she noticed, had been polished to a high gloss.

The vicomte was not as tall, nor did he have shoulders so broad, but he was nevertheless handsome in the more refined Continental way. His auburn hair had been smoothed back to curl at his nape.

She supposed The Rogue must be intending to capture a lady's attention, though she didn't recall seeing Countess Lieven on the invitation list. Doubtless he would attract any number of ladies. Did all rogues have that sparkle in their eyes? That dashing smile of white teeth? Likely so. Else how did they beguile every female in which they took an interest?

"Good evening, Sir Robert," she said in formal welcome as he turned toward her.

His hazel eyes glistened as he took in her gown from the mounds of her breasts to her claret slippers, making her pulse race. "And to you, Miss Reynolds. Enchanting as always."

Chastity returned him a brief smile with her thanks and, leaving him to converse with Rose and the vicomte, sallied forth into the parlor, lifting a glass of champagne from the footman's tray as she did. Disarmed by Sir Robert's bold appraisal, she took a deep drink of the sparkling wine and gazed about the crowded room, determined to find someone for Rose.

In one corner, a small group played chamber music, adding to the ambiance.

As she ventured deeper into the crowd, she noted that the guests were not all over the age of sixty, as she had expected. Instead, she found herself surrounded by both young and old engaged in lively conversations.

Judging by appearances, the guests seemed to be enjoying themselves. Her great-aunt's reception would be counted a huge success and, for that, Chastity was grateful. She wanted Aunt Agatha's kindness to be recognized.

She was about to seek out Letty when a gentleman Chastity had been introduced to at the front door approached her.

She recognized the handsome man immediately. "Mr. Henry Cairo, I believe?" With a name like that and a winning smile, she could never forget him.

"Indeed, I am, dear lady, and grateful you have remembered me."

"Your name is so unusual. Is it too obvious to ask if your family is from Egypt?" His ruffled cravat hinted of the Continent, but there was nothing foreign about his speech and his curly dark brown hair framed a fair complexion.

He gave out a chuckle. "No, indeed. I'm from Coventry in the north."

She peered into his dark eyes with genuine interest. "Why, that's not far from my home in Northampton. What brings you to Brighton?"

"I was planning to summer in London, handling some business for my family, when I met Sir Bellingham at a showing of our latest designs. He persuaded me to come to Brighton for a visit as his guest." Mr. Cairo fixed her with an intense gaze. "I am thinking it was a wise decision."

The man was fascinating and might prove an acceptable suitor for Rose if he were unattached. "If I might inquire, what business has you displaying designs in London?"

"I like to think of my family as 'artisans in time'."

She returned him a puzzled look. "Artisans—"

His laughter interrupted her question. "That's what everyone does when I use that expression."

His speech was animated in a way that conveyed his excitement for the subject and Chastity leaned in, listening with great interest to hear him over the noise around her.

"To put it in common terms, Miss Reynolds, we make fine watches and clocks, and have since our family's early beginnings in Italy."

"But you have no Italian accent," she said, speaking aloud her thought.

He grinned. "Not for generations, I suspect."

"I have always admired a good timepiece," she said. "I'm fascinated by clocks of all kinds."

He took his pocket watch from his gold brocade waistcoat and, placing it on his palm, offered it to her for inspection. "This is one of my favorite designs. Unusual, don't you agree?"

She stared in amazement at the open face pocket watch, its offset hour dial in white with gilded hands. The larger face had been painted with a scene out of classical Greece: a lady in a bright red cloak over a white gown held an urn as she stood in front of a domed stone building. "Why, it's positively masterful! Truly, a work of art."

"My father and brothers design the mechanism and I paint the faces. I am delighted it's to your taste."

Seeing no ring on his finger, she smiled up at him, a plan forming in her mind. "Did you have an opportunity to speak with my good friend, Rose Crockett?"

"The dark-haired young woman I met at the door? I did not."

"You simply must have a chance to show her your watch! She, too, is from Northampton."

Chastity glanced around the room. Rose had drifted to the far corner, still speaking with Mrs. Fitz. "Come, I will take you to her.'"

He swept his hand before him. "Lead on, my lady."

To get to Rose, Chastity had to skirt the crush of people. As she was doing so, she passed her great-aunt, who was chatting with Sir Robert and M'sieur Donet.

Over the noise of the many conversations, Chastity heard Sir Robert say, "Please forgive our late arrival, Lady Sanborn. We were unavoidably detained."

"I'm so glad you came," replied her great-aunt. "I was quite worried you might not. I am gratified you are here at last." Aunt Agatha smiled at them. "The footmen will get you any drink you desire and there are plenty of hors d'œuvres to enjoy."

Chastity was aware of Sir Robert's gaze following her and Mr. Cairo as they continued toward their destination.

"My friend has accompanied me from Northampton," she told Mr. Cairo. "She will be most interested in hearing of your family business."

Finally reaching Rose and Mrs. Fitz, Chastity begged permission to speak to them of her new acquaintance.

"Mr. Cairo comes from a most talented family," she said. "Ask him to show you his remarkable watch," she urged the two women.

Rose and Mrs. Fitz greeted Mr. Cairo with expectant gazes.

"I will see you a bit later," Chastity said to him as she left the three of them and walked into the crowd but not before she looked over her shoulder and winked at Rose. *Now there is a suitor for you.*

Standing with Jack and Lady Sanborn, Robbie had observed Chastity Reynolds staring enraptured into the face of a man he had never met. His attire was that of a successful gentleman, his coat cut by a skillful tailor. Robbie must know more of this man before the evening was done. After all, he had promised The Grand Countess to look after The Girl Who Needed Watching. That he no longer thought of Chastity Reynolds as a girl, but a ravishing young woman, mattered not. He had a duty to fulfill.

Lady Sanborn excused herself and moved toward her other guests.

By his side, Jack sipped his brandy, casting a glance around the large room. "Have you noticed that every man in attendance under the age of seventy appears to be smitten with the lady you would have me believe is a virago?"

"Miss Reynolds?" Robbie watched as she passed through the room, men's heads turning to follow her as she led the man with curly brown hair through the crowd. In that glimmering red silk gown, she was something to behold. Her pale skin was nearly translucent as if glowing from within like fine marble. A rare beauty even by London standards. "Perhaps 'tis just that she is new on the Brighton scene."

"Even you don't believe that," Jack chided. "It was the same at the Pavilion the night we dined with the king. Miss Reynolds passes through a room like a bright candle in the darkest twilight. *Un rare spectacle.*"

"There you go again, Jack," Robbie teased, "spouting that French romantic gibberish."

"You need a bit of French gibberish in your life, Nephew. Just ask your mother."

"My mother, née Claire Donet, can be quite fierce when she speaks French. It's the language in which she chooses to discipline her sons, so I hardly think of it as romantic."

"What a waste of good words," said Jack.

"However, I agree with you that Miss Reynolds is unusually attractive." In London, Robbie had noticed that some ladies of the *ton* walked with an arrogant stride, their noses ever in the air. Not so Chastity Reynolds. It was as if she were unaware of how beautiful she was or how men watched her. *A beauty who is all fire and cheek.* A woman, he suspected, who would be passionate in bed.

With her mission to find Rose an acceptable suitor at least partially successful, Chastity squeezed her way through the throng in the parlor looking to see if she recognized anyone.

"Miss Reynolds," said Sir Robert, suddenly appearing at her side. He and the vicomte each held a glass of brandy. "Might you have a moment?" His amused expression suggested he thought she might try to avoid him altogether which, truth be told, had been her intention at the outset of the evening.

"Of course," she said, finishing off her champagne and handing her empty glass to a passing footman. "With so many things to entertain you in Brighton, it is kind of you to attend my great-aunt's *soirée*." What she didn't say was that she was surprised her great-aunt had invited him. Well, perhaps it was due to his association with her countess friend. Then, too, the vicomte made for an unusual guest. "Have you met many of Aunt Agatha's friends?"

The vicomte cast a look around the crowded parlor. "Not all. But, from those I have met, this appears to be a gathering of some of the most interesting members of Brighton's society."

"I expect it is," said Chastity. "At least the ones who summer here. My great-aunt seems to know everyone."

Sir Robert glanced toward Rose. "Who is the man conversing with your friend?"

"Oh, that's Mr. Cairo, whom I only just met. A fascinating fellow. With them is my aunt's good friend, Mrs. Fitzherbert. Have you perchance met her?"

"Is Mrs. Fitzherbert the one associated with the king?" asked the vicomte.

Chastity thought "associated" an interesting choice of words. "Yes, in his distant past. She is a wonderful woman." Another controversial woman, thought Chastity, one she was proud to call friend.

"I shall look forward to meeting her," said M'sieur Donet. His accent was a soothing balm to her senses disturbed by the presence of Sir Robert standing so close. She detected a subtle smile forming on The Rogue's face as if he were aware of her discomfiture and found it amusing.

"I'm sure my great-aunt would be pleased to introduce you to the young women here. I scarce know any of them or I would do so myself." In truth, she didn't want to introduce the vicomte to any lady who might draw his interest from Rose. She would feel herself successful if, after tonight, Rose had many suitors in Brighton competing for her hand, one of whom was the vicomte.

"What of your cat, Miss Reynolds?" asked M'sieur Donet. "I have heard so much about him."

She glanced at Sir Robert, a twinkle in his eye. "I daresay you have."

"Is the feline about?" inquired M'sieur Donet.

"Crispin doesn't favor crowds. I expect he is lounging on my bed at this very moment."

"What an appealing thought," said Sir Robert with a wry smile that made her suspect he was not speaking of the cat, but her bed.

Turning to M'sieur Donet, he said "The cat and I are now friends, Jack. I shall introduce you myself should the feline condescend to make an appearance."

The vicomte chuckled.

Chastity probably should have remarked on Sir Robert's rescue of her cat but his smug look drove that thought from her mind. Fighting a huff, she wished them a good evening and went in search of another glass of champagne.

Sometime later, Lady Sanborn stopped to chat with Robbie, asking him if he and Jack were enjoying themselves. The grand feather adorning her many-colored turban wafted in the breeze coming through the door to the parlor.

"We are," Robbie offered. Seeing Chastity Reynolds glide past them with her friend and Mr. Cairo, he added, "Your great-niece seems to be delighted with your many friends."

Lady Sanborn watched her great-niece for a moment and then turned back to him. "Yes, and they appear to adore her. Why, Lord Alvanley has been seeking her attention all evening but she has yet to pause long enough for him to catch up with her."

"The music is quite nice," observed Jack, darting a glance at the small group of musicians.

The older lady sighed as she let her gaze drift around the room. "One cannot very well have a *soirée* without music, but the musical group does take up space. Alas, I could have wished for a larger parlor, but I do believe the press of all my guests has not diminished their pleasure."

Having been curious about some of the men he'd observed, Robbie asked, "My lady, do you know all of those here tonight?"

"Goodness no, not all," she said, shaking her head, causing the feather to flicker above her. "Some have come with those I invited. I never mind such additions. They are often the most interesting people." She turned toward her guests. "Have you met Mr. Cairo?"

"I have not had the pleasure," said Robbie.

"A splendid fellow. He came with Sir Bellingham." Leaning in to be heard, she said in a lower voice, "I believe the young ladies find him very attractive, as they do the two of you."

"You are most kind to say so. Where is Cairo from? With a name like that, one thinks of Egypt."

"Oh no, not so far away. I believe his family originated from Italy, but he lives in Coventry, near where my great-niece and her friend reside in Northampton. How fortuitous is that?"

"Fortuitous, indeed," said Robbie. He would have to be more attentive to Miss Reynolds, lest she become infatuated with some man of whom The Grand Countess would not approve.

Examining the other men in attendance, Robbie wondered if any of them could be among the ones who had been following him. Such a man could have slipped into the reception as supposed friends of the invited guests. After all, Arthur Thistlewood had been a gentleman and he led the conspirators.

Chastity was engaged in conversation with Sir John and his wife Letty as the guests began to depart and Sir Robert and his uncle took their leave. Surprised to feel a sense of loss at The Rogue's departure, she turned back to her new friends, knowing she should have been relieved he was gone.

The man had gotten under her skin with his sparkling hazel eyes and handsome face. He had even charmed her cat! Still, his constant amusement at her expense was tiresome. Without speaking a word, he could tease her unmercifully, no doubt in an attempt to remind her of their first encounter. She was not immune.

Sir John and his wife had indulged in several glasses of champagne yet they were hardly affected by the wine. Letty towered over all of the women in the parlor and half the men. Even at her age, she stood erect with the same elegant air with which she sat a horse.

Chastity inquired if Letty might like to ride again with her.

"Hell, yes. Another race if you're up for it. Damn good jaunt the last time." At Chastity's happy nod, Letty said, "I can't ride tomorrow, but perhaps the day after?"

"Indeed, yes!" She would allow Letty and a high-spirited ride to divert her thoughts from Sir Robert.

Chapter 9

The next morning, Robbie strode past the king's stables to the green lawn in front of the dense stand of trees on the Pavilion's grounds where he was told he might find his uncle. Narrowing his eyes, he glimpsed the sun flickering off a silver blade as it flew from Jack's hand to lodge in a knot in the broad trunk of an old oak with a "thwack"! Another joined it seconds later. Then another. The distance was far and the accuracy deadly.

Jack never missed.

Robbie crossed the lawn to join him. "Tiller gave me your message. Why did you ask me to join you with my pistols loaded?"

"I thought we might practice." Jack said over his shoulder as he strode to the tree and pulled the knives free.

Robbie came alongside him. "Here on the king's grounds? Not likely." He gestured to the large domed building some distance away crowned with a cupola. "The stables, Jack. Think of the horses. Why, Zeus and Apollo would be shrieking in their stalls were I to send off shots within their hearing. And why now? It's not as if we need to polish our skills." Robbie had hoped the two of them might take his curricle for a jaunt around Brighton to exercise the grays before breakfast. With the sky portending rain, he was anxious to leave.

"It occurred to me a worthy display of skill might serve to warn any who would be watching us that we are armed."

Robbie let his gaze travel over the grove of elm trees at the edge of the lawn, so dense he could not see through the branches. If there were eyes staring back, he neither saw nor sensed them. "I suspect anyone who would plot against the king's ministers cares not that we can defend ourselves. Cowards rarely face a man head on. They act with stealth, always at one's back, waiting for the moment to strike."

"*Très bien*," said Jack, sliding his knives back to their hiding places, the last fitting neatly into his boot. "Is it your wish to ride before breakfast?"

"I thought perhaps we might exercise the grays. I asked Tiller to have a groom ready my curricle."

"I like that idea."

The stables were only a short walk away. When they arrived, a groom awaited Robbie alongside his curricle. The grays snorted, impatient to be off. He stroked their necks, whispering soothing words to remind them he was their master and knew well their preferences. A gentle touch helped to quiet the spirited horses but did not rob them of their eagerness to run.

Climbing into the vehicle, he slid his pistols into the compartment beneath his feet he had designed for his weapons.

"A clever hiding place," remarked Jack as he climbed in beside Robbie.

"One never knows when a scurrilous thief will attempt a robbery. I have an extra set in my chamber."

Robbie took great pleasure in the taut reins of his matched pair as they moved with alacrity down the Steyne and turned left onto the Marine Parade. Once there, he let the horses have their heads on the deserted stretches. The breeze from the sea smelled of salt and fish. He never tired of it, for the sea had been the smell of home for many years.

Few people were out walking this early, for those coming to Brighton from London generally kept city hours, rising late. It was rare, however, that Robbie slept to midday. His years at sea had given him the habit of greeting the sun as it rose in the sky.

Moving along at a good clip, Robbie inquired, "Did you enjoy your jaunt in my curricle with the lovely Rose Crockett?"

"Indeed, I did. She was quiet at first, but when I took off at some speed, she held on to her bonnet and laughed, her dark eyes sparkling with delight. Beneath her quiet demeanor lies a woman who dearly loves to have fun."

"She is lovely," said Robbie, noting the pensive look on his uncle's face.

"I have been thinking your mother may have the right of it in urging us to find wives. My father would urge the same of me. You don't have the need to produce an heir as I do; still, knowing how you adore your nephews, I think you will find yourself married one day. As for me, since my mother is English, a bride from England would be well accepted into the Donet family."

"You are thinking of Miss Crockett?" asked Robbie, not realizing his uncle had been so taken with the girl.

"Let me just say that I find her reserve attractive, especially when she sets it aside. She is thoughtful and does not engage in idle chatter, and she is a great observer of people. Her remarks are often astute."

Inclining his head to better view his uncle, he noted a wistful look in the man's eyes. Perhaps he was smitten with the country lass. "You could do worse than a gentle country girl."

As he turned the horses back toward the Steyne, Robbie saw folks gathering on the beach some way down the Parade. "'Tis the fish market," he remarked. "Here's where the early risers go." Robbie slowed the grays as he recognized Chastity Reynolds and her friend just stepping onto the beach. "Look, Jack, 'tis Snow White and Rose Red. Shall we greet them?"

"By all means," said Jack.

Robbie slowed the curricle to a stop.

Jack hopped down, a broad grin on his face.

Robbie tied the reins to a nearby post and took in the scene on the beach where the denizens of Brighton who had managed to rise early had flocked to buy fish. Beyond the wives of the fishermen who sat beside large baskets hawking their fish, the boats had been pulled up on shore, their nets hoisted to dry. Tiller had told Robbie that on any given day a hundred ships might return to Brighton bringing fish to the local market and beyond. From what Robbie could see, less than half that number was arrayed on the shore today.

As they approached the two women, Robbie tipped his hat, asking if he and Jack might join them.

Miss Crockett spoke with excitement. "Please do. We were just about to venture into the mass of shoppers." Her eyes scanned the beach. "Have you ever seen so many fish?"

"On the Isle of Guernsey, certainly," said Jack, "though mostly oyster boats and cod fishermen."

Seeing the basket Chastity held over her arm, Robbie inquired, "Have you come to buy fish?"

"Indeed, we have." She turned her bonneted head toward the women selling fish. "We are shopping for Lady Sanborn's cook."

Cries went up as the women sitting by their baskets yelled out the fish they had for sale.

Miss Crockett smiled up at him. "It seems that mackerel have come into season, Sir Robert, and the fishermen's wives want to be certain we know of it. And just there," she said pointing, "I see turbot."

"Shall I help you select some good fish?" Jack asked Miss Crockett. "I think I see prawns over there." He pointed farther down the beach.

"I would welcome your assistance," said Chastity's friend, "Cook said to bring back prawns if there were any to be had."

Jack offered the girl his arm and the two strolled off toward that part of the beach. Robbie turned to Miss Reynolds with a bemused smile, wondering if she would deign to allow him to accompany her. "Is there some fish you favor?" The sky was overcast but her pale golden hair glistened beneath her straw bonnet and her bright blue eyes shone like the sky on a clear day. The peach-colored spencer jacket she wore over her morning gown brought a blush to her cheeks. Altogether, she presented an alluring sight.

"My great-aunt's cook mentioned dories. I would be obliged if you might direct me to those. The River Nene in Northampton is not home to that fish."

"I'm sure we can find some here as they are among the breakfast selections at the Royal Pavilion. Come," he said, offering his arm, "let us hunt for them together."

With what he recognized as reluctance, she took his arm. Whatever the cause, at least for this morning, she had called a truce and he was glad of it. Curling her fingers over his arm, he held them in place with his hand. The feel of her delicate hand, even through the gloves she wore, brought to mind how soft she had been when pressed against his chest the first night he'd encountered her at Grillon's Hotel.

They passed the various impromptu stalls and wove their way around large baskets of fish set on the shingles. She gazed into each one, clearly captivated by so much on display. "I love how the vendors cry the names of the fish they have for sale. It makes the market quite lively, don't you think?"

"'Tis one benefit of being on the coast," he replied. "It's the same in the South Pacific on the islands where fish and turtles are caught in great abundance."

"Have you often sailed to the South Pacific?"

"Aye, with my father and brothers, though these days they sail mostly to the east for tea and spices."

"It sounds exotic, like the Pavilion."

"It can be a worthy adventure, especially for young lads as we were when my brothers and I first went to sea. On a balmy day when the sun is setting into the horizon and dolphins are leaping under the bow racing with the ship, there is no more magnificent sight. But there are other times when pounding waves crash over the deck and the weather calls for a man's courage. My eldest brother once had to fight his way out of a hurricane in the Atlantic."

Her frown cast her beautiful eyes in shadow. "I wouldn't want to be on a ship then. Still, travel holds much interest for me."

She gazed up at him with an innocence he was certain was not feigned. Her blue eyes sparkled and, for a moment, held his gaze. Then he shifted his attention to her perfectly shaped lips. Lips, he reminded himself he had once sampled. Jack's assessment had been correct. Miss Chastity Reynolds had no idea of her effect on a man and Robbie was only beginning to realize how devastating was her effect on him.

She turned away, her bonnet hiding her face but the peach-colored ribbons lifted in the breeze, making him want to turn her toward him to look again into her eyes. He was certain she would not welcome the gesture.

Robbie scanned the beach, spotting baskets full of dories in the distance and, taking her elbow, he guided her toward the odd-looking fish.

Suddenly, she lost her footing on the shingles and began to fall. He reached his arm around her waist, steadying her. His hands on her soft flesh caused a desire for more to sweep through him. She was slender beneath her gown and more delicate than her personality would suggest.

"Oh!" she exclaimed, righting herself. "Thank you," she said with a flush of embarrassment.

An overwhelming need to protect her from anything that might cause her to fall surged through him. Such feelings for a woman were new to him. He tried to make light of it, returning her a wry smile while slowly letting go of her waist. "Anytime."

"You are a scoundrel, Sir Robert. If I didn't know better, I would have thought you arranged that stumble."

"I would never be so obvious." But he couldn't hide his pleasure at having had her so close. He would have more if he could.

They arrived in front of a sun-bronzed woman who sat on a stool surrounded by baskets of dory fish. On her head was a faded blue plaid scarf and around the waist of her plain gown was tied an apron, spangled with fish scales glittering like sequins.

Robbie focused on the unusual fish, flat and nearly round in shape, but with striking markings. "These are fresh caught," he told Chastity. "You can tell by their brilliant stripes, nearly orange. In time, the color will fade."

She pointed to the fish the woman held out for inspection. "What is that black spot in the center?" She was a child full of wonder at nature's oddities, curious and innocent. So unlike the young women of London, who were either empty of ideas or full of simpering affectations to gain a man's interest. He watched her, captivated.

Unwilling to let her see how enamored he was, he adopted a formal yet teasing tone. "Why, Miss Reynolds, I'll have you know that is God's protection against predators who mistake the spot for the fish's eye, giving the dory time to escape."

She laughed up at him, seeming to enjoy the formal manner he had pretended for her benefit. "Well these didn't escape!"

"Ah, but man is the ultimate predator."

The wizened fishwife selling the dories obviously wanted to get to her business as she looked up at him with an inquiring gaze. "How many will ye be wanting, sir?"

He turned to Chastity. "Did the cook say?"

"No, but I should think enough for the household, and the servants would not turn away a meal of fine fish."

"We'll have a half-dozen," he told the fishwife. She smiled, pleased with her sale, and proceeded to wrap up the fish. She handed him the package and he paid her in coin.

"I could have paid her," insisted Miss Reynolds, her lips forming into an attractive pout.

"Consider it my gift to Lady Sanborn." He reached for her basket. "Allow me to carry this. As long as we are here, we should procure some sole. That's a fish that often accompanies other dishes."

She agreed and they thanked the woman and proceeded to where the sole were being offered. The ordinary task of shopping for fish in which Robbie rarely indulged had become a morning of unexpected pleasure. He relished this new amiability between them as they walked on, speaking of their childhoods.

"I played with the neighborhood boys when I could," she said. "The only activities in which the girls engaged were sewing and painting. I guess that's why I spent so much time with my father. He was more interesting."

"And that's how you became a designer of shoes?"

She blushed attractively. "Yes, I suppose it was. My father is ever so clever. He designs boots for the finest bootmakers in Northampton. His designs are unusual and are even coveted in London." Her face glowed with admiration for the man who had taught her the craft.

"You are very proud of him," he observed.

"I am." From beneath her bonnet, she asked, "And you? What about your youth?"

"When my twin, Nash, and I weren't at Eton, we were at sea. It was an ideal life for a boy but often lacking in schooling us in social graces. Seamen are hearty souls but can be a rough lot."

"Well that explains your boldness," she said. "Is your twin the same?"

He thought about his soft-spoken twin who Robbie had protected from bullies. "Nash is the serious one."

"I'm sure your parents thank God for that."

He laughed, unoffended. She only spoke the truth. He could hardly be offended when her eyes glimmered like sun on azure pools, so vividly blue they were mesmerizing.

By the time they had finished their shopping, Jack and Miss Crockett had returned to find them. They compared purchases, laughing, for much had been bought, more than could be eaten in a few days.

Jack smiled broadly. "I think Lady Sanborn's cook will have to salt some of this fish to preserve it."

"I'm certain the servants will appreciate some of this seafood for their dinner," put in Miss Reynolds. "And then my great-aunt may invite the neighbors to dine with us over the next few days. She likes to entertain."

"Prawns for breakfast, anyone?" Miss Crockett inquired with a smile.

Jack chuckled. "Why not?"

"Please consider yourselves invited for dinner tonight," said Miss Reynolds. "Aunt Agatha will have need of your male appetites to help consume some of this."

Robbie was surprised at the invitation coming from her but he was not one to turn away such an offer. "That is most gracious," he said with an amused grin. "We accept."

"'Tis only fair that you should help us eat what you have helped to acquire," agreed Miss Crockett. She had obviously enjoyed her brief excursion with Jack and the two of them exchanged warm smiles.

"Our neighbor, Maria Fitzherbert, whom you met at the reception, will be joining us," said Miss Reynolds. "Mrs. Fitz is a lady of impeccable character and my great-aunt's particular friend."

"Sounds delightful," he said. "If you are amenable, I suggest Jack convey Miss Crockett and our purchases to Lady Sanborn's in my curricle, and I will escort you home by way of a fly." He looked up at the threatening clouds, noting the wind had picked up. Rain was not far away. "If we hurry, we might just miss the deluge."

"A fly?" asked Miss Crockett.

"Those are the small covered carriages you see around Brighton drawn by a man and an assistant. Very convenient and with room for two. The ones that Prinny and his noble friends use for midnight excursions are dubbed 'fly-by-nights'."

"I am not even surprised," said Chastity. Turning to her friend, she added, "You go with M'sieur Donet, Rose. I am happy to share a...a fly with Sir Robert."

Robbie handed their packages to Jack and offered his arm to Miss Reynolds, guiding her from the shingles to the road. He suddenly realized he'd been so absorbed in their time together, he'd paid little heed to the men gathered on the beach.

Any one of them might have been watching him.

Chastity and Sir Robert arrived as the rain began to descend. Once he had seen her to the door where the vicomte waited, the two men raced for the curricle as the clouds burst forth their well of water. Undaunted by the foul weather Sir Robert shouted, "I've endured worse at sea!" His beaver hat caught the rain as he grabbed the reins and urged his grays into a run. Even the thunder and lightning did not dissuade him from his course. "We'll return for dinner!"

He and the vicomte sped away, but they were already drenched.

She did not doubt he would hold to his word and return. Rogue he might be but Chastity recognized in him a strength of character that was even more attractive than his face. And that morning as he'd guided her over the shingles, her resistance to the man's charms had begun to fade as she leaned on his arm, drawing from his strength. The ride back to her great-aunt's home in the fly had been another experience where his intense gaze had dwelt on her.

"A chance to be alone with you," he said. "But I assure you I will take no advantage. Though I'd rather be sitting next to you, in deference to the two carrying us, I thought to balance the fly."

Chastity stood at the parlor window, watching the rain turn the

Steyne into mud. Rubbing against her skirts, Crispin sounded a loud "Meow." Even he had softened to the man. Or, did the cat merely mirror her mood toward him? "To my great surprise, he did act the gentleman, Crispin."

True to his word, later that day, as the rain subsided to drizzle, Sir Robert returned with his uncle. After sharing drinks in the parlor and a reacquaintance with Mrs. Fitz, the six of them ventured into the dining room.

Above the mahogany table a gilded chandelier cast glowing candle-light on Aunt Agatha's elegant Wedgwood china, a pattern that featured feathers circling the rim.

As the first course of asparagus soup was served, her great-aunt proudly announced, "The asparagus for the soup came from my kitchen garden."

"Agatha is very industrious," said Mrs. Fitz. Dressed in a pale green silk gown, the older woman was the essence of aging royalty. Aunt Agatha, in contrast, was dressed in vivid mustard yellow trimmed in cinnamon colored ribbon.

"'Tis very tasty," offered the vicomte.

Chastity forced her gaze from Sir Robert, who had been regarding her above his soup spoon to consider his uncle. "Do you not have kitchen gardens on Guernsey?"

"*Mais oui*, we do, and I greatly admire them. Guernsey grows many vegetables." His manners were elegant and his features aristocratic, whereas his nephew was the kind of man men seemed to favor.

When the soup was taken away, a footman served sole prepared in lemon butter. The flavor was delicate, the fish fresh from that morning.

"This is delicious," remarked Mrs. Fitz, sitting at one end of the table. "Your excursion to the beach this morning has proven a grand success."

"We did acquire a bounty of fish," said Chastity. She had chosen a gown of Calamine blue that reminded her of a robin's egg. She hoped the color didn't drain her face of color.

"Cook was pleased with the many purchases," said her great-aunt. "She promises more fish to come. Tomorrow's dinner will feature dory fish."

As she savored the sole, Chastity's mind returned to her morning on the beach and how well she and Sir Robert had done together. She remembered laughing as he explained the strange-looking dory fish, his patience in selecting the sole to get just the fish he wanted and his bold grasp of her waist to keep her from falling as she tripped on the shingles. It had been so natural to be with him.

While her great-aunt and the others were eating their soup, he had been staring at her over his spoon, his gaze so intense it was as if she weren't wearing anything at all. The knave! Perhaps his manners of the morning proved too great a strain. He might appear the gentleman but beneath the veneer, he was still a rogue who dallied with married women and tavern wenches. She feared if she didn't guard her heart, she would fall for him like so many other women had. She vowed she would not be seduced.

"I collect you young people enjoyed yourselves this morning," said Aunt Agatha from the end of the table opposite Mrs. Fitz.

"We did," Rose said. "M'sieur Donet was ever so helpful in selecting just the right prawns."

"I'm certain Cook will bring some of them to the table in due course," said Aunt Agatha. "When I left her, she was studying a recipe involving prawns and truffles."

A chuckle issued from Mrs. Fitz. "Agatha told me she was tempted to ask Cook to compose the entire menu from what you brought back as there was so much fresh fare."

Chastity's great-aunt shook her head. "I could not persuade her. She insisted on having the chicken fricassee and a haunch of lamb added to our menu."

"Dining with you, Lady Sanborn is like dining at the Pavilion," said the vicomte, one auburn curl falling to his forehead as he focused on his sole. "I must pace myself if I'm to arrive at the puddings with any appetite at all."

"You remind me," put in Aunt Agatha, "you know the king has been in London for that dreadful hanging of the men who meant to murder the Cabinet. I am told he will soon return to Brighton, coming in his yacht, the long way from London. No doubt the whole town will turn out to see him standing on the deck."

Knowing to speak of the king might raise a sensitive chord for Mrs. Fitz, Chastity thought to involve her in the conversation. "Have you sailed on the royal yacht, Mrs. Fitz?"

"Not the one the king sails today, my dear. I sailed with him on the *Royal Caroline* many years ago before he became regent."

"I should look forward to sailing," said Chastity. She gave Sir Robert a hopeful glance as he had promised to include her should he receive an invitation from the king, but he was lost in his thoughts.

As the plates were removed and the next course served, her great-aunt said, "My friends tell me there's to be a ball at the Royal Pavilion celebrating the king's return. I imagine you will be invited, Sir Robert, as well as M'sieur Donet, since you are his guests for the summer."

"A ball at the Pavilion!" exclaimed Rose. "I can only imagine." Her eyes glistened with excitement.

Chastity was a little excited herself. Except for the Winter Assembly in Northampton, which didn't really count, she had not been to a ball since her failed first Season in London. Perhaps this ball would provide a better memory.

"You must go if you can," said Mrs. Fitz to Chastity and Rose. "The balls held at the Pavilion are something to see and the music grand." Chastity was pleased to observe that the woman who was once Prinny's favorite held no rancor for her erstwhile husband but unselfishly delighted in the possibility of Chastity and Rose enjoying themselves at his Pavilion.

"I wonder when such an event might occur," Sir Robert said, but he appeared distracted. She puzzled over the cause. A moment later, he leaned toward Chastity. "Even with all those years on my family's ships, I did manage to learn to dance. Of course, 'twas most often the sailor's hornpipe we danced to, not a waltz."

She was tempted to utter a "Humph" but kept silent in light of the company. She was familiar with the rollicking fiddle music but could not imagine dancing to its tune. Then again, on a ship's deck, she might be persuaded.

The vicomte turned to Rose. "I learned to dance in Guernsey, the same place I learned to fence. But since a Bourbon now sits on France's throne, I can again dance at the Tuileries."

Rose smiled at the Frenchman. "That sounds very romantic, M'sieur. I imagine you are a very good dancer."

In a deeper French accent than typically characterized his speech, he replied, "You will have to allow me to show you, Mademoiselle."

"Well," said Mrs. Fitz, "it strikes me you will certainly have a grand evening should the ball come to pass."

After dinner, they retired together to the parlor where tea was served for the women and brandy for the men. "You may rest assured, M'sieur Donet," said Aunt Agatha, "that the brandy you drink is the finest French cognac."

"I will have to bring you some from my family's estate," said the vicomte.

Chastity took that opportunity to urge Rose to entertain them with a song.

"If you're sure you would want me to," Rose said shyly.

"Of course we do," said Aunt Agatha. "We'll sit here enjoying our drinks and listen to your lovely voice."

Rose nodded and took her place at the pianoforte. Setting her fingers on the keys, she began to play. Soon she was singing a haunting melody. Her voice had an unusual quality, a throaty, pleasing sound that brought much emotion to the music. The song she chose was the Irish tune "Robin Adair", one she often sang in Northampton to great effect.

What made the assembly shine?
Robin Adair.
What made the ball so fine?
Robin was there:
What when the play was o'er,
What made my heart so sore?
Oh! It was parting with
Robin Adair.

Chastity watched the vicomte as he listened, enraptured, his eyes never leaving her beautiful dark-haired friend. Glancing at Sir Robert to see his reaction, she was surprised to observe he had fallen into brooding silence, drawn into his thoughts. His eyes were downcast as he pensively twisted the glass of brandy in his hand. What could have brought about such a change—from smiling rogue to brooding dinner guest—in so short a time? Whatever was he thinking?

Robbie had not been able to take his eyes off Chastity Reynolds as they dined. A vision in blue, her eyes the color of a calm sea in tropical waters, he recalled the feel of her body as he'd reached for her waist that morning on the beach. Now, staring into his brandy, his mind considered the danger surrounding him in Brighton, a danger that could plague her as well.

Since the day he'd been followed on North Street, he'd not experienced the uncanny feeling of being watched. Nor had he observed anyone hiding in the trees that morning on the grounds of the Pavilion. But someone could have been there, watching. Distracted as he was by Miss Reynolds, it was possible he'd failed to detect eyes upon him. The crowded fish market had contained all levels of society. While the people perused the fish, they also watched each other. Surely he and Chastity Reynolds had been observed. Again, he worried that the enemies of the Crown would turn their eyes on her or even her great-aunt.

The friends of the conspirators could have shot him many times over. The note had said *"...when you least expect it, ye will suffer."* That could be at any time his back was turned. Yet they had not taken action. What was their intent? Why did they wait, only observing? He could only hope Chastity Reynolds was not with him when their attack came. Perhaps he should set another trap, this time for his pursuers.

Standing in the shadows of the rooms he had rented just off 4th Street, Aaron Ings studied the men he had chosen to exact his revenge. They were a rough lot, the kind who would do murder for a price with nary a concern. It helped his cause that they regarded a spy for the Crown to be the worst of men, a loathsome wretch. Powell was just such a one, the only one who'd been there at the beginning with Aaron's brother, James, when Thistlewood had first spoken of the need for action, but who'd not been there at the end. It had taken time, but Aaron had tracked him down.

Once Aaron knew where the spy was headed, he followed him to Brighton, arranging to meet his hired men a few days later. That Powell was the guest of the king and staying in the Royal Pavilion made things difficult as it was well guarded. But Aaron would have his revenge, even if it took him the summer to see it done.

He leaned against the planks of the wall in the dismal lodgings, listening to his men discuss how he might go about it. With the shades drawn over the windows, he and the men he'd hired in London were left in near darkness, save for the two tallow candles burning from the sideboard. The shabby surroundings were not up to his standards but the entrance in the alley off North Street enabled them to come and go without notice. It was on North Street he had first discovered the despicable spy strolling along with his companion as if he had not an ounce of guilt for betraying good Englishmen to the gallows, including Aaron's own brother.

Aaron was curious to hear what his men had to say since they had just returned from the seafront where they had been watching Powell that morning.

"Ye should have seen him eyein' the chit," said Duffy. "No sister that one. A real looker she were, too I seen him with her the night I trailed him from the king's palace to that fancy house on the Steyne."

"Aye," agreed Augie. "Whoever she be–sister, friend or roll in the hay, he were careful of her, quick to help her over the stones and carryin' her basket."

Pete rubbed his hand over his bristled chin. "Is it just killin' the bastard ye're after, Guv? Or would ye care to make him pay in kind for what he done? I say take from him, like he took from ye!"

Aaron uncrossed his arms and pulled away from the wall. "You may have a point, Pete. Touching the object of his affection would prolong the agony. But I will not kill a woman."

"Who said anythin' about killin' her?" asked Pete. "We could have a bit of fun with her and return him used goods. He might even thank us. A skirt is like a horse, better when they're broke in some."

Augie licked his lips. "I've always had a hankerin' to try a piece of high-born tail. Ye know, just to see what 'tis like."

Pete grinned. "Skirts are all the same. Strip off them fine clothes, there's no way to tell Lady Lah-de-dah from Easy Sally Slattern."

"You are correct." Aaron lifted his fine boot onto the seat of a chair and crossed his arms over his thigh, his eyes narrowing at the thought. "Society's passport is reputation. To truly burn that blackguard's heart, the girl must be worse than used. She must be soiled beyond redemption. She must become Easy Sally." He nodded to himself as the plan formed in his mind. "I know of a brothel my brother frequented when he moved among the gentry. I assume the madam will accept donations, and won't be overly particular about the source. How fitting if Powell's lady were to join the ranks of the courtesans there."

"Right," said Augie with a sneer. "We drop him a note and send him half out of his mind searchin' for her. Meanwhile, we give her to yer fancy London brothel. Even if he manages to find her...she'll be ruined."

Pete smiled, his blackened teeth forming a most unpleasant sneer. "She might as well be dead."

Aaron stared into the candle's flame thinking about all he must do. "I'll need time in London to take care of things," he muttered. "While I'm away, keep your eyes on the prey. I wouldn't want him to leave Brighton before we are ready. But, remember, he's a spy and will be wary, so be on your guard."

Chapter 10

Several days later, Chastity made her way to the breakfast room to discover Rose happily chatting with Aunt Agatha. "Good morning." Drawn to the sideboard by enticing smells of the morning meal, she fixed herself a plate of eggs and a hot bun flavored with caraway seeds.

Taking her seat, she waited for the footman to pour her chocolate as a feeling of melancholy swept over her. The message she'd received from Letty that said she would be unable to ride this morning was certainly a part of it. It was a shame as the weather promised a glorious day and a fast race would have taken her mind off Sir Robert. Her thoughts had often drifted in his direction recently. She actually missed him, which would never do.

"I trust you both slept well," said Aunt Agatha. "I had a terrible night, tossing and turning with vivid dreams. Too much wine, I suspect. But then one is only old once, *n'est-ce pas?*" She laughed at her own humor.

Rose chuckled.

Chastity took a long drink of her chocolate. "'Tis too early for that, dear Aunt." She ate her eggs in silence thinking about the other reason for her somber state of mind. The day before, Henry Cairo had left his card when she and Rose had gone for a stroll. Lord Alvanley, too, had paid them a call while they were gone. Chastity regretted the missed opportunities since both would make fine suitors for Rose.

With little to occupy her for the rest of the morning, she thought of the circulating library on the Steyne she had yet to visit. Perhaps Rose might wish to join her. Or, she might attempt a new design for a lady's half boot she'd been thinking about. She liked to stay busy, surrounded by friends, which made her wonder how well she would do when servants and the occasional visitor to her estate would be her only companions. Of course, Crispin would be with her. He had followed her downstairs and now sat looking up at her attentively. He was a wonderful companion but woefully lacking as a conversationalist and she did so love lighthearted raillery. Alas, Sir Robert was very good at banter.

"Now that you are both here," said Aunt Agatha, "I must ask, have you noticed the weather has turned decidedly warmer?"

Chastity glanced at the sun streaming through the paned windows. "Well, yes, one can hardly miss that. We don't even need a fire this morning."

Her great-aunt's eyes sparkled with mirth. "The good weather gave me an idea. What do you two think of our indulging in sea bathing today?"

Rose's brow furrowed. "Will it be very cold?"

"Undoubtedly," said Chastity's great-aunt. "The cold seawater is thought to be beneficial to one's health. 'Tis not just a cold bath, Rose, but a cold *medicated* bath, good for the circulation."

"I would definitely favor such a venture," said Chastity, quite taken with the idea. "I have been anticipating the delicious feel of seawater against my skin." Letty had told her swimming naked was a sinful delight. "Must we wear clothes?"

"Chas!" scolded Rose. "Of course, you must."

"Indeed, no," Aunt Agatha corrected. "'Tis true those small wooden bathing machines that are towed to the water will contain loose-fitting linen gowns for us to put on should we choose, but some women prefer to bathe in no clothing at all."

"It sounds scandalous," said Rose, her cheeks turning red.

"It sounds marvelous!" said Chastity. "Did you never bathe in a river in the summer as a child?"

Rose shook her head. "Papa would never allow it."

"Oh, very well. You wear the gown if you must," said Chastity. "But, as for me, I want to feel the waves on my bare skin. Besides, we'll be private, won't we?"

"Why, of course!" said Aunt Agatha. "There are separate bathing areas for men and women and the women who act as dippers helping us into and out of the water keep it that way."

"Letty doesn't wear a bathing gown," said Chastity, knowing Letty would never impose cloth between her skin and the sea.

"Well, that is Letty," said Rose.

"I have seen her bathing naked," Aunt Agatha said. "She is of a height and weight that cause her no worry for the waves. But unless you are a strong swimmer, I do recommend you accept the tether the dipper offers you so that you do not drift away. The current can be strong."

Chastity wondered if The Rogue engaged in sea bathing. Since he came from a family of shipmasters and had sailed to the South Seas, she rather thought he could swim where an ordinary sailor might not. How she would like to sail to faraway islands where she imagined lagoons so clear one could see through the water to the sand. She tried to imagine him naked and diving into a lagoon but, since she'd only ever seen her sisters naked, the image her mind conjured was his masculine form in a gentleman's clothing submerged in blue water. Ridiculous! A rake would be quick to doff his clothes. And no doubt just as quick to accept the favors of the island women.

After the morning meal, Chastity and Rose donned their simplest gowns and climbed into her great-aunt's carriage that would convey them to the ladies' beach. "A carriage is best," explained Aunt Agatha, "as we won't want anyone to see us on the way home. Our hair, though hidden beneath a bonnet, will surely be wet and our gowns damp, although the dippers do provide drying cloths."

They arrived at the beach to see women flocking to the bathing machines lined up at the shore waiting for the horses to pull them to the water. The small wooden structures on wheels had one door facing the beach and one on the opposite side facing the sea. A short set of stairs led up to each. Chastity and Rose chose to share a compartment so they could help each other undress. Aunt Agatha brought her maid who would perform the same service for her.

Once inside their bathing machine, Chastity and Rose settled onto the benches and braced themselves for the tow to the sea. When the small conveyance came to a halt, Chastity shed her clothes and, urging Rose to hurry, emerged through the back door. A dipper helped her down the few steps to the water where she paused, looking out to sea, feeling the sun on her bare skin and the small waves lapping at her toes. Her skin turned to goose flesh in the onshore breeze. Rather than stand there and shiver, she gathered her courage to jump.

From behind her, Rose's voice quavered. "Are you sure you want to swim without the gown?"

"Very sure," Chastity said. "It will only weigh me down." Refusing the tether the dipper offered her, Chastity plunged into the surging sea. She gasped as the icy cold saltwater embraced her tender flesh, sending a chill to her very core. Ignoring the frigid temperature, she began to swim. Soon, she became used to the cold water and found it invigorating.

Other women were leaving their bathing machines. Chastity swam past them. Even though she kept her head above the water, the spray swept across her face causing her to experience a sudden exhilaration. She loved the freedom of swimming naked. It reminded her of other times when she had defied convention, the times she had galloped across the hills of home.

Turning around in the water, she glimpsed Rose stepping cautiously down with the help of the dipper, a sturdy woman who tied a tether to Rose's wrist.

"Just jump!" Chastity urged. But her reluctant friend raised her nose in the air and shouted, "I shall enter in my own way." Chastity laughed at the picture Rose presented yet she admired her friend for her insistence on entering the water at her own pace.

Not far off, Aunt Agatha ventured into the water. She was a sight with her plain bathing gown and her feathered bonnet.

"You wore a gown, too?" Given her great-aunt's penchant for the unusual, Chastity was surprised to see her fully clothed.

"Were I your age," Aunt Agatha said, swimming toward Chastity, "I would not have done so. But at my age, one needs all the covering one can get."

Chastity laughed and looked toward Rose, who came as far toward them as she could with the tether. "So, what do you think?"

"I'm cold," said Rose, "but I am trusting the seawater to do me good as Lady Sanborn assured us."

Chastity's great-aunt stood, the water churning around her. "You will soon find yourself enjoying the water, my dear. It will be a memory of your visit to Brighton that will last your life long."

Chastity silently agreed. When she returned to the slower pace of life in Northampton, she would have many memories. But were memories all she would have?

Robbie's instincts told him he was being followed. Tempted to glance over his shoulder, he resisted. It would only tell the brigand Robbie was aware of him. Somewhere in the distance on North Street, behind them both, Jack would be pursuing, ever watchful. It had been their plan to find out who was tracking Robbie and the location of his hiding place.

For surely such a man would be holed up in some loft over a tavern or a shed at the edge of town. What Robbie really wanted to know was the identity of the one who had written the note, for Robbie's instincts told him the miscreants numbered more than one.

He had worn a light overcoat for the effort in order to hide the small percussion pistols he had purchased from James Purdey of London. Purdey had developed a new firing mechanism for sporting guns that deprived birds of an early warning by avoiding the initial puff of smoke from the flintlock powder pan. It also had a shortened interval between the trigger pull and the shot. Adapted to pistols, the mechanism served well a spy's needs.

Robbie made the quick decision to enter Woolbridge's cigar shop, hoping Jack would expect him to exit onto the alley as they had done before. He waited for a moment but no one entered the shop after him.

Mr. Woolbridge glanced up from the counter expectantly and Robbie said, "Just passing through."

"Again?" the shopkeeper said, perplexed.

He smiled apologetically. "Can I help it if I like the scent of fine tobacco?"

Once in the alley, Robbie looked around, seeing nothing save old packing crates. The alley led him to Ship Street where he paused, taking in the shoppers and those coming and going from The Old Ship Inn a short way down the street. No one paid him any mind. He was about to continue when footfalls behind him caused him to turn, his hand on his pistol.

"*C'est moi,*" said Jack.

Robbie breathed out a sigh of relief.

"I followed the man down North Street until he went to ground ahead of me in one of the alleys."

"They may have lodgings there. We should examine the boarding houses off North Street. But why did he stop following?"

Jack ran a hand through his auburn hair in a frustrated manner. "I suspect he became aware of me."

"No matter. Tell me what he looked like."

"His appearance tended toward the ordinary. He was of middling height and weight. Whatever clothes he wore were covered by a chestnut-colored cloak, likely weighed down by pistols heavier than yours judging by his drooping pockets. His boots were brown and worn. Beneath his sloppy top hat, I saw a fringe of red hair. I didn't get a look at his face but when he turned to look down an alley, I detected no beard or side-whiskers."

"You did well. Red hair distinguishes him from many others. And such a one coming and going from North Street narrows it further."

"Would I make a good spy, *peut-être*?" Jack inquired with a grin.

Robbie chuckled. "We both come to the profession honestly given our sires, but you will have a better life if you keep to your vineyards and your ships."

"Aunt, would it be all right for Rose and me to walk to Lulham's, the shop where we ordered our shoes? They should be ready by now." Seeing her great-aunt purse her lips as if pondering the request, she added, "We could pick up your order, as well." Chastity wanted to retrieve the pair of slippers she had designed for Aunt Agatha with no one save Rose aware.

"I think that would be permissible," said her great-aunt where she sat by the fire, tending her stitchery. "After all, North Street is not far and 'tis early. But don't linger overlong. There is tea to think of and Cook has made a special tart."

With Rose by her side, Chastity donned her pelisse and bonnet and set off, crossing the Steyne to North Street. A short way on, she spotted Sir Robert and M'sieur Donet coming toward them.

"Perhaps they are returning to the Pavilion," suggested Rose. It was a reasonable thought since the Pavilion was just to the north but Chastity was inclined to think of something else.

"More likely they have just left their favorite tavern," she said, remembering the comely wench who had thrown herself at The Rogue.

"Miss Reynolds, Miss Crockett," said Sir Robert, tipping his hat. "How fortunate we are to encounter you. Might I ask what brings you two out this afternoon?"

"We are going to Thomas Lulham's shop to pick up our order of shoes."

"'Tis a surprise for Chastity's great-aunt," Rose informed them. "A pair Chastity designed herself."

"May we accompany you?" asked the vicomte. "I'd like to see the shoes."

"Certainly," said Chastity, noting the fond look the vicomte gave her friend.

Sir Robert's buckskin overcoat, draped loosely over his broad shoulders, made them appear even larger than when he wore only a tail coat. Beneath the overcoat, he wore a white shirt and neckcloth, a dark green waistcoat, and a black coat and breeches. His black boots, she noted, were unusually scuffed. She wanted to ask if he'd been striding through muddy streets but did not wish to appear rude.

The two men fell in on either side of them.

"I've news that should interest you, Miss Reynolds," said Sir Robert. "The royal yacht is expected to anchor off Brighton late this afternoon."

"Really?" asked Chastity, delighted.

"Indeed, and we have been invited to dine on the king's yacht tomorrow."

Chastity met his hazel gaze, wondering if he would say more. It wouldn't be the done thing to invite herself. But, oh, how she wanted to go.

"Don't tease them, Robbie," said the vicomte, a hint of amusement in his dark eyes. "We have inquired, dear ladies, and been advised you are welcome to accompany us."

"Oh, Chas!" exclaimed Rose. "Just think! We shall dine with the king on his yacht!"

Chastity beamed her pleasure. "It will be our pleasure to accept your invitation."

"Good," said Sir Robert. "I believe several other invitations are being sent out today, including one to your great-aunt."

They had nearly reached the shoemaker's when Rose asked, "Is the king's yacht very large?" Chastity could see the fear in her friend's eyes for she was not sure she could manage a smaller vessel that might be tossed about by the tide.

"Over a hundred feet on deck," replied Sir Robert. "The royal yacht is a full-rigged ship, large enough for the king to entertain a fair-sized group of guests for dinner. But a smaller rowing boat will convey us to the yacht."

"Oh," said Rose.

"Have no worries," put in M'sieur Donet. "The trip to the yacht will be short and I will be with you."

Rose gave the vicomte a warm smile. "Yes, that is a comfort."

They entered the shop and Chastity asked if the shoes she had ordered were ready.

"I believe your entire order is complete," said Mr. Lulham. He passed through a curtain that led to the back of his shop and returned with several packages.

Chastity paid the man for his service and opened the package with her name on it. The brown paper unfolded to reveal the orange silk slippers with yellow satin ribbon cross straps. On the toe was an embroidered sunflower. "I do hope Aunt Agatha will like these."

"Oh, she will," said Rose. "This may be the loveliest pair you have designed."

"Do you design men's boots?" asked Sir Robert.

"My father is the one who designs men's boots," said Chastity. "I fear my attempt would not be so masculine as to please the male gender."

"Alas," said the vicomte, "that is a loss, for the French do love decorated shoes, be they for a lady or a gentleman."

"I hadn't thought of that," said Chastity, noticing the vicomte's shawl collar, and his lace-edged cravat. He also wore pantaloons, not breeches, revealed by his low boots. All decidedly French in style. "I shall think on it, M'sieur."

Pleased with their purchases, Chastity allowed Sir Robert to escort her back to the Steyne. Behind them, absorbed in conversation, walked Rose and the vicomte.

Chastity's own conversation with Sir Robert was sparse. Again he appeared distracted, studying every person on the street, or was it just the men? That she had become so attuned to his moods she would notice such a small change annoyed her. *Why should I care what concerns him?* But the truth was, she did care. She wanted to know what lurked beneath his ever-charming exterior. She sensed a depth she had missed in their first encounters. She might not trust him but he intrigued her.

At her door, he bowed slightly. "A most enjoyable meeting, Miss Reynolds. I will send word tomorrow with the time we must depart for the yacht."

Since the walk to the shore from Lady Sanborn's house was not long, Robbie intended he and Jack would escort the ladies on foot to the place where a boat would be waiting to transport them to the king's yacht.

As the two of them ventured forth from the Pavilion, Robbie gazed up at the summer sky, which would not see sunset for many hours. Clouds drifted lazily in a field of blue, changing shapes with the wind. "At least the weather is with us and the onshore breeze mild."

"The ladies will be happy that dinner should see no glasses rolling on the deck."

"Except for Lady Sanborn, I doubt the other two have sailed before," said Robbie. "It will be a good introduction to ships for them to be on a vessel of that size."

"The largest yacht ever built to date," said Jack. "At least according to our breakfast waiter."

Robbie tried to imagine the deck of the yacht he'd seen only from a distance. Its length made it the size of some of his family's schooners.

"I've heard the yacht described as *élégant*," said Jack.

Robbie fought a chuckle. "Prinny never does anything by half when he is decorating. I expect his yacht will be exceptional."

They arrived at Lady Sanborn's to find the ladies ready and excited for the dinner that lay ahead. "What a glorious evening," said Lady Sanborn, looking very much like a flower in a brilliant orange and yellow silk gown and a feathered turban of the same colors. "The king will be so pleased."

Ever since he'd known Chastity Reynolds, he began noticing people's shoes. On the countess' feet were slippers that featured a sunflower.

"I am thrilled to be going," said Miss Crockett. "I've never been on a royal yacht, or any ship for that matter."

"*Très bien*," said Jack, "tonight that will change, Mademoiselle."

Miss Crockett smiled at Jack, her brown eyes sparkling.

Robbie had to admit they made a handsome pair but what might come of it, he had no idea. Like himself, Jack was a mixture of French and English, but Jack had a poetic, romantic side Robbie lacked. And Jack had another side that insisted on the utmost propriety. Robbie seldom gave lip-service to propriety unless it was for the benefit of others.

Chastity Reynolds, in her frothy sea green gown reminded him of a decoration on a marchpane-covered cake. Delectable enough to make him want to taste her.

As they made to depart, the red-haired butler held out her shawl. Robbie took it from him and draped it over her shoulders, brushing his fingers over her warm skin as he did so. A slight shiver accompanied his touch. *Good.* He liked to keep her off balance. She had the strength of character to easily dominate a man, but she'd not be happy if he allowed her to rule him.

The huge black cat that had previously been his enemy ambled down the stairs and rubbed its body against Robbie's boots, meowing loudly.

"Is that your cat, Miss Reynolds?" said Jack. "I have yet to meet him."

"Yes," she said, watching the cat with a frown, "though you might not know it to observe his lavish display of affection for Sir Robert." She tightened her paisley shawl around her shoulders and looked down at the cat. "Traitor!"

A chuckle escaped Lady Sanborn. "It seems the knight has tamed the dragon, dear."

Jack laughed and reached down to scratch the cat behind its ears. "Hardly a menace, Nephew."

"To my great relief," said Robbie, "Crispin has become a devoted follower." Robbie couldn't decide if the cat's new affection for him was a good thing when there was a distinct possibility the animal might soon be licking his boots, the same boots Tiller had spent hours cleaning and polishing.

Robbie consulted his pocket watch. "It's time we were off."

As they set off down the Steyne, Robbie's spirits rose to think he would soon be standing on a ship's deck. It might be anchored in the harbor but a ship that size was familiar territory.

The captain's gig was waiting for them where the water met the shore. In the distance, he glimpsed the *Royal George* at anchor, its three masts rising high above the hundred-foot deck. Above the main mast flew the Royal Standard. Instead of gun ports, thirteen large windows marched along the side of the hull overlapping the ocher-colored strake.

Other guests of the king had already gathered, including Lord Alvanley, Sir Bellingham and his wife Harriet, Lady Graham, and Henry Cairo, the gentleman from Coventry who designed timepieces. Citizens of Brighton stopped to ogle the *Royal George* and the passengers waiting to be taken aboard.

"The marchioness and Sir John and Letty are already aboard," Alvanley informed them. He turned and climbed into the gig after Sir Bellingham and his wife.

Robbie offered his hand first to Miss Reynolds to help her into the boat, but she declined. "Please assist my great-aunt first, if you will."

"Of course." As he was helping Lady Sanborn, Henry Cairo offered his hand to Chastity Reynolds and proceeded to assist her into the boat where he quickly claimed the seat beside her. Robbie's brow furrowed with his displeasure.

He waited for Jack to help Miss Crockett over the gunwale and take a seat beside her on one of the forward benches. Seeing the other guests had claimed seats, Robbie climbed in and gave the bow oarsman a nod of polite acknowledgment as he joined him on the forward-most bench. The oarsman tugged his forelock in a gesture of respect.

Robbie sat with his back to the bow like the boat's crew so he could watch the passengers, one in particular. Cairo leaned close to Miss Reynolds to whisper something in her ear that made her cheeks flame. Robbie pressed his lips together, resisting the temptation to throw him over the side.

The crew took to the oars and soon they were looking up at the yacht's black hull. The crew shipped the oars and waited as a bos'n's chair, rigged to the end of a spar, was lowered to the gig to allow the ladies and anyone else who wanted to use the chair to be hoisted onto the main deck. It was evident to Robbie that the crew had done this many times for the king and his friends, because they executed the maneuver with flawless efficiency.

He watched Chastity Reynolds, wondering what her reaction would be. He smiled to himself when she quite happily slipped into the chair and beamed her joy as she was sent aloft, like a child experiencing her first swing. Her friend, however, was a bit skittish until Jack convinced her it was safe and, though it swung about, would not dump her into the sea.

Except for Robbie and Jack, the men who had come with them also ascended to the deck via the chair. It was certainly the easier path, but where was the fun in that?

When the others were securely onboard, Robbie said to Jack, "Our turn," and grabbed the knotted manrope hanging next to the steep boarding steps built into the side of the ship. Even as a boy, his father had expected him to scale the steps. Had he not learned quickly, his older brothers would have ridiculed him.

As he began climbing, he looked up to see Miss Reynolds peering down at him from the rail, her eyes wide and her brows uplifted. He smiled to himself. If this impressed her, he could show her more.

Like Robbie, Jack was accustomed to climbing the rigging, so he grabbed the manrope and followed Robbie up the steps and through the cutout in the gunwale to join him on deck.

Letty, standing nearby, let out one of her famous oaths. "Hell and damnation, Powell. If only I had on breeches, I would have joined you."

Robbie grinned. "I do believe you would."

Letty turned on her heels and strode off toward her husband, grumbling about the restrictions of a lady's attire.

The king, who, with his mistress, was in the process of welcoming his guests, left them to cross the deck to Robbie and Jack, a satisfied smile on his face. On his chest, the king wore the ribbon and Star of the Order of the Garter. "I might have known you two would come up the side. Well done!"

Chastity felt the yacht shift with the incoming tide as she watched the king greet Sir Robert. By all appearances, they were on very familiar terms. Not for the first time, she wondered what The Rogue had done to earn the king's favor and a baronetcy. The hereditary honor had sometimes been awarded to returning soldiers who had distinguished themselves in the war with France. He would have been in his mid-twenties then. Perhaps it was something to do with a battle on the sea that helped defeat England's enemy. Jack had mentioned their fathers had been privateers. Yet neither of them was called "Sir". The vicomte's father had been the comte de Saintonge even before the French Revolution and Aunt Agatha had referred to Sir Robert's father as Mr. Powell.

She and Rose stood next to the rail as Aunt Agatha crossed the immaculately clean deck toward them. "Come, dears. Lady Conyngham is asking the ladies to go below." Then as a gleeful aside, "We're to dine in His Majesty's great cabin!"

Chastity followed her great-aunt and the other women, wondering what a "great cabin" looked like. Over her shoulder, she glimpsed the men, Sir Robert among them, lingering behind, talking with the king. Of what did they speak? Possibly something more interesting than the women would offer.

She paused at the companionway leading to the lower deck. The polished mahogany with its gilt moldings was something she would have expected in a fine townhouse in Mayfair. She thought it opulent for a seagoing vessel but then, this was Prinny's own and, if the Pavilion was any example, the king never scrimped when spending the government's money.

"Mind your head, Miss," a sailor cautioned, as Chastity stepped onto the ladder leading down. "You will find the ladder is wider than the ordinary by the king's orders."

The angle of descent was still uncommonly steep to Chastity's mind and, though there was another sailor at its base, she would have to transverse the length of it alone. As Rose was behind her, Chastity wanted to show courage, for her friend was already looking peaked. Turning to face the ladder, she braced herself with one hand on the side rail while lifting her gown with the other, and carefully made her way down.

It was the first time she had been on a large vessel of any kind. The small boats they used in the summer on the River Nene in Northampton for fishing and pleasure were half the size of the boat that had conveyed them to the yacht.

Relief flooded her as her feet touched the deck. She looked up and encouraged her friend, "'Tis not hard, Rose. Just go slowly."

Rose had decided to descend with her back to the ladder. Halfway down, the sailor reached for Rose's hand. "Here, Miss, let me assist you."

Rose accepted with a grateful smile.

The great cabin where they were to dine occupied the entire stern from side to side. The panel work in the cabin was carved in a dark wood with gilt moldings.

The windows, both stern and side, were of plate glass, flooding the cabin with light. Through the clear glass, she glimpsed the water on three sides with the shore beyond. Above, a skylight shed more light, illuminating a Brussels carpet beneath Chastity's feet.

A ship's lantern hanging from the skylight added a glow to the long mahogany table that was set for fourteen. White china, banded in gold and imprinted with the royal arms, made a regal statement. Chastity had never seen a table setting so fine except for that in the Pavilion. Crystal glasses for water, wine and cordial were set at each place.

The chairs surrounding the table were covered in red velvet casing, in addition to which ottomans and sofas were placed about the large cabin.

On a sideboard, decanters of liquor filled a polished wooden box, the kind that could be secured when at sea.

Against one side of the great cabin, to her amazement, stood a pian-oforte.

"My, but this is lovely," Aunt Agatha remarked to the dark-haired Lady Conyngham bedecked with jewels for the evening. To Chastity's chagrin, neither lady had experienced difficulty navigating the ladder. It gave her some comfort to realize her great-aunt was always up for an adventure and likely had sailed before, and the king's mistress had doubtless descended those same steps many times.

The king and the gentlemen joined them shortly. The steward poured the king and each of the guests a drink of their preference. Chastity accepted a glass of sherry. A musician slid onto the bench at the pianoforte and began to play.

Brandy in hand, Sir Robert came to her side, very handsome in his dark green coat and ivory satin waistcoat over buff-colored breeches. When he had arrived at her door, she had been surprised at how glad she was to see him. "What do you think of the king's yacht, Miss Reynolds?"

"It displays the same opulence as the Pavilion, yet I never would have imagined so elegant a dining room was down here."

"His Majesty likes to travel in style. I can assure you, my family's ships are not so magnificent belowdecks. More functional, I would say."

"The difference between a merchant and a king?"

His white teeth flashed a smile. "Just so."

The king spoke from where he stood at the head of the table. "Allow me to suggest a seating arrangement. My lady," he said to his mistress, "here on my right, as always. Alvanley," the king continued, "on my left, if you will, and Lady Sanborn next to you. At her side, let's have Sir Robert and then Miss Crockett, Mr. Cairo and Lady Lade. Across from Lady Sanborn, next to my lady, I would suggest Sir Bellingham, Miss Reynolds, Monsieur Donet, Lady Graham and Sir John. At the end of the table opposite me will be our captain, Sir Edward Berry, who I have asked to join us. Along with Admiral Nelson, he is remembered as a

'Hero of the Nile'. Welcome, Captain."

Sir Edward, standing behind his chair, erect in his dark blue uniform with gold braid and brass buttons, white waistcoat and pantaloons, inclined his gray head to the king. "It is my honor, Your Majesty."

Chastity judged him to be in his fifties. No longer at the side of Lord Nelson, who was long dead, the captain nevertheless appeared to have a lively interest in everything around him. His blue eyes shone with the pride of having served his king and country with distinction.

The king beckoned them to take their seats, and the gentlemen promptly assisted the ladies. On Chastity's right, the vicomte pulled out her chair for her. Once seated, she found herself meeting the amused gaze of The Rogue directly across from her. He looked very pleased with himself, as if he'd arranged their seating with the king. It vexed her to think he could rattle her with only a look from those stunning hazel eyes.

The first course was a white soup, well seasoned and tasting of chicken in cream. Chastity did not lift her head as she bent to dip her spoon for she felt Sir Robert's eyes still fixed on her. *Seductive charm such as his should be kept under lock and key.*

"How was your time in London?" Lord Alvanley asked the king.

Prinny huffed. "Clouded by the hanging of those 'desperate fools' as Lord Byron has called them, the 'awkward butchers' who would see my ministers dead." He gave Sir Robert a knowing look. "Still, we can be glad justice is done and they are gone from this world, eh?" He raised his glass of champagne and proposed a toast to the demise of all those who plotted treason.

Chastity sipped her champagne, wondering what had passed between the king and his subject. It had to be some knowledge they shared about the Cato Street debacle she had only read about in the newspapers.

"It is good to have you back in Brighton, Sire," said Aunt Agatha, gracefully changing the subject. "The town mourns your going and celebrates your return."

The king smiled, his cheeks reddening. "How gracious of you to say so, my lady."

"Will you open the Brighton races?" asked Sir Bellingham.

"Indeed, I will," said the king. "And soon."

The soup bowls were taken away and the fish course promptly served.

"My cook has prepared this dory fish a new way," said the king. "With mussels, spinach and apples. Appears appetizing enough, don't you agree? But do give me your good opinions."

Chastity raised her eyes to catch a glimpse of Sir Robert, an expression of mirth on his face as he glanced at the fish just placed on his plate. She had eaten dory fish more than once since their morning at the fish market.

"The fish is excellent," said Sir Bellingham. His wife, Lady Graham, nodded her agreement. In truth, Chastity liked mussels so she was quite happy to see them paired with the fish and its delicate flavor.

Henry Cairo was speaking with Rose when the king addressed him. "Mr. Cairo, I understand from Lady Sanborn you are a master of timepieces. What have you to say?"

"My family business in Coventry, Your Majesty, is making fine watches and clocks, some quite unusual with painted faces."

"Painted faces, you say? You must come 'round to the Pavilion and show us some. We can always use more clocks to track the hours. Might you have some with a Chinese theme?"

Henry Cairo directed his comment to the king at the other end of the table. "I can paint anything on the face of a timepiece, Sire, including a scene from China, if that be your desire."

"Ah! So, *you* are the artist?"

"I am."

"Have him show you his pocket watch," put in Aunt Agatha. "Truly extraordinary."

"Tomorrow, then," said the king to Mr. Cairo. Turning his attention to the vicomte, the king said, "Monsieur Donet, did you travel from France to holiday with Sir Robert?"

"My family has vineyards in France, Your Majesty," he added with a smile. "There we make fine cognac. But my home is on Guernsey. I frequently travel between the isle and England as my uncle is the Earl of Torrington and his estate is in West Sussex."

At his statement, Rose's eyes widened and she cast a glance at Chastity, who nodded briefly, pleased. Her friend's father could hardly object to a suitor who was the nephew of an English earl.

"I know Richard well," replied the king. "He and I have weathered together many battles in Parliament." The king stared at his wine glass as he rotated it in his hand. "The earl was a great friend of Prime Minister Pitt before he died. Pitt was a devoted Tory who gave to England the years God gave him."

"Hear, hear," said Lord Alvanley. "Well said."

Chastity remembered her father saying that Pitt and his friend, the king, as well as Alvanley, were all Tories.

Cold sliced lamb followed the fish course. Chastity, already feeling full, took very small bites and sipped her wine sparingly. She observed her great-aunt, across the table, did the same.

The king lifted his wine to his lips and inquired of Aunt Agatha if her great-niece and her friend were enjoying themselves.

"Oh, Lord yes. You were kind enough to invite them to the Pavilion, which they thoroughly enjoyed and, since then, they have indulged in riding, shopping and sea bathing."

Across the table, Sir Robert's dark brows rose in question. Did he wonder if she bathed without clothes? She indulged in a small smile. *Let him wonder.*

"Did you enjoy the seawaters?" the king asked Chastity.

"I did, Your Majesty. Very...ah, stimulating." Though Chastity could tell Rose was less enthusiastic, she managed a nod in the king's direction.

"Sea bathing in only one's skin can be diverting," remarked Letty, from where she sat on the captain's right. This caused Lord Alvanley to sputter into his wine and Sir John to chuckle.

"I would expect nothing less of you, dear Letty," said the king.

"I prefer to wait until warmer weather to sea bathe," said Marchioness Conyngham. Chastity gave the king's mistress a sideways glance, admiring her necklace of emeralds and diamonds, sparkling in the lantern's light. The necklace was dazzling. *But at what price?* What means honor when a king can take another man's wife to his bed with impunity. Prinny had done so more than once, but what husband would defy the king?

Under her lashes, Chastity sneaked a glance at The Rogue. She had never learned the outcome of his flirting that night at the Pavilion with the married Countess Lieven but he expressed no disapproval of the open invitation in the countess' seductive eyes conveyed over her fan at the concert. The king and his subject, she reminded herself, were much alike.

Lady Graham on the other side of the vicomte, availed herself of a pause in the conversation to ask the captain if he and the king's yacht would be in Brighton for some time.

"I serve at the king's pleasure," said Captain Berry, nodding in the king's direction. "But were I to guess, I would say unless the king is called back to London, we'll be here for the summer."

That seemed to please the guests near enough to hear the comment.

Sweetmeats followed dinner. The king and the men indulged in several glasses of port, the king reminding all it had been the favored drink of William Pitt.

Lord Alvanley made a toast in his honor. "To a man who served his country well!"

As they rose from the table, Sir Robert came to her side. "Do you have a hankering to sail?"

"Indeed, I do. Being on a yacht, especially a large one such as this, while in the harbor is grand, but to feel the wind on my face and the billowing sails above me would be grander still." Chastity had no fear of seasickness, and doubted Rose had any as they had ridden together in a closed carriage from Northampton to London over rocks and through mud with no ill effect.

His hazel eyes sparkled. "I shall keep that in mind should my ship's course divert to Brighton."

Chapter 11

The king wasted no time in bringing the social whirl back to Brighton. It was as if all of London realized the place to be was the seaside town and, wishing to be seen among fashionable company, flocked there in great numbers. This made Robbie's job of discovering the hiding place of the conspirators' friends more difficult. Several attempts had produced no results.

Meanwhile, horse racing had begun in earnest. Robbie and Jack attended each afternoon, wagering with Alvanley, Sir Bellingham and Sir John. On occasion, the king joined in, adding to the atmosphere of celebration. Sir Bellingham's guest, Henry Cairo, made several appearances. That is, when he wasn't pursuing Lady Sanborn's great-niece and her friend. His calling on the two young women had become a frequent event.

One afternoon, Robbie had glimpsed the clockmaker strolling down the Steyne with Miss Reynolds and her friend. A wave of jealousy had swept over him. It was an entirely new experience, one he did not enjoy.

Each Monday, the Castle and Old Ship Inns hosted balls. He and Jack attended a few and, each time, encountered a bevy of young women looking for husbands; however, Miss Reynolds had not been in attendance. Robbie thought the evenings greatly diminished by her absence. The brilliant spark she added to any gathering was missing.

"Perhaps it is time we paid Snow White and Rose Red a visit," he said to Jack at breakfast as he pushed his eggs about his plate with his fork, thinking of some excuse to look in on his "Ward for the Brighton Season", as Lady Claremont had called her.

Jack paused, holding his coffee between his hands. "I am not opposed to the idea. What did you have in mind?"

"I am certain Lady Sanborn would insist the two young women attend church on Sunday. Though I'm not sure which one is her preference, the closest to Lady Sanborn's residence is the Chapel Royal. We might offer to escort them to the service."

Jack grinned mischievously. "You devil."

Undaunted, Robbie sent an invitation to Lady Sanborn offering to accompany the three ladies to the Chapel Royal that Sunday. Robbie's mother, Claire Donet, had been raised a Catholic in France but, after her marriage to Simon Powell, she had become a devout Methodist. Thus, she had insisted her sons attend church. Even on their ships, a service of sorts was held on Sundays, officiated by the captain, which, in some instances, had been Robbie. He smiled to himself, trying to imagine what Miss Reynolds would think of that.

As he returned to his chamber to dress for dinner, Tiller approached with a sealed message. "This just arrived, Cap'n."

Robbie thanked him and broke the familiar seal. With more anticipation than he might have expected, he unfolded the single sheet. Lady Sanborn's script elegantly conveyed her short reply. "We'd be delighted. You may call for us a quarter hour before ten o'clock."

"A rogue in church?" Chastity asked her great-aunt, intrigued. "Whatever for? Penance?" She poured Aunt Agatha and Rose more tea, then subsided onto the sofa, lifting her cup to her lips.

"Perhaps that is the best place for a rogue," said Aunt Agatha, leaning forward to take a biscuit from the silver tray. "If indeed Sir Robert is a rogue." With a pensive expression, she added, "As I recall, the king used to attend the Chapel Royal until several years ago when the curate preached a sermon titled, 'Thou art the man'. You can well imagine Prinny's reaction."

"I know that story from the Bible," said Rose, a small bite of pastry lifted on her fork. "Wasn't that the one where the prophet confronted King David for taking another man's wife?"

"Indeed, it was," said Aunt Agatha. "Though David did worse than that. He ordered the husband into the front line of battle to be killed. Of course, he eventually repented of the deed and God forgave him. But there were consequences."

"I don't think King George has repented," said Chastity. "He's still taking other men's wives to his bed. But there is the consequence that he is left without a legitimate heir."

Her great-aunt's eyes took on a sad look. "The death of his only child, Princess Charlotte, was a tragedy, for her husband, who loved her, and for England. Had she lived, one day she would have been queen."

"So one rogue has forsaken Sunday services while another takes his place. How fitting it should be Sir Robert." Chastity tried to imagine sitting with The Rogue in church and failed.

"I think you are too harsh on Sir Robert," her great-aunt gently chided. "He has been nothing but a gentleman as far as I have seen."

Chastity didn't want to stoop to gossip, even if it was based on her own observations, nor would she tell Aunt Agatha about their first encounter, so she did what any proper lady would do. She took a sip of her tea and conceded politely her great-aunt might have a point.

Robbie gazed up at the tall, highly decorated pulpit as the singing ended and the reading from the Old Testament began. The five of them took up an entire pew in the spacious and lofty Chapel Royal at the corner of North Street and Prince's Place. The church near the Pavilion had been designed to encourage royal attendees. It had thus far failed in that mission if the current king was any example.

Robbie sat on the aisle with Miss Reynolds next to him. Lady Sanborn had placed herself between her charges and Jack was on the other side of Miss Crockett. Altogether, given the limited space, it was a cozy arrangement, one that Robbie favored. Chastity Reynolds' faint scent of flowers drifted to his nostrils and her warmth burned into his sleeve and breeches where their bodies touched ever so slightly.

"Our reading from the Old Testament today is from Proverbs 31," intoned Reverend Wagner. As he began to read, Robbie turned to glance at the profile of The Girl Who Needed Watching. Indeed, she did. Inclined to adventure, even mischief. He imagined her bathing naked in the waters off Brighton, her golden hair wet and flowing behind her. He was certain, like Letty, Chastity Reynolds would have foregone any kind of bathing attire. Rather than the frigid waters off Brighton, he preferred to think of her swimming in a warm lagoon on some distant shore, far from the stuffy atmosphere of the *ton*. There, he would show her the ways of love.

An elbow jabbed into his ribs and her whispered "Woolgathering?" jarred Robbie out of his reverie.

"Who can find a virtuous woman?" the good reverend went on. "For her price is far above rubies. The heart of her husband doth safely trust in her, so that he shall have no need of spoil. She will do him good and not evil all the days of her life."

Robbie pondered the advice of King Solomon. Such a woman was just the kind he wanted to begin the legacy he had in mind. He shifted his gaze to Miss Reynolds and allowed a subtle smile to cross his face. Ah, yes, a virtuous woman. Fair of face with an intelligent mind and an unusual creative talent. And she was kind, putting others before herself. In his experience, there was no other woman like her. Chastity Reynolds might not know it now, but, one day, she would be his. And once he had set upon a course of action, he saw it to the end.

Augie left the chapel well ahead of the swell and returned to report to the others. "Ings returns tomorrow," he said as he studied the alley from the window in their upper story lodgings. "He'll want to hear about what I saw today."

"I wouldn't have thought ye'd be steppin' into a church," said Pete, "not after the nights ye've been keepin' with the tavern wenches. Didn't ye fear bein' struck dead?"

Augie gave him a reproachful glance. "Are ye daft? No one questions a sinner's right to attend services. 'Tis expected. My head might have been hurtin' after last night's ale, but I wanted to watch him with her in that place."

"And what did ye see?" inquired Duffy, running his fingers through his red hair. The man's hair had always been a concern to Augie; it didn't blend well with the rest of the guvnor's men who could melt into a crowd in a moment. His concern had grown when Duffy returned one afternoon with a tale of being followed.

"Powell and the chit were close as two peas in a pod, sneakin' looks at each other while the parson was speakin'. She's the one, all right."

Pete sneered, a nasty flicker in his dark eyes. "We'll have to be watchin' for a chance to nab her." Augie stared at the man, who concerned him as much as Duffy. He didn't trust Pete to follow orders. Somewhere he had a screw loose.

"We'll not touch her until Ings is here," Augie said in a tone that brooked no dissent.

"I see the two of you have received several invitations from gentlemen of good report with whom you might attend the king's Fancy Ball," Aunt Agatha said excitedly. "I shall act as chaperone, of course. So, who will be the fortunate men?"

Chastity shuffled through the messages Featherstone had handed her on the salver. "Alvanley, Cairo, some gentleman I barely recall from the reception and then there is this one, Rose. An invitation for the two of us to attend with Sir Robert and M'sieur Donet."

"I, too, have a collection of gentlemen offering to escort me," said Rose, looking up from the pile in her lap with a happy expression. "All are gentlemen I met at your reception, Lady Sanborn. While I would be please to attend with any of them, I would prefer to go with Chas."

"Then the decision is made, yes?" Aunt Agatha lifted her brows as she faced them.

Chastity could not deny Rose a chance to spend the evening with a very fine suitor like the vicomte, especially when she herself had looked with favor on the invitation from Sir Robert. "Very well. I agree."

"Now that you have decided on your escorts, you must consider costumes. Having been to His Majesty's Fancy Balls before, I can tell you all manner of beings will populate the Music Room, so you have many ideas to choose from. If gowns from an earlier age appeal, the attic holds many."

"What fun!" exclaimed Rose. "I love looking through clothes from the time when ladies dressed in elaborate fashion."

"Not me," said Chastity with a grin. "I've an idea to wear a sheet."

"A bed-sheet?" inquired Rose, incredulous.

"My dear great-niece, whatever is your intention?"

"I would dress as a Grecian goddess." Seeing their confused expressions, she explained, "Oh, I shall be fully clothed in a white gown, a toga, I think they are called."

"That was the dress of the Roman men, dear," said Aunt Agatha.

"Well, you know what I mean," said Chastity, "and I'd add a golden shawl."

"You can adapt a toga-like gown to your purpose," said Aunt Agatha. "And we can do better than a bed-sheet. Such a simple style can be made in a few days. We will go to my favorite dressmaker and see about it. And for you, Rose, a trip to the attic is in order. You will look lovely in a silk brocade gown I had made a score of years ago. It was the earl's favorite and very lavish. I think it just may fit you as I was considerably more slender then."

That afternoon, after a visit to the dressmaker and an excursion to the attic with Aunt Agatha and Rose, Chastity sat down to write polite rejections to the invitations she had received, all except for the one from Sir Robert and M'sieur Donet.

Sir Robert, Monsieur Donet,

My dear friend, Miss Crockett, and my great-aunt, Lady Sanborn, and I are pleased to accept your kind invitation to accompany you to His Majesty's Fancy Ball. In truth, we quite look forward to it and are planning our costumes!

Sincerely yours,
Chastity Reynolds

Robbie smiled at the note and looked up to meet Jack's inquisitive gaze. "I daresay we were lucky to be the ones they accepted. I know for a fact Alvanley was hoping to take Miss Reynolds. But since each of the two young women needs a chaperone and there is only Lady Sanborn, our invitation to them both had an advantage."

"Except for Cairo, who must have sent them an invitation as well. Since he will most certainly be attending with Sir Bellingham and his wife, Lady Graham, there is a chaperone in that group."

"So there is. Yet still we prevailed. Obviously, Miss Reynolds is coming to see the wisdom of my suit."

"Is that what it is? I rather thought you and she were at odds most of the time."

"She resists my charm, 'tis true, but she is not indifferent to me. It's just that she finds it easier to speak of my faults rather than to admit a growing fondness for one she believes to be a rake. Only consider her cat, who now welcomes me with contented purring. Miss Reynolds, too, will come to see she is fated to love me."

"Love?" Jack coughed a laugh. "I wish you well with that venture, Nephew, though I have my doubts. Meanwhile, what costume will you be wearing for the king's ball?"

"Whatever we choose, the costumes must allow for weapons. I am not at all sanguine that only the king's guests will attend. Such an event is likely to attract the men who mean me harm. I thought of a pasha, complete with turban and bejeweled sword. I expect there is such a costume to be had in Brighton where masked balls occur fairly often, but it might prove cumbersome. Then another thought came to me...from the fairy tale I told you about. Why not a bear?"

"If you do that, should I go as the mad dwarf who stole the prince's gold?"

With a smirk, Robbie said, "That would hardly win the heart of your lady, the fair Rose Red."

"I'd rather go as a *chevalier*, now that I think on it. Ladies like knights and such a costume would provide an excuse to take my long knives."

"On second thought," said Robbie, shaking his head, "I'm afraid we cannot don either. With the chainmail and the helmet in the heat of the Pavilion, you'd roast. And I cannot go as a bear. There would be no good place to hide my pistols and 'twould be like wearing a rug. I would suffocate."

Jack sighed. "You are right. I could never endure a knight's armor as hot as the king keeps the Pavilion. However, it might do for me to go as the pirate my father once was, dressed all in black with a sword at my side, all my knives tucked inside my clothing and one of your pistols secured at my belt. What say you to that?"

Robbie smiled. "Splendid. As for me, I've another thought, too. The musketeers in France guarded the king. How fitting it would be for me to dress the part I have most recently played. I would wear the old uniform of the *Ancien Régime* with lace collar, a sword hanging from a belt across my chest, tall bucket boots and a cavalier's plumed hat. It will require a wig of longer hair. Too, I must find a blue cloak."

"*Alors*, where is all that to be obtained?"

Robbie shook his head at his uncle. "I can see you have yet to realize all of Tiller's many talents. He is a magician who can conjure up most any disguise. He has done so for me many times. I'll ask him to scour Brighton for us and, failing that, he can dig into my chests."

Aaron Ings leaned back in his chair in the smoke-filled Albany Tavern on West Street, drinking ale with his men and listening to Augie's report of the government spy and his lady friend

His time in London had been well spent, his plans now set in motion. Soon, he would have his revenge for his brother's lamentable death. He had secured a set of rooms in a shabby, not quite squalid, part of London where he could hold the woman before delivering her up to the brothel. He would need a few hours' sleep before seeing to that errand. The rented quarters had been his headquarters while he was in London, allowing him time to identify the brothel his brother had frequented and to obtain access to a carriage that would attract no attention.

"You saw them together again?" he asked Augie who had risen to a place of leadership among the men in Aaron's absence.

"Aye, I did. Cozy as two church mice sittin' on a pew in the Chapel Royal."

That such a man could sit in church and not feel regret at his actions that had led to good men's deaths angered Aaron beyond all reason.

"We've been watchin' for a chance to nab her," said Duffy. "Looks like the king hisself has handed us what ye swells call 'an opportunity'."

Aaron fixed his eyes on Duffy, waiting to hear more. His brother had wanted the death of the king and his ministers. While Aaron had no such goal, he had no qualms about using the king to get to the man whose death he wanted. If the king provided an opportunity, he would take it.

Duffy smiled. "There's to be a masked ball at the Pavilion."

Aaron raised a brow. "A masked ball, you say? That can work to our advantage." Aaron thought back to the times he had visited Brighton. "Whenever the prince gave a ball, the crowd that rushed forward included many who were not invited. Bounders, scoundrels and ladies of easy virtue always attend along with the costumed aristocrats."

"By scoundrels, ye mean us, Guvnor?" asked Pete.

Aaron nodded. "If you prefer to think of yourself that way. As for me, I will attend in disguise, not a scoundrel but as a man of the earth, a poor man full of righteous indignation."

Pete responded with a malicious grin. "This is soundin' better all the time. I always yearned to go partyin' with the swells."

Chapter 12

The fading rays of the sun drifted in through the window, casting a warm light around Chastity's bedchamber. The rain had stopped some time ago, but she was glad they would have a carriage to convey them to the Pavilion, as the Steyne would be muddy.

She paused before the long mirror, certain she was looking at a stranger. The white silk gown draped from one shoulder to a high waist that was banded by golden cords. From there, it flowed in soft folds to the floor.

The face that looked back at her could have belonged to Helen of Troy.

Her large blue eyes, adorned for the first time with a tasteful application of cosmetics, were framed by blonde curls piled on top of her head, some left to dangle by her cheeks. Golden cords circled the curls like a crown. Her only jewelry was a pair of small gold earrings. Golden slippers, her own design she had been saving for just such an occasion, graced her feet. The final touch had been the diaphanous golden shawl with Greek fret trim draped loosely across her bodice.

In the mirror, she saw Crispin lounging on the bed behind her. "I don't believe it's me," she said to him.

"Of course, it's you, Silly. It's always been you, only now you are more strikingly beautiful than ever."

Chastity peeked around the mirror to see Rose standing in the doorway, adorned in a gown of luminescent pale green brocade silk, the sleeves billowing to her elbows and falling beyond in long, lace-trimmed folds. The tight-fitting bodice above the skirt featured five rows of claret silk frogs descending to the narrow waist. "Oh, Rose, you look like you stepped out of Versailles a century ago."

"Lady Sanborn said the same thing." Rose entered Chastity's chamber, her skirts swishing about her ankles as she did. "Do you like my hair this way?"

Rose's raven curls had been swept off her face and woven with strands of pearls, one long curl left free to fall to her back. "I think it's lovely, truly."

"I'm so glad you like my costume. Your great-aunt has found us both masks we can hold before our eyes. She said they wouldn't be as hot as the ones that are tied against the face. Isn't that sweet of her?"

Just then, Aunt Agatha appeared with three masks mounted on sticks. "My, but you two are stunning! The suitors will be hovering around you like bees."

"And what about *you*?" Chastity asked her great-aunt, a picture of elegance in a shimmering royal blue caftan embroidered with silver flowers. Tiny silver-covered buttons descended in a long line from the bodice to the floor. "I have never seen such a costume as yours. It's magnificent!"

"It's in the Moroccan style," said Aunt Agatha. "Exotic yet large enough to give my aging body ample room."

The cuffs of the long loose sleeves were adorned with the same silver embroidery. Around her shoulders rested a hooded silk burnouse, the same blue as her gown. Diamond pendants hung from her ears, glistening in the candlelight like tiny chandeliers.

"I do love dressing in costume," said Aunt Agatha. "I feel like a girl again! And, seeing you, it's a good thing Sir Robert intends to come for us in a carriage. I cannot imagine walking the streets of Brighton like this." Chastity's great-aunt handed them each a mask. "Take these and I will see you both below. Do hurry."

Sir Robert and his uncle were standing in the entry hall with Aunt Agatha as Chastity and Rose descended the stairs. The jaws of the two men dropped in a most satisfactory manner, telling Chastity her instincts for the Greek goddess costume had not been amiss, nor Rose's for her choice of the French gown that only enhanced her beauty.

"It seems we are to have at our side a pirate and a musketeer," she said to Rose in an amused tone.

Her eyes had been drawn at once to Sir Robert's beguiling costume. His dark hair was now long to his shoulders, a wig but very convincing, and he sported a thin mustache and chin whiskers in the French fashion. His piercing hazel eyes shone from beneath his black cocked hat that sported a panache of feathers. His white shirt, left open at the collar, was garnished with lace and across his chest was a wide leather belt to which was secured a very convincing sword. Over his left shoulder, he wore a dark blue cloak lined in red. Black breeches were tucked into bucket boots with leather cuffs folded down. She had to wonder where he had found them.

M'sieur Donet was more simply dressed, all in black as a pirate. He wore a dueling shirt with full sleeves, a fringed red silk sash knotted low around his hips and a tricorne hat that shadowed his features. He removed his hat and swept it to the side as he bowed before them in grand gesture. "*Mesdemoiselles*, I stand in awe of your beauty. You will cast all other women into the shade." He glanced at his companion and added, "Observe my nephew, unable to speak."

The vicomte pulled back one side of his coat to reveal a pistol stuffed into his waist. On his other side, Chastity glimpsed a sword with a gilded hilt. "You see I am well armed to defend you."

"Are we going to war?" asked Chastity, impressed with the weapons she could see and thinking there were likely more she could not see.

"Not at all, Miss Reynolds," said Sir Robert, finding his tongue. "But with such beauty to protect, we dare not take our job as escorts lightly. Surely Lady Sanborn," he said, glancing at her great-aunt, "expects no less."

"Indeed, you are correct," said Aunt Agatha.

"And may I add, Lady Sanborn," said Sir Robert, "you are clothed most elegantly this evening, a lovely chaperone. We'll be pressed into guarding you, too, before the evening is done."

"You'll be doing nothing of the sort," Aunt Agatha fired back with a grin. "Now, let's be off."

Chastity, Rose and Aunt Agatha were handed into the carriage to sit on one side. The two men climbed in behind them and sat with their backs to the horses. "We've retained a driver for the evening who will take care of the carriage," Sir Robert informed them. "Our only task is to enjoy ourselves."

Her eyes were luminous as their gazes met across the carriage. Robbie could not have looked away even if he'd wanted to. He recalled her slow descent from the top of the stairs, a goddess leaving Mount Olympus. Deprived of speech, he had stared up at her in shocked admiration.

Sitting across from him, she appeared a serene goddess in a gossamer white gown that left one ivory shoulder bare. He longed to reach out and touch her glowing skin, to kiss again her lips he knew to be soft. To explore her honeyed mouth. He had wanted her when she was the hoyden spitting fire. Even more so now that he saw her as a picture of divine femininity.

Once they arrived at the Pavilion, he and Jack handed the ladies out of the carriage and the five of them strolled into the Music Room where they drew many curious gazes. Already, the large room was filled with hundreds of people, their conversations blending with the lively music.

Fancy Balls to Robbie were timeless events as the costumes could be from nearly any era. While most of those attending had chosen to wear a costume, there were always those who wore their usual attire or, as in the case of military men, their dress uniforms.

A short way into the room, Robbie caught sight of the Duke of Wellington who had chosen to wear a nobleman's clothing and a black cape lined in gold silk. Now that he was Governor of Plymouth, he would not be wearing his red field marshal's uniform that had been made so famous with Waterloo. The duke was said to be a frequent guest of the Prince Regent and so Robbie was not surprised to see him here tonight at the invitation of the king.

A parade of scantily clad wood nymphs, satyrs and assorted fauns and fairies frolicked about the room, joined by a Sultan's genie in a turban and loose flowing silk pajamas, a Russian serf with a full beard and a Highlander in a kilt and sporran. An odd mixture to be sure.

"Is that Mr. Cairo dressed as a Spanish matador?" asked Miss Reynolds, who had taken Robbie's arm. She was remarkably docile this evening. Perhaps it was his disguise as a musketeer. Did she envision him as a valiant hero whose only goal in life was to defend the king? All things considered, she would not have been far from the truth if she did.

"Indeed, it is. I only recognized him because he is standing next to Sir John who is in his usual riding clothes. And Letty, who, even garbed as an Amazon—which is her nickname, by the way—with leather jerkin, gauntlets and wicked looking long knife, is still discernable as herself. Few women are that tall."

"Shall we greet them?" she asked.

Robbie nodded and let Lady Sanborn and Jack know of their destination.

It took some effort but Robbie and Miss Reynolds finally made their way through the crowd that ebbed and flowed like the sea, to arrive in front of the threesome.

"Good evening," he said.

Letty looked him over, amused. "Don't you look dashing, Sir Robert. I like the long hair on you and the trim mustache. Very gallant."

"You are lovely as always, Miss Reynolds," said Sir John, "that costume becomes you."

Henry Cairo had eyes only for Chastity Reynolds, causing Robbie to curl his fingers possessively over her hand. He had begun to think of her as his and didn't much like other men acting as if she were available to be courted.

The matador bowed ceremoniously before her, sweeping his hat from his head. "Miss Reynolds, you come dressed as I have always pictured you, a goddess." Straightening, he said, "Might you be Aphrodite, the goddess of love?"

"Hardly that, Mr. Cairo," she replied, "but I do thank you. You must see my friend, Miss Crockett. She is dazzling in her costume from the French court."

"I will certainly make a point of finding her before the evening ends."

Robbie turned to Sir John's wife. "Letty, I see you make up for your husband's lack of costume. How fierce you look!"

"If they are to call me 'Amazon' for my height, by Jove, why not dress the part?"

Sir John blithely shook his head. "Long ago, I gave up trying to restrain her. Letty must be Letty."

"Which is exactly as you like it," said Letty, planting a kiss on her husband's cheek.

Robbie felt a presence behind him and turned to see Dorothea, Countess Lieven, smiling at him. She was garbed as one of the nymphs in a pink and green sheer fabric that left little doubt as to her charms. A wreath of leaves circled her dark red hair left free to flow to her shoulders. "Good evening, Countess." He would be polite but would give her no encouragement.

"What a romantic figure you make as a musketeer, Sir Robert."

Miss Reynolds tightened her hand on his arm, which told him much. He thanked Countess Lieven for the compliment and wished her a good eve before turning back to his friends.

"She still seeks your company," observed Miss Reynolds in a soft whisper.

"'Twill do her no good," he replied.

A short distance away, two Celestials greeted the king, inclining their heads in grave courtesy. The king exclaimed his delight at their costumes that blended well with the Pavilion's Chinese décor.

Both the king and his mistress wore costumes. Robbie was suddenly thankful that he had decided against a pasha costume, for that is what the king had chosen. The elaborate flowing green robe and inner tunic, both embroidered in gold thread, circled the king's girth. Affixed to his side was a long bejeweled sword sheathed in gold. On his head was a white turban with a large emerald shining from the front with a plume rising above. The king had donned facial hair, which, like Robbie's, was not his own. Robbie suspected the full beard, though fitting for a pasha, would be dreadfully hot.

Not surprisingly, the marchioness was dressed as one of the pasha's harem, in filmy silk scarves of many colors, her neck adorned with diamonds and rubies. She wore no mask but a thin veil over the tip of her nose that covered the bottom half of her face.

"Come," Robbie said to Miss Reynolds, "we must greet our host." Anxious to take her from the watchmaker's bold stares, he bid the Lades and Cairo a good eve and crossed the short distance to the king.

"How very appropriate, Sir Robert!" said the king in open admiration. "My very own musketeer. And you, Miss Reynolds, are a vision."

Robbie greeted the marchioness, reminding her she had met Miss Reynolds on the king's yacht. The older woman appeared to be enjoying herself, unthreatened by the beautiful younger woman before her. She knew well the king's tastes did not run in that direction.

Bidding the king a good eve, they went on to exchange pleasantries with Sir Bellingham and his wife, Lady Graham. Sir Bellingham, an imposing figure in any clothes, was even more so in the black domino and half-mask, his tall figure an apparition come to haunt the ball. His wife, a pleasant woman, wore a subdued costume that reminded Robbie of a shepherdess.

They chatted briefly with the Grahams and then Robbie turned to Miss Reynolds. "We must dance at least one waltz."

She smiled up at him. "I do love to dance."

Taking their leave, Robbie swept her into his arms and twirled her about the room, joining in the others who were dancing. Never before had he enjoyed a waltz so much. She was weightless in his arms and followed his steps without missing a beat of the music. "You dance expertly, Miss Reynolds."

"I should," she said, "considering the time I spent with my French dancing instructor."

"Should I be jealous?" he inquired.

"That would only be so if you had some claim on me, which we both know you do not."

"As I said, I am a patient man. All in good time, my lady."

She laughed at that, no doubt thinking he was jesting. He was not.

When the music stopped briefly, Robbie suddenly felt the heat of his costume. The wig, the jacket, the cloak, even the boots had become oppressive. "Shall we get some air?"

"That would be most welcome."

"But first, let us get something to drink. I'm sure the king's servants have put the icehouse to good use and whatever they are serving will be chilled."

They indulged in a glass of iced champagne. Then, he found Lady Sanborn and told her they were just going into the gardens. "We will return shortly."

Though the chaperone studied him closely, she gave her consent.

"Not long, mind."

Once outside the Pavilion, he guided Miss Reynolds to the green lawn and took a deep breath of the air that was laden with the remnants of rain and the breeze from the sea. The sweet smell was only enhanced by the flowery scent of his companion.

"Finally, we have escaped the heat and the noise," she said.

The descending twilight now colored the sky lavender with streaks of gold, but Robbie could still see her slender form clothed in white. "Are you cold?"

"Just a little," she admitted. "After so warm a room, I think it's the change that has me shivering."

He untied his cloak and set it about her shoulders. "There, this will keep you warm, unless, of course, you are reduced to shivering by my mere presence."

"You are such a rogue," she chided, the light from the Pavilion falling across her face.

"Do you know that when you are trying to be angry with me, your eyes become intensely blue? I noticed it that first night I kissed you at Grillon's."

"How despicable of you to recall that incident I have been trying to forget."

"But you can't forget it, can you?" A blush suffused her cheeks, giving him the satisfaction of having correctly judged her feelings. "Just as I thought," he said. "Neither can I."

He turned her cloaked shoulders toward him and drew her close, bending to kiss her. It was no light kiss, for the taste of her created in him an overpowering desire for more. She pressed her palms to his chest but did not push him away. Instead, she began to respond, her lips softening beneath his, kissing him back. Reaching her hands to the back of his neck, she held his head to her.

"There," he said, breaking the kiss. "Now you see what lies between us."

She removed her hands from his chest and took a step back. "I see nothing of the kind! And I did not give you permission to kiss me."

He fought the urge to laugh. "No, I suppose you did not. Still, those eyes of yours told me you would welcome my kiss. And you did." He reached for her. "Don't fight me, Chastity."

"You would seduce me?" she asked, incredulous.

"Nay, I would marry you! We belong together, you and I."

"You are boldly presumptuous, sir!"

He let out a sigh, searching for the words to get through to her. "I admit I've been at loose ends. It took me some time to find my bearings but, now that I have, I know the woman I want for my wife. And that woman is you, Chastity Reynolds." In a softer tone, he called her by the name he would always prefer. "Darling."

"Darling? You jest! You are forever finding amusement at my expense. How could I marry such a one as you? A rogue!"

"The description might have fit me at one time but since I met you that evening in London, I have reformed."

"Again, you would bring up that embarrassing episode."

"But I must," he protested. "From that day on, I have not been able to get you out of my mind. You can imagine how delighted I was to discover you were the one the Countess of Claremont had asked me to call upon. She may have conceived the match but I am pleased to follow through. You would not be happy married to a man who always gives you your way."

"Why should I marry at all? I have no need. At my twenty-first birthday, not long from now, I come into a family legacy, an estate of my own in Northamptonshire. Already there is an estate manager and servants to see to my needs. The manor is not large, but it is quite adequate."

"Perfect! When we are not in London or on my ship, we can live there. Children do better with a home on land breathing country air."

"Children? Aren't you getting ahead of yourself?"

"Possibly," he said. And, with a smile that might have been a smirk, he added, "But I do plan."

She turned and dashed away into the night.

"Chastity!" he called across the lawn, as she disappeared into the trees. He would give her a moment alone and then go after her. He had taken her by surprise. Once she had time to reflect, she would see reason.

Chastity leaned back against the trunk of an oak, her hand pressed to her racing heart. Sir Robert's kiss had stirred something deep within her, something she did not want to admit. She had run not just from him but from herself and from dreams she had allowed to die long ago.

For weeks, she had hidden her heart behind her anger, anger at the audacity of the man being so free with her person. She had thought his teasing manner spoke of his lack of respect but perhaps she was wrong. The rogue was slowly winning her heart. She had not resisted his lips upon hers. No, she had shamelessly responded.

He couldn't be serious about marrying her, could he? And why her? Why not Rose or countless other beautiful women he had known? Doubtless some were more highborn than she.

He had made no avowal of love, no proposal on bended knee. And, if he were serious, could she ever trust such a man to be faithful? Could she live with a man who wasn't?

Before she could answer her questions, she was suddenly aware she was not alone. Dusky shadows beneath the trees crept toward her.

"There you are!" said a man's voice she did not know. As he stepped out of the shadows, she recognized the costume of a Russian serf she had observed among those attending the ball. The dark beard and mustache beneath his peasant's cap were likely not his own but his clothing, the long white shirt belted over loose-fitting trousers tucked into his boots, was convincing.

He stalked closer. There was something sinister about his approach as if the shadows still clung to him.

Fear gripped her and slowly she backed away, drawing Sir Robert's cloak tightly around her as if to conjure the man himself, knowing somehow he would defend her with his life.

"Grab her!" the man hissed to another.

She screamed and turned, running as hard as she could, desperate to get away.

A hand caught her arm and wrenched her back, making her drop her mask. "Got her, Guvnor."

She yelped in pain at the vise he had on her arm and turned to kick the man's shins and beat his head with her fist. "Let me go!" The man smelled of unwashed skin. He wore no costume but the simple clothes of a dockworker. Her slippers were not much of a weapon, but she kicked as hard as she could, relieved when the man shouted an oath and loosened his grip. She hit him again in the face with her fist, breaking his hold on her arm.

Again she ran. "Help!" she yelled. "Sir Robert, help!" Heart pounding, she ran from the trees and had just reached the clearing when she was seized from behind.

A scarf was lashed around her mouth and tied at the back of her head. "No sense in yellin', Sweetin'. Yer lover cannot hear ye. Seems he's taken a blow to the head and is…indisposed."

The men chortled, finding humor in her misery.

Who are they and what could they want with me?

She turned to fight, swinging her fists and kicking out, until the Russian serf grabbed her hands and tied them behind her. "Quickly, get her into the carriage," he ordered.

There were three of them now. Two were dragging her toward the Steyne. She dug in her heels but they were stronger, lifting her from the ground to carry her. As they were about to leave the Pavilion grounds, she left the only clue she could and let one of her slippers fall from her foot. The men were so intent on getting her away, they failed to notice.

One of them tossed her into the waiting carriage, a plain black affair that, even in the dim light, looked worn. A driver sat on top.

"Pete, you sit up top with Duffy," said the leader. "We'll drop the two of you at the lodgings to take care of our remaining business. Augie and I will meet you in London at the tavern."

London? She had no idea why these men had abducted her or why they were taking her to London. She would have asked if her mouth had not been gagged. Men didn't abduct a young woman for a noble purpose. It could be a kidnapping for ransom. Her family would be desperate to recover her. But it could be worse; it could be rape. Quavering, she prayed Sir Robert lived and would come for her. But what if he were too late? What if he never found her? Dread settled into her chest along with a feeling of impending doom as she imagined the worst. *Oh, God, help me.*

Voices around Robbie roused him from the deep blackness. "Robbie! Robbie!" Jack's voice. A slap on the cheek brought him awake.

He moaned as a terrible pounding in the back of his head grew worse. "What…what happened?" The grass beneath him was damp and had seeped into his clothing. "Why am I on the ground?"

"Here, let me help you sit," said Jack.

Robbie rose to a sitting position. The world swam around him.

"Where is my great-niece, Sir Robert?" asked a concerned Lady Sanborn whose face suddenly appeared before him.

"Where is Chastity?" demanded an unusually fierce Miss Crockett.

Robbie tried to leap up only to fall back. Jack caught him and helped him to stand. Robbie pulled the wig from his head and ran his fingers through his hair, feeling the back of his aching head where a huge lump had formed. "What do you mean, 'where is Chastity'? Isn't she here?"

"No," said Jack. "You were the last person to see her."

"We were talking," Robbie said, trying to remember. "We had a bit of a tiff and she ran off. I was just going after her when…oh, God. I was struck from behind."

"Oh, no," Lady Sanborn said on a gasp, covering her mouth. "Someone has taken my great-niece."

"What time is it?" asked Robbie. "How long has she been missing?"

"It's after midnight," replied Jack.

"This is all my fault," lamented Robbie. "I should have seen it coming. I should have known they would strike at her."

"Explain yourself," said Lady Sanborn.

"Let's get him into the Pavilion," said Jack. "He can explain there."

"No," said Robbie, his mind clearing as guilt assailed him. "It lies to me to find Chastity. I will search."

"You and Lady Sanborn wait for us in the Pavilion," Jack said to Rose. "I will go with Robbie."

They strode into the trees, looking for any clue. The darkness didn't help them but Robbie caught the glitter of gold and reached down. "It's her mask."

"Over here!" shouted Jack.

Where the lawn met the Steyne, a slice of gold shimmered from the ground. "'Tis Chastity's!" he exclaimed, picking up the slipper. "She was wearing these."

"If they left from the Steyne," said Jack, "they likely had a carriage. Come, let us return; the ladies will be anxious."

Inside the Pavilion, Robbie subsided onto a sofa in the Music Room Gallery that, thankfully, was devoid of all but a few servants.

When Rose saw the slipper and the mask, she blurted, "Those are Chastity's!" and took them from him.

The two women took a seat on either side of him, wringing their hands. Jack stood in front of him, a look of concern on his face.

Plagued by regret and his thoughts scattering to the wind, Robbie tried to determine his next step. The woman he would take as his wife, the woman he had—against all odds—come to love, had been abducted. He must get her back before any harm could come to her. He looked up at Jack. "It could be North Street. I have to try."

"You are not making any sense, young man," said Lady Sanborn in a tone that spoke of authority. "I would know what this is about and why someone would want to abduct Chastity."

He turned to see the worried expression in her brown eyes. "I am, my lady, or have been, His Majesty's spy. Because of my work ending the Cato Street conspiracy, men in sympathy with those hanged for the crime have been following me."

Miss Crockett gasped.

"There was a threatening note, but their hatred was directed at me. Jack and I have tried to identify the culprits on many occasions but have not been successful. We were prepared for an attack but not on Miss Reynolds. They had rooms somewhere near North Street. I will comb that street tonight and at first light, I will follow the clues to where she has been taken. In the meantime, I will ask the king for help."

Robbie was escorted with Jack, Lady Sanborn and Miss Crockett to the small anteroom near the king's chambers where Robbie explained all he knew to his sire.

"We will have the traitors strung up as we did the others!" said the king, who had shed his pasha costume. "What can we do to help you catch them and return Miss Reynolds?"

"If you would spare me a few of your guards, I would go to North Street and scour it for any evidence that she has been there. And we may expect a note demanding a ransom."

"You shall have whatever you need, Sir Robert." The king turned to the nearest footman and gave an order.

Worried for the time that was lost while he lay unconscious, Robbie set off on foot accompanied by Jack and three of the king's guards.

North Street was dark, the merchants' shops closed for the night, except for a few taverns at the other end of the street. But this part of the street with its narrow alleys was where they had spotted the redheaded man.

"Spread out and check the alleys!" he urged. "And look for any carriage."

There were stables off North Street but before he would resort to checking them, he wanted to see if the evildoers had returned to their lair. He refused to allow himself to think what they might do to a young innocent like Chastity Reynolds.

An hour later, it was clear there was no carriage anywhere on North Street or hidden in its alleys. "Damn," he said, "there has to be some sign they were here."

"They may have taken her out of Brighton," suggested Jack.

"Aye, they might. We can ask about carriages headed to London." They were about to leave when Robbie spotted a light coming from a second story window. Most people would be in bed at this hour.

He drew the men to him and whispered to the three guards, "Wait here should any run from this door. Jack and I will see what keeps this lodger up so late."

Pistol drawn, Robbie opened the street door and slowly crept up the stairs. Jack, a knife poised in his hand, followed closely. Robbie listened for voices but heard none until he was in front of the door on the upper floor.

Men's voices drifted to his ear.

"A tidy piece of work," said one.

"Neat as a pin," said another, deeper voice.

"The guvnor should be in London by mornin' with his baggage wrapped up and ready to deliver."

"Aye, and in that getup she wore to the masked ball, he should have no trouble unloadin' the goods."

His pistol cocked, Robbie kicked the door open. The two men scrambled to grab a weapon. "Don't move," he said with ice in his voice, aiming his pistol at the redheaded man just laying his hand on a pistol.

In a very unwise move, the man decided to lift the pistol. Robbie fired, knocking it out of his hand.

"Ye shot me!" said the wounded man, clutching his bloody hand to his chest.

"I'll do worse if I don't get some answers." Robbie laid aside the used pistol and drew another.

Boots pounded on the stairs behind them and one of the king's guards stuck his head in the doorway. "Everything all right here, sir?"

"Yes," said Jack, "We're just ridding the place of these vermin."

The three guards entered and took up a stance behind them.

Robbie aimed his pistol at the other man. "Now I want answers. Where is the girl?"

The two men shared a glance. "We don't rightly know."

"That won't do," said Robbie. "There were more of you, yes?"

The redhead nodded.

"And a carriage?"

He nodded again.

"Give me their destination," he demanded.

Neither man spoke a word. Without turning, Robbie said to Jack, "It appears they want a display of your skills with a blade."

Jack threw his knife, pinning the wounded man's hat to the wall. "I can come closer, you know, *much* closer. Neither of you would miss an eye or an ear."

"We don't rightly know where the guvnor is," blurted out the redhead's companion whose eyes looked a bit crazed. "We're to meet at The Prospect in a week's time. That were the place he hired us."

"The tavern on the London riverfront?" Robbie knew it well as it was a favorite haunt of the crews of his family's ships.

The man nodded. "Aye, that one."

"And between now and then?" said Jack, a second knife glinting in his hand.

The wounded redhead cringed away from the knife. "He never told us the one he's takin' her to."

Robbie frowned, his teeth grinding in frustration. "What do you mean 'the one'—the one what? Spit it out."

The man had the audacity to smile. "Which nunnery in London, yer lordship. All we knows is that it were a fancy one."

Dead silence filled the room as Robbie considered what they were saying. He had expected them to hold Chastity for ransom but this he had not imagined. "He is taking an innocent to a London brothel?"

"Aye," said the redhead, blood dripping down his wrist. "The guvnor knew ye were soft on the chit." He added with a snigger, "He knew ye wouldn't like it. O'course, he wants ye dead, too."

Robbie's eyes narrowed on the sniveling creature. "I want his name."

"Ings is all we know," said the other man.

The leader, this man "Ings" had planned well, not trusting his hired men to know his whereabouts or his precise destination. Robbie hated to ask but he needed to know to be prepared for what he might find. "Did any of you touch her?"

The two men exchanged a look. The unwounded man stuck out his chest. "Oh, she's a rare plucked 'un, she is, but I had her singin' a song…"

Robbie crossed the room in one stride and struck the man with his pistol. The man recoiled. "Now, here, there ain't no cause fer that."

"There is," Robbie said, pointing the pistol at the man's head. "I'd as soon as blow your head off as listen to your blathering. Now give me a straight answer!"

The pathetic creature's eyes grew large and he whimpered, pleading for his life. "No, no, we never touched her. The guvnor wouldn't allow it. Said she's worth more unsullied. He said a drab house can sell fresh baggage for a pretty penny."

Robbie's gut twisted. He was sorely tempted to end their sorry lives here. "How many are taking her to London?"

"Two."

Robbie could not wait for the meeting at the tavern. He must find Chastity now before her innocence was taken and she was terrorized. Turning to the king's guards, he said, 'I leave these two to you and the king's justice. I must go to London. Except for the king, tell no one what you have heard." He might yet be able to save Chastity from a terrible fate.

The king's men agreed and prodded the two brigands down the stairs.

Jack pulled his knife from the wall, hiding it on his person.

"Before we leave," said Robbie, "let's search the place. We might find a clue as to the name of the brothel."

The search was a short one as they found only clothes, the makings of disguise and food. There was no paper of any kind, save an old newspaper. He doubted the two men he had met could read but the leader would have. He had obviously been the one to write the threatening message to Robbie.

"We were lucky," said Jack as they hastily retraced their steps to the Pavilion. "Now we just have to find her before a brothel's customer does."

"I pray we do," said Robbie. "We can change while the curricle is readied. If we are to be calling upon the best brothels in London, we had best dress the part."

"We wouldn't get far dressed as we are." They still had on the remnants of their costumes.

"We must hurry. She's alone and frightened and at their mercy." Robbie dared not think of the danger Chastity faced. "I will kill anyone who touches her." He knew then that no matter her condition, as long as she lived, he would claim her as his.

Chapter 13

Exhaustion overcame her but Chastity refused to give in to it. Instead, she concentrated on the jarring she endured as the carriage bumped over the rutted road and surreptitiously watched her captor, willing him to sleep so she could work at the bindings around her wrists.

The Russian serf stared at her from the shadows across the conveyance. She felt his hatred and the cold determination he wore like a mantle. His dark eyes were hard as if steeled to some distasteful task. The man scared her to death but she would not let him see her fear.

Finally, he drifted into a fitful sleep and she went to work on the bindings in earnest. She could feel the knot beginning to give way when her captor roused, looked at her, and then returned to sleep. She breathed out a sigh and returned to the bindings. This time, they loosened.

With her hands free, she removed the gag around her mouth and, with a last look at her sleeping captor, opened the carriage door and leapt out. She hit the ground hard with a grunt but the vegetation along the side of the road softened the blow. She picked herself up and turned back toward Brighton. At first, her steps were slow but then she picked up speed and ran, her one slipper the only protection against the stones of the road.

The carriage slowed and she heard a shout behind her. The sounds of running feet followed. She ducked behind a bush, her heart racing in her chest. Forcing her breathing to slow, she prayed they would not find her.

They passed the spot where she was hidden. She thought they had missed her, but one man carried a lantern and he turned and came back, slowing as he neared her. "The footprints stop here," he said, lifting the lantern. It was the voice of the leader. "There she is. Grab her!"

"Thought ye'd get away, did ye?" asked the one who had been driving. "Old Augie weren't gonna let that happen. He bound her hands again, this time much tighter. When that was done, he began to paw her, his rough hands moving over her body.

"You disgust me," she spit out. "Take your hands off me!"

Gripped in his one hand, he slapped her hard across the face with the other, leaving her skin stinging. "Where ye're goin', ye'll learn to like a man's touch, Sweetin'." Then he hit her in the mouth, splitting her lip.

"Enough!" said the leader. "I want her undamaged. Retie the gag and return her to the carriage."

By the time the man Augie had dragged her to the carriage, she was aching all over, bruised from her fall to the ground and her face swelling and sore from the impact of his fist. She held on to the hope that whatever had led to her kidnapping would soon be discovered. Her father was a landed squire who could well afford to pay a ransom. But what she heard in Augie's words and saw in the leader's cold pitiless eyes in the lantern's light as he took the seat opposite her told her she was not to be ransomed.

Despairing, she sank against the side of the carriage, tears running down her battered face.

When dawn began to creep into the sky, the carriage jarred to a stop in a part of London she had never been in. It had to be the East End of London from the descriptions she'd heard. A place of dilapidated tenement houses in which poverty and disease flourished and the stench of open sewers hung in the air and rats scurried from the shadows.

The carriage door opened. Her captor stepped down and, grabbing her by the shoulders, wrenched her out. "How unfortunate you have muddied your costume and lost your shoe." He reached down and pulled off her one remaining slipper, muddied from her attempted escape, and stuffed it into his pocket. "Barefoot might suit you better where you're going, but we'll have to clean you up a bit."

He left her to Augie and turned toward the building. The growing light reflected in the polish of his boots, a design she recognized as her father's. At the base of the outside shaft tooled in the leather was a small stylized "R", a symbol of his fine workmanship. This man was certainly a villain of the worst sort but he had means to buy expensive boots and hire brigands to do his dirty work.

He yanked her toward the door. She glared at him, grunting her disapproval. She was terrified to enter such a place and could only hope wherever he meant to take her was not so bleak. Her hands were cramped and her arms ached from being tied behind her. Her mouth was tight from the cut lip and her throat so dry she could barely swallow.

She stumbled up the stairs they ordered her to ascend, nearly falling more than once as she tripped on her gown and the cloak. She wasn't freed of her bindings until they shoved her through the door to a bedchamber at the top of the three-story house.

"Guvnor, what say ye to lettin' me test the goods before we deliver her to the madam?" said Augie. "One tumble for good luck?"

She could see the leader was tempted. What better way to sully a virgin than to compromise her?

"No," he said to Augie. "It would not serve my purpose. She's worth more as a maid."

Cold fear crept up her spine as Chastity listened to them talk. She had been right to think it was not ransom they sought. She was merely a piece of goods to be traded, perhaps to the highest bidder, or handed off to some place of ill repute. The thought caused her to shudder.

Once the scarf around her mouth was removed, she turned on her captors, anger welling within her, vowing they would not see her quaking before them. "Are you such worms that a woman must be bound, trussed up and forcibly taken?"

"Shut up!" spit the Russian serf.

"Why should I? What cowards you are! For shame, beating a mere woman."

The one called Augie raised a hand to strike her but the leader grabbed his arm. "No more bruises."

"Why have you kidnapped me? Why am I here?"

"'Tis the company you keep," was the gruff answer the leader gave her. His speech was more refined than the man he called "Augie", who had driven the carriage, but instead of Augie's lust, the Russian serf gave her a look of utter disgust.

"I keep no bad company," she said, drawing Sir Robert's cloak tightly around her.

"Oh, but you keep the very worst of company, and he is a wretched traitor to all good Englishmen."

"Surely you are wrong. I know no such man."

"Why, 'tis your lover, Powell," said the Russian serf.

Sir Robert? He might be a rogue but she could never imagine him a traitor. The king and he were close. "I do not believe it," she said, turning away.

"What you believe is unimportant," he said dismissively. "I will deal with your lover later."

"My father can pay a ransom," she offered, hoping he could be persuaded.

He gave her no answer. She hated to show them any weakness but her throat was as dry as dust. "A drink of water?"

The leader nodded to Augie who poured her a cup of ale. "We've no water."

She took a long drink. He waited until she was finished and returned the half-full cup to Augie, who left them alone.

She stared out the window. The light had grown stronger. Soon, there would be people on the street. Turning to face him, she asked, "How long am I to be here?"

"Not long," he said striding toward the door. Again, she noticed his boots and the telltale mark of her father's design as he disappeared through the doorway, closing the door behind him.

The room was cold, the fireplace clean and devoid of wood. They would not trust her with fire. Had Sir Robert not given her his warm cloak, she would be suffering terribly given what she was wearing. But his cloak, like the memory of his kiss, kept the chill at bay and gave her hope he would find her.

She went to stand at the grime-covered window that looked down on the dirty street below. Her heart sank to discover the window was nailed shut. Even had it been open, she could not jump so far without grave injury. She cast a look toward the bed. It was a mere frame with a thin mattress and no bedding.

She saw no people on the street but it was still early. She vowed to scream at the first person she saw, breaking glass to be heard, but, given where she was, she doubted any Good Samaritan would come to help her. She sank to her knees and asked God to help her.

Robbie and Jack were hours behind the man called "Ings". But at least the curricle was faster than the carriage they were following. Robbie gave the grays their heads and prayed the good weather held. Chastity's feisty nature would serve her well in this. He loved that about her for it would mean their life together would never be dull, that is, if she survived to speak to him again. It was his fault, all of it. He should have seen it coming. The thought of some man touching Chastity made him grind his teeth.

"I seem to recall the name Ings from the newspaper," said Jack. "It belonged to one of the conspirators. Do you think—"

"No, that one is dead. It's likely a relation. I don't suppose you have visited any high-class brothels recently?"

"Not in London but if we were in Paris, I could give you names of half a dozen, *mon ami*."

"I can think of several in London frequented by the aristocracy," said Robbie. "We will have to call upon all of them. In the meantime, sleep if you can."

They arrived mid-morning and, while he stabled the grays to be cared for and fed, Jack procured them meat pies from the nearby tavern to sustain them. From there, Robbie hailed a hackney and they set off, visiting every bordello of note he could recall ever hearing mentioned. They had to be the kind who would take a young woman against her will. It was not the kind of brothel he ever frequented but he knew some had less than stellar reputations.

Hours later, they had been to houses on Newman Street, Queen Anne Street, Princess Street, Cavendish Square, Pit Street and even one in Soho. All with no luck.

Robbie grew sick at heart when he recalled the reaction of the madams, the abbesses who ran the brothels. When he'd given them a description of Chastity and what she was wearing, the response often was "Blonde hair, blue eyes and fair skin dressed as a Greek goddess? Oh yes, she would do quite well here. Do let us know if she desires to join our ladies, won't you?" He dared not reveal Chastity's name. They would laugh at her Christian name, finding it highly amusing, and remember all too well her surname. No, he must seek her in anonymity. His eyes were scratchy from no sleep and his stomach growled, reminding him he lacked food, but he pressed on. Faithful Jack uttered no word of protest, knowing they raced for a girl's life.

Chastity had no opportunity to summon a stranger's help. That same morning, they bound her hands under her cloak they had brushed free of dried mud and forced her into the carriage. Her face was now wiped clean but she was certain her bruised cheek and damaged lip could be seen.

As they set off across London, she felt like a captive bird thrust into a cage. She clung to the hope Sir Robert yet searched for her. But how could he know where they were taking her?

The carriage came to a stop in a much better neighborhood, lined with trees, where large houses drew her gaze. This, too, was a section of London she'd never been in before.

The leader of her abductors leaned across the carriage in an intimidating matter. His dark eyes were like windows into hell. "Don't say a word about your situation else your lover will find a ball in his back."

He no longer wore the Russian serf costume but the clothes of a gentleman. The facial hair remained the same and his hair overlong for the style in vogue, convincing her at least a part of his appearance remained a disguise.

Chastity shrank from his intense perusal. His threat was real. For some reason, unknown to her, this man was convinced Sir Robert was a traitor. She would waste no words trying to convince the madman he was wrong. She believed him when he said he would kill Sir Robert if she told anyone of her abduction.

The man named Augie opened the carriage door to reveal an ornate iron gate behind which stretched a path with a green lawn on either side. The path ended in an elegant white manor surrounded on one side by weeping willow trees. A pond lay on the other side where pink and red rose bushes bloomed. There was no sign indicating the name of the place or its purpose. She needed none to understand they had arrived at a brothel.

Augie untied her hands and warned her to silence with his glare. He remained by the carriage as the leader walked her up the path. Her one foot that had been unshod was sore from the road she had walked trying to escape. She rubbed her aching wrists, red from the bindings, and looked back at the carriage where Augie watched her with a menacing expression.

As they drew closer to the front door, Chastity's mind conjured ideas for escape. No matter where they took her, she would sneak away.

At the front door, black with a brass knocker, a well-attired butler with gray hair beckoned them enter. The villain beside her muttered a name in the butler's ear and handed a footman his hat.

Apparently, they were expected for the butler asked no questions. He offered to take her cloak but she declined, unwilling to give up the one thing that reminded her of Sir Robert. She fixed the butler with a steady gaze. "I shall keep my cloak, thank you. I do not intend to stay." They had brushed the cloak clean but there were still smudges of mud on her white costume.

The butler frowned in puzzlement.

Her bearded captor forced a harsh laugh. "She's a playful minx, always jesting. Aren't you, Sweetheart?" He dug his fingers into her arm, pinching her so hard she cried out.

The butler shrugged and walked on.

"Stop! Wait, please…I feel faint. Would it be possible to sit?"

The butler paused and turned, looking down at her bare feet.

"You just sat an hour in the carriage, dear girl," said her captor. "Now cease your teasing and behave." He gave her a shake that rattled her teeth.

The butler turned away. "Follow me, please."

They crossed the black and white tiled floor of the entry hall, passing a wide staircase leading to the next story. At the base of the stairs stood a large man with blond hair looking straight ahead unmindful of their presence. There were no women present but then she wouldn't have expected them to be awake at this hour having worked the night.

They walked down a corridor, passing several rooms with impressive furnishings. This was no ordinary brothel. Finally, the butler stopped and bade them enter the well-appointed parlor. The first thing Chastity noticed was the crystal chandelier hanging above two brocade sofas flanking a marble fireplace. A gilded mirror set over the mantel made the room appear much larger than it was. The colors were subdued, a light blue and a soft rose.

When the butler departed, a young maid, plump with blonde curls beneath her mobcap, sallied into the room and introduced herself as Emma. "Welcome to Willow House," she said, giving Chastity a warm smile. "Miss Abby will see the gentleman in her office. You may remain here, Miss."

The door was shut as they left. Chastity tried the handle. Locked. A second door on the other side of the parlor beckoned. As she stepped close to it, she heard the leader speaking with a woman, their voices lowered.

"Not our usual..." said the woman.

"Untouched..." the man replied.

"I would see her alone," said the woman in a voice that forbade argument. "Wait here."

The side door opened and a woman entered, closing the door behind her. Chastity did not know what she expected but certainly not a stately woman in her late forties with dark brown hair pulled back into a tasteful knot and appraising hazel eyes that reminded her of Sir Robert's. She might have been an aging governess, so proper was her gray-blue morning gown.

In a whispered voice, Chastity said, "Oh, please, Ma'am. I am in terrible trouble. You must help me!"

The woman gave her a polite smile but her gaze took in Chastity's face, dwelling for a moment on her torn lip. "Perhaps, my dear. Everything in its proper time. First we make our introductions."

She led Chastity to the far side of the room where a small table with two chairs was set in front of a window looking out at the willow trees. "I am Abigail Darkin, but you may call me Miss Abby. And you are?"

"Miss Chastity Reynolds."

The woman gave her an assessing look before asking, "Would you like to shed your cloak? The fire burns well in the grate and I believe the room is quite warm enough."

Chastity held the cloak to her. "No, thank you."

"We can be private here," said Miss Abby. She glanced toward the side door. "He cannot hear us. Tell me what brought you to Willow House. I'm quite certain his representations are not all there is to the story, if, indeed, they are accurate at all."

The woman's eyes were kind and her manner sincere, so Chastity decided to disregard the warning she'd been given. If he never knew, then he would not harm Sir Robert because of her. Tears flowing from her eyes, she said, "Please do not tell him I have told you this, for he threatened to kill a friend of mine if I did. I know he would do it, too."

The woman nodded.

"It was horrible. I was at a costume ball in Brighton where he and his hired brutes abducted me. I had gone to the gardens for a bit of cool air and three of them came out of the trees, grabbed me and stuffed me into a carriage."

"Poor dear, you must have been terribly frightened."

"I believed they would rape me. Then I feared they would kill me, but it seems they only meant to shame and ruin me. I tried to escape and, for that, I was beaten."

"I see the bruises on your face. We can tend them. Meanwhile, did they—"

"No...no, I was spared rape, thank God." Chastity's cheeks flamed with embarrassment at having to discuss such a possibility.

"I see," said Miss Abby, her eyes full of pity. "As you might imagine, I have heard such tales before. Not every young woman brought to me arrives unscathed, I am sad to say. Was the man who abducted you the man who brought you here?"

"Yes."

Miss Abby went to the sideboard and poured a glass of wine and handed it to her. "A few sips will do you good."

Chastity sipped the rich red wine. It calmed her frayed nerves. Now that it seemed she was safe, she could not stop shivering.

"Have you eaten?"

She shook her head.

The woman went to a tasseled bell pull and summoned a footman. "See that some food is brought for our young guest, Raymond. Some cheese, bread and fruit and tea. And ask Emma to bring the basket of salves."

"Yes, ma'am," said the footman before retreating.

"Now then," said Miss Abby. "Let us sit and you can tell me what happened."

Finally experiencing relief, Chastity drew Sir Robert's cloak around her and began to recount all that had befallen her since her arrival in London.

The woman's face took on a look of grave concern. "For your sake, I will tell the man who brought you that you did not object to entering my house and that I have decided to accept you. He will think you are joining my ladies, but it will not be so."

"Oh, thank you," Chastity said, tears of relief cascading down her bruised cheeks.

The woman handed her a handkerchief. "Here, dry your eyes."

Chastity gratefully accepted it.

"Perhaps it would help you to know that I did not seek to become the madam of a bordello and I take my responsibility to the young women here seriously. A distant uncle bequeathed Willow House to me when my position as governess to two young women ended. I always had a tender for girls in trouble and my reputation for showing them kindness drew to me young beauties who wanted a safe place away from the bawdy houses of Covent Garden or worse. Any girl who comes to me wishing for a different life is helped on her way, some to domestic service, and those who are educated to more. Only the most beautiful, well-spoken and gracious are allowed to join those who live and work at Willow House, if that is their desire and there is an opening. Some of those eventually find a relationship with a particular man."

Chastity felt safe for the first time since she'd been taken. "Thank God that horrible man brought me to you."

Miss Abby patted her hand. "He is not aware of my reputation. He knows only that Willow House is the most elegant brothel in London, which it is. Members of the *ton* and their wealthy friends are our only clientele."

The food arrived and Miss Abby urged her to eat, which she did, surprisingly hungry all of a sudden. The maid, Emma, entered with a basket and came to apply salve to her face. "Poor thing and ye have such beautiful skin, too."

The kind madam poured tea. "While you are eating, I will dispense with the man." She handed Chastity a cup of tea.

"What will you tell him?"

Miss Abby gave her a knowing smile. "Why, that you are beautiful and intelligent and will fit in perfectly with the ladies of Willow House." She looked at Chastity's bare feet. "Emma, find Miss Reynolds a decent gown and some shoes."

Robbie was growing desperate and exhausted. His eyes burned for lack of sleep but he had no intention of stopping. As a spy he had, at times, forced himself to go on little or no sleep. He would do so now to find Chastity.

He and Jack had spent all day searching only to find Chastity was not in any of the bordellos they had visited, unless the madams had lied which, all things considered, might be a possibility. A young woman of Chastity's quality would be a prize they would not easily surrender.

He glanced at Jack, recognizing the lines of fatigue but knowing he would never complain so great was their mission. Robbie had decided to stop at The Guardsman public house for food before going on. As they entered, he smelled the familiar scent of ale and smoke. The light from several large paned windows fell across a dozen scattered wooden tables, half of them occupied with customers.

"I've never been here," said Jack. "A recent favorite?"

"Until last year, my twin brother and I were frequent customers. It was once home to the First Regiment of Foot Guards and only in recent years has become a public house. Were he not in Brighton, you might glimpse the Duke of Wellington raising a pint with the fellows at the bar."

Robbie and Jack claimed a corner table where they could talk undisturbed. It was still late afternoon so many tables were yet to be filled. The air smelled of the fare one found in a tavern. They ordered coffee and mutton stew, which arrived with bread and cheese.

"I'm famished," said Jack, breaking off a piece of bread and a hunk of cheese and stuffing them into his mouth.

Robbie lifted a mouthful of stew to his lips as Sam, the rotund proprietor in his fifties, came to their table. He waited until Robbie swallowed. "'Tis good, isn't it?"

Robbie nodded. "Very good."

"My Amy's been makin' it fresh each day. Can I get ye anythin' else, Powell?" As an aside, he added, "I won't be askin' which one ye are as I could never tell ye and yer brother apart."

"It's Robbie." He was about to tell the man they were fine with what they had when he thought to ask, "Sam, can you think of a high-class brothel in London where one can find exceptional women?"

"Oh, ho! Are ye askin' for yerself or yer friend?"

"Neither, however, it's an urgent matter of great importance."

Sam nodded. "I don't look for other women with my Amy to come home to, but I do recall ye once speakin' in glowin' terms about a place named after a tree."

Robbie screwed up his face in concentration, his weary mind grasping for what he had missed. "A tree?"

"Aye. I can't remember the name."

"Willow House!" Robbie exclaimed, the name suddenly coming into his mind.

"That's the one."

"Bless you, Sam. Based upon what we were looking for, that name had quite slipped my mind. But 'tis a possibility."

Jack dove into his stew.

Sam walked away and Robbie's mood picked up. "I can't imagine they would be foolish enough to take Chastity to Willow House. Abigail Darkin has a reputation as a kind-hearted madam who helps girls in distress. She would see through a ruse in a trice. But she might be able to help us. She'll know where they may have taken Chastity."

Robbie had lost his appetite for anything but finding the woman he loved. "Finish up; we must be off to Willow House."

Chastity stood before the fireplace in the bedchamber Miss Abby had given her, looking into the flames burning cheerfully. She was finally warm after being chilled for so long. Light from the paned windows flowed into the room. The furnishings, like the parlor, were tasteful in shades of green, the bed hangings silk. Above the mantel was a painting of a great lady of an earlier century.

A thousand things ran through her mind as she waited for the gown the maid, Emma, had gone to retrieve. As much as she had once loved her costume, Chastity had gladly shed it when she'd been given a hot bath and a robe. She had not allowed them to take Sir Robert's cloak but had laid it carefully across the chair.

She had narrowly escaped a terrible fate and thanked God it was to Willow House she'd been taken. But what about Sir Robert? He, too, was in danger. Was he, even now, searching for her? The man who had abducted her said he intended to deal with him. She could not bear for her rogue to be hurt, or worse.

Emma burst into the bedchamber. "Here you are, Miss. This is one of the new gowns Miss Abby just received from the dressmaker. She said you might have it. And there are slippers to match!"

"That is so very kind of her," said Chastity, taking the gown from the maid and holding it up to her. "She has been my savior." Chastity did not doubt her reputation was in tatters as word would spread throughout Brighton she was missing, if not kidnapped. But at least her innocence and her life had been preserved. It could have been so much worse.

The maid helped her to don the gown of pale blue silk, pulling the laces taut. The slippers were a little large but fit well enough. "Thank you, Emma. Should I go down?"

"Oh, no, Miss. The young ladies will soon be gathering in the parlor and the gentlemen will arrive after that. You wouldn't want to let them see you. I will bring up a tray and some wine for you. Tomorrow, Miss Abby will find a way to return you to Brighton."

Aunt Agatha would be frantic with worry. Rose, too, would be frightened, thinking the worst. "I do appreciate your lady's help," she told the maid.

"Miss Abby likes to help. You might find some books on those shelves to enjoy," Emma said, pointing to a bookcase on the far side of the chamber. "I will return soon."

Chastity went to the shelf of books, novels every one, and took a likely one from the selection. *"Sense and Sensibility* sounds like a book I should read," she said, chiding herself for the predicament she was in. It was all those hours she had spent with Sir Robert that had made her a target of a madman's vengeance. And, in the Pavilion's gardens, she had succumbed to his kiss. Perhaps if she'd had more sense, none of this would have happened.

Robbie leapt up the short set of stairs to the front door he had stood before at other times when pleasure had been his only purpose. He was vaguely aware of Jack following at a slower pace. It seemed as if years had passed since he'd last been here, so much had changed. He had changed. Now, he wanted only to be assured the woman he had asked to be his wife was safe. He dared to hope the outlaws had brought Chastity to Willow House and not some less worthy place, else she would already be on her back serving the brothel's clientele. He could not bear to think of it. But Abigail Darkin would recognize an innocent in an instant.

The butler, who was familiar with his face, took his hat and allowed him entry. "Mr. Powell, you were not expected this evening." Jack followed him in and the butler shut the door. Inside the entry hall, the doorman, a blond giant stood like a sentry, his only purpose to deter any unruly guest, of which there were few.

Robbie handed the butler his new card. "Wilson, I come not as a customer but my uncle and I are here on an urgent matter. I would see Miss Abby in her office at once. A young woman's life may depend upon it."

"Very well, Sir Robert, follow me."

"I'll wait here for you," said Jack.

"There is a small waiting room just through that door," said Wilson, pointing to a door off the entry hall, "where there is brandy and wine."

"You will find me there," Jack assured Robbie.

Abigail Darkin insisted on formalities, so Robbie waited outside her office for Wilson to present his card and explain the urgent nature of his mission.

A moment later, the butler opened the door and beckoned him enter.

Miss Abby stood behind her polished cherry wood desk, her head bent over his card. Behind her, a fire crackled in the stone fireplace. She smiled as she looked up. "Sir Robert is it now?" Her sharp eyes fixed him with a steady gaze. "You must have done some worthy deed for His Majesty, yes?"

He averted his gaze. "A favor, no more."

"May I offer you a brandy? 'Tis French."

"That is kind of you, but no. I come on an urgent matter."

"Yes, Wilson mentioned that. What is it that brings you here?"

With hope in his heart and scrambling for words, he said, "Do you…have a young woman?"

She smiled. "We have many, as well you know."

"Not one of the girls who live here. Another. Hair the color of pale honey with skin like the purest cream and striking blue eyes like a sea on a distant isle. When she smiles, she lights up the room."

"Does this paragon have a name?"

"Chastity," he choked out. "Miss Chastity Reynolds." Distraught, he added, "It may be that a man brought her here asking you to take her into your house. I pray it was so for any other place does not bear considering."

Abby fixed him with an intense look, one that he had seen before on her wise face.

"I have combed all of London, calling at every brothel to which he might have taken her. I cannot allow myself to think how desperate her situation might be, how scared she must be." Robbie pleaded, "Tell me you have her or I shall be a man most miserable."

"I do."

His brows lifted, hardly believing his ears. "You do?"

She studied him with careful assessment. "Who are you to Miss Reynolds and what is she to you?"

"I am sometimes in great disfavor with her but the truth is I...I love her and would make her my wife. She was abducted because of me and my work for the Crown."

"I see." Given her clientele, Abby likely did see all too well. His older brother, Martin, had once patronized Willow House and he, too, had been a government spy.

Robbie leaned forward over her desk. "You haven't—"

"No, I have kept her apart."

He let out a deep sigh. "May I see her? I wouldn't want her to stay any longer."

"I will have to ask if she would welcome your visit. Chastity has had a great shock, a scare that her upbringing did not prepare her for. Had the wicked man not brought her here, I can well imagine what might have befallen her. She has imagined it, too, I daresay."

"I cannot thank you enough for taking care of her."

"Wait here. I will ask her."

Chapter 14

The door opened and Chastity looked up from her book. Miss Abby stepped into the room, closing the door behind her. "Did you get a nap? You appear more rested."

Chastity nodded. "I did nod off for a few minutes but, mostly, I think it's feeling safe at last. Thank you for the gown. It is lovely."

"That blue quite becomes you." She came closer. "I have come to tell you there is a man downstairs who wants to see you."

A cold chill ran up Chastity's spine as the fear returned that had been her constant companion since her abduction. "Who is he?"

"His name is Sir Robert Powell."

She leapt from her chair, the book falling to the side. "Sir Robert is *here*?"

"From the look on your face, I can see that is good news."

"Oh, yes. I have been praying he would find me."

"He has been searching all of London for you."

"How did he know to look here?"

"He didn't. But he has visited Willow House before."

"It would not surprise me. He is a rogue and doubtless would find your ladies attractive."

"My ladies are effusive in their praise of his kisses," Miss Abby said with a subtle smile.

"I can well imagine that," she said, her cheeks flaming at the memory of his last kiss.

"Chastity, he says his intentions are honorable. You can be sure I asked. He told me seeks your hand in marriage."

She frowned recalling their last conversation. "He has not asked me to marry him, more like informed me."

Miss Abby chuckled. "Yes, I can see him doing that. Sir Robert is a bold one, but a gentleman for all that and, in this instance, quite sincere, I believe."

Lifting her chin, Chastity said, "I have not consented."

"Are you willing to see him?"

"I would not turn him away. Besides, I must warn him. His life is in danger."

Robbie bounded up the stairs and brought himself to a halt in front of the door. He wanted to burst in, so eager was he to be assured she was safe, but in deference to her modesty, he knocked softly.

She wrenched open the door and fell into his arms. "Oh, you came!"

He kissed the top of her head and held her tightly to his chest, relieved she was safe. "Darling, I will always come. I only wish I'd found you sooner but I did not know where he'd taken you." He kissed her then, long and hard, assuring himself she was real and unharmed, assuring her he was her defender.

She pulled back and, for the first time, she appeared vulnerable, a beautiful woman in need of a protector. "That horrible man who held me captive told me you are the reason I was abducted. He said you are a traitor to good Englishmen. How is that possible?"

"Come, let us sit, and I will explain."

They sat on a settee. He held her hands in his, getting a good look at her face for the first time. "You are hurt!" He gently touched her bruised cheek with the back of his hand.

"The man named Augie hit me when I tried to escape."

Robbie frowned. "He will die for that."

"I'm all right now," she said, squeezing his hand.

Making a note to dispense with the man who had hit her, he described his role in the capture of the Cato Street conspirators and his service to the Crown in the past few years. He hoped she did not see his missions as less than honorable. Disguise—and he had donned many—implied deceit. He needed her to believe him worthy.

"However did you become His Majesty's spy?"

"I come by it honestly. My father and my brothers have all undertaken intelligence work for the Crown, that is, in between their lives as shipmasters. In fact, the latter work was key in the assignments we accepted early on."

"A family of spies…" she muttered. "So that is how you earned the baronetcy?"

"A reward bestowed by a generous sovereign. My brother, Martin, was also made a baronet for his work in France during Napoleon's reign."

"And what do you know of the man who abducted me?"

"By his surname, I assume he is somehow related to one of the conspirators who was hanged. When I first arrived at the Pavilion, he sent me a threatening message but it was unsigned."

She visibly shivered.

Concerned for her, he squeezed her hands to remind her he was here to guard her. "What is it?"

"I was just remembering his cold, dark eyes. The man was dreadful. He said he intends to deal with you, too." Her blue eyes clouded. "You must be careful. He means to harm you."

"Don't worry. I will be on my guard. I carry my pistols with me and Jack is very good with a blade."

She stared at him a moment as if trying to understand. "Do you know why he took *me*? He said only it was the company I keep, meaning you."

"He and his men have been following me for some time. They would have seen me with you and were obviously keen observers. In all our banter, Chastity Reynolds, you quite failed to discern my tender feelings for you. But the villain did not. He meant to hurt me through you, and would have struck a devastating blow had he succeeded."

"Oh." She looked down at their joined hands. He hoped she now realized how much he cared for her, how much he loved her. She looked up. "Will he return to Brighton, do you think?"

"Not if I have anything to say about it. His business with me is unfinished but he no longer has lodgings near North Street. Jack and I saw to that. Two of his men are in the king's custody. They told us their leader expects to meet them in a riverside tavern in a week's time. Jack and I will be there."

"Oh, do be careful, won't you?" Her blue eyes looked up expectantly. Perhaps she did care for him more than a little.

"I will. And that reminds me, were there four of them?"

"At the Pavilion, yes. The leader was different than the others. They were lecherous, but his speech was more refined and his manner cold, even arrogant. Remember the Russian serf at the ball?"

Robbie nodded. As a spy, he had taken in all those attending the ball and remembered the Russian serf.

"That was him. But when he brought me here, he was attired as a gentleman, though he retained the beard. I don't think it was his."

"He is clever enough to have at least that much of a disguise. But you have given me the look of the man, his height and his general demeanor."

She chewed her lower lip as if in concentration. "The man who drove the carriage to London was the one named Augie, or at least that's the name by which the leader called him. And there is one other thing I noticed that might help you."

"What?" Robbie would be happy for anything that would identify the man.

"The leader wears fine black boots that bear my father's insignia, a stylized 'R' on the base of the outside shaft. It is the mark of the Reynolds design and highly coveted. He could have purchased them in London, of course. A few bootmakers have them for purposes of taking orders. But he also could have acquired them in or near Northampton."

"That will help, thank you."

She rose and retrieved his musketeer cloak from a chair. Handing it to him, she said, "You cannot know what having this meant to me. It was the only barrier between the lust of his men and me. At night, it kept me warm when I would have shivered."

He accepted the cloak and pulled her down to sit beside him. "I hope it reminded you of me, that I would come for you."

"It did." She slipped her hand from his. "I must return to Aunt Agatha. She will be terrified for me."

"I agree. But I cannot be the one to take you. Our returning to Brighton together after your absence would have tongues wagging, unless you are willing to announce our engagement."

"Definitely not."

He chuckled. "Very well then, as long as you resist, I have an idea. The Countess of Claremont owes me a favor. Since they are such good friends, I believe I could persuade her to pay a visit to Lady Sanborn. Your return in her carriage would provide the perfect excuse for your absence."

"Do you think she would do that for me?"

"There is only one way to find out."

Later that evening, Chastity watched from the window as Sir Robert brought his curricle to a stop in front of Willow House. Her gaze lingered on his lithe form, his broad chest and his handsome face beneath his top hat. He had come to her rescue, winning her admiration, yet, for all that, he was a rogue, experienced and worldly. Could he ever be a man she could trust with her heart?

She had said goodbye to Miss Abby, who only let her go when she had learned of the plan to restore Chastity to Brighton, hopefully with her reputation intact. In deference to that reputation, Miss Abby had agreed with Sir Robert that she should not spend a night in Willow House. As a result, their departure had been from the rear of the house, Chastity covered in Sir Robert's musketeer cloak.

While she had waited for him to call for her, she had reflected on her life. Living in the shadow of her beautiful mother and sisters, her expectations for love had been meager. In truth, she had not believed to ever find it after the young man she had wanted turned out to be unworthy of her trust. Still, when she thought of the women of Willow House, she had to be grateful. She had so much more to live for. One of them might become the mistress of a great man, treasured at first but then discarded, like the parade of women who amused the king. Few could look forward to a legitimate marriage and children. If she were willing to change her intention for the future to live alone, she could.

Emma had come to tell her Sir Robert awaited her. She thanked the maid and followed her down the servants' stairs to see his warm smile. "Good evening!" he said, holding out his hand. He appeared tired and worn but happy.

"And to you."

They walked to his curricle and he helped her to climb in. His touch gave her confidence to face Muriel, Countess of Claremont, a woman Miss Abby had told her was respected by all of London.

Above them, the twilight sky was cast in shades of dark gray. She wore the blue gown Miss Abby had given her and hoped it would not rain, as the curricle would afford them little protection from a downpour even with the hood up. She wanted to look like a lady when she met the countess. Emma had fixed her hair so that it was restored to good taste and, for that, she'd been grateful.

Sir Robert snapped the reins and the grays stretched out away from Willow House. He was attired as a gentleman in an olive-green velvet coat, gray waistcoat and breeches. The green of his coat brought out the green in his hazel eyes. His cravat was simply tied but impeccable, a shock of white against his tanned face. He had shaved and trimmed his side-whiskers. And his boots were polished to a high gloss. Was it for her or the countess he had taken such pains with his appearance?

When she asked about the vicomte, he told her his uncle had stayed behind to see about his collection of knives. "I'll return to him later. He awaits me at Grillon's Hotel."

"Grillon's?"

"I do not wish to stay at my family's house. There would be too many questions." With an amused expression, he added, "Besides, I have such fond memories of the place, you know, particularly the lobby." He laughed then and she realized he was trying to take her mind off the past few days.

"Ah, yes, the lobby," she said, lifting her eyes skyward.

Some minutes later, the curricle came to a stop in front of an imposing four-story house with tall columns and rows of windows on each floor. He handed her down from the curricle, and Chastity stood in awe, taking in the impressive edifice and the gardens she could just glimpse through the iron fence. Would the countess welcome her? Or, would she consider her a pale image of the woman she had imagined Sir Robert would meet in Brighton. The elderly countess might have preferred Rose.

"So this is Claremont House," she said gazing up at the mansion.

"Indeed, it is," said Sir Robert. "The home of the dowager countess or, as I call her, The Grand Countess. The two of you remind me of each other, you know. Both formidable women."

She didn't know what to make of that. She had never thought of herself as such. Willful and independent, yes, even impudent. But hardly formidable. Still, since she was certain he had meant it as a compliment, she returned him a smile. "To be compared to your Grand Countess is high praise, indeed."

A waiting groom took the reins of Sir Robert's grays and he opened the gate and escorted her to the front door. She was glad he was beside her; she wouldn't want to meet the countess alone.

At the sound of the brass knocker, the door opened and an aged butler greeted them, taking Sir Robert's hat. "Welcome. I delivered your message to Lady Claremont, Sir Robert. She is expecting you and Miss Reynolds."

"Thank you, Cruthers."

Chastity had only begun to look around the grand entry hall with its magnificent chandelier and gilded staircase winding to the second story, when the butler beckoned them to follow him.

The parlor they entered was fashionably decorated yet understated in pastel colors and ivory. The silk brocade drapes were a beautiful shade of pink and the Axminster carpet featured a geometric design with pink roses. The room was feminine yet somehow regal in effect.

From one of the ivory sofas, a silver-haired woman wearing a pearl-gray gown rose and smiled at them. Chastity kept her head enough to curtsey before one dubbed The Grand Countess.

"Good morning, Sir Robert. And this young lady must be Chastity Reynolds, great-niece of my dear friend." The countess lifted the quizzing glass that hung around her neck and peered through it at Chastity.

She tried not to fidget and forced herself to remain calm. "Yes, my lady," she said, inwardly quaking at the countess' careful examination of her person. She had not cowered before the men who had taken her captive, but she felt like doing so now before this grand lady. She feared she would be judged and found wanting.

The countess gestured them to the sofas and asked the butler to see that tea was served. "I have heard much about you from Agatha, Miss Reynolds, which is why I asked Sir Robert to call upon you in Brighton. I am so glad he did."

A knowing look passed between the countess and Sir Robert, which produced a smile on his face. "You remain wily as ever, Lady Claremont."

"Now," said the countess, ignoring Sir Robert's comment, "why are you two together in London and to what do I owe this visit?"

Chastity glanced at Sir Robert, hoping he would explain. She couldn't bring herself to describe her abduction or the night she'd spent in London as a captive and the day in a bordello. Though she remained a virgin, few would believe it.

"My lady," Sir Robert began, "you know of my recent work for the Crown." He did not look at Chastity as he said this, nor did he elaborate.

"Yes, that dangerous spy business you engaged in that brought those traitors to justice. I know of it."

"What you don't know is that some of the brigands connected with the Cato Street conspirators have learned my identity and are bent on revenge. They followed me to Brighton. Not to put too fine a point on it, but they have me in their sights. My uncle, the vicomte de Saintonge, whom you have met, and I, have been trying to ferret them out but with no success. We did not anticipate that a part of their revenge would be aimed at Miss Reynolds, with whom I have recently been keeping company."

The countess smiled and shifted her gaze to Chastity, a pleased expression on her face.

He was a spy who served the king, a shipmaster from a fine family and a close enough friend of The Grand Countess that he could tease her. No longer could Chastity think of him as The Rogue. Though rogue he might be when it came to women, in truth, he was so much more.

A footman entered with a tray on which was set a pot of tea, three cups and a plate of sweetmeats. Chastity accepted a cup of tea, glad for something to hold in her hands.

"What has transpired in the last few days," Sir Robert said, as the footman departed, "has not, in the smallest degree, been brought about by any action of Miss Reynolds."

Chastity sipped the hot tea, which she found soothing. Beside her, Sir Robert took a drink from his own cup, then set it down.

"And what, exactly, has transpired, Sir Robert?" asked the countess. "Do get to the point."

Sir Robert then explained Chastity's kidnapping, how she ended up at Willow House and his concern for her reputation were he to escort her back to Brighton.

"The villain took you to Abigail Darkin's house?" the countess asked Chastity. "How very fortunate for you, my dear."

Chastity nodded. "Yes, my lady."

"You know her?" asked Sir Robert, a perplexed expression on his handsome face.

"I know *of* her. She is well thought of by the ladies, including me, who have benefitted from the girls she has placed in service."

"I had no idea," said Sir Robert.

"Nor should you," said the countess, shaking her head. "Moreover, I will expect you to treat them no differently now than you did before."

"Of course."

The countess set down her cup. "I begin to see what is needed here. I agree, you cannot very well return Chastity to Brighton. But I can, accompanied by the explanation she has been visiting the dear friend of her great-aunt, yes?"

"Exactly," said Sir Robert. He took Chastity's hand and gave her a fond look. "You should be aware that I have asked Miss Reynolds to marry me."

"Told, not asked," corrected Chastity. "And I have not accepted."

The countess chuckled, which was remarkable given her straight posture and refined manner. "These men are all alike, my dear. They get a notion in their heads of the women they would have to wife and expect us to fall in with their plans straightaway. Though you could hardly do better than Sir Robert, the choice is yours. I, for one, am pleased he has come up to scratch."

Chastity was taken aback. Did the countess approve his desire to marry her?

The countess leaned forward as if sharing a secret. "He is the last of the Powell brothers to marry. His mother and I were near to giving up hope. You, my dear, may be an answer to prayer." Facing Sir Robert, she said, "Leave this dear child in my care. I have been thinking of paying Agatha a visit anyway. I will send a message to let her know she may expect us tomorrow at teatime."

Robbie bowed before the two women. "You have my eternal gratitude, Countess." Rising, he said, "I will leave Miss Reynolds' portmanteau with Cruthers." He had kept the small valise Abby had packed for Chastity in the curricle, not wishing to appear presumptuous, though he had harbored few doubts about the countess accepting the task of returning Chastity to Brighton. Muriel loved a challenge.

As he was about to take his leave, Chastity stepped close to ask, "Will you remain in London then?"

"I must. This is not yet finished and the villain remains in the city."

Knowing she was in good hands, he kissed her on her forehead and took his leave. The Grand Countess would have outriders as well as an armed coachman to guard the women. Too, he did not think the leader of the brigands, the man he knew only as Ings, would return to Brighton anytime soon, not when he planned to meet his men at The Prospect in a few days' time. The question was, did the leader foresee Robbie discovering his Brighton lodgings and thus obtaining the information concerning the tavern meeting? If he were very clever, he might have anticipated a spy would do just that. In which case, Robbie would be expected.

When he returned to the suite of rooms he and his uncle would share at Grillon's, Jack was honing his knives. Six blades of different sizes were laid across the table. Jack's shifted his gaze to Robbie as he took a seat across from him.

"Did the countess accept her mission?" Jack inquired.

"She did. Now we can turn to the task at hand. And, for that, I am thinking I might call in a few friends."

Jack paused in his polishing. "Which friends might those be?"

"Well, it occurred to me that since the villain thinks to meet his men at The Prospect, and that is a favorite haunt of the Powell Shipping crews, why not enlist a few to our cause? One of the ships is certain to be in port. It might even be my own."

"Do you really think we need them when there are two of us and we are better armed?"

"It's merely a contingency. You see, I've been thinking he set this up from the beginning to lure me to him. Oh, he meant to hurt Chastity, I've no doubt about that, but he must have known I'd track the two he left in Brighton to their nest. It was an easy way for him to dispense with the two he didn't need while pointing me to the place he wanted to be found."

Jack began hiding his knives on his person. Two went into sheaths inside his boots; one went into a loop inside the back of his breeches; one he slipped down inside his shirt along his forearm; and two lodged at his hips.

Robbie watched, fascinated. "Do you always carry so many knives?"

"*Pas toujours*. But since you told me we were being followed about Brighton, yes. Now, as for these troublesome pests who would lurk in the shadows and seek to ruin young ladies of good breeding, I say let's away with them and quickly." Jack swept his index finger across his throat. *"Comme ça."*

Robbie had to laugh. "There are times, Jack, when you quite amaze me."

"Those devils interfere with our *vacances, non*? And they would hurt the lovely virago?"

"They did, though, thank God, not as badly as they intended. I shall send a message to Tiller who will ascertain the whereabouts of the crew. It might be that the leader of the brigands has yet more men of which we know naught."

Being the guest of the Countess of Claremont had its advantages. She had more servants than Chastity would have imagined for one lady and a cook. In a few days' time, Chastity had gone from a beaten and starved captive, threatened with ruin, to a lady of leisure dining with a denizen of the *ton*.

But she had not forgotten the terror of her capture nor joy in the arms of her saviour.

The dinner they had that evening was one she would remember and not just for the food. Branched silver candlesticks graced the mahogany table set with sparkling crystal, some colored blue, and porcelain in a pattern she recognized as one by Spode, which her mother greatly admired. In the center of the table sat a squat vase full of white roses. Above the flowers hung a brilliant crystal chandelier with a multitude of candles.

The countess claimed the seat at the head of the table and directed Chastity to the chair on her right, which a footman pulled out for her. The food served them was sumptuous. It began with vegetable soup. "The vegetables are from Cook's kitchen garden," said the countess. "In the summer there are so many to choose from."

"'Tis delicious," remarked Chastity. "My mother has an extensive kitchen garden."

"In Northampton?"

"Yes."

"Do you miss your home?" the countess asked.

Chastity thought of what she might say that did not sound ungrateful. "Our home is not so grand as yours, Countess, but it is old and stately and has a beautiful setting. I do love the countryside and think of it often. But I must tell you I have enjoyed the visit with Aunt Agatha. We get on as the best of friends. She is always full of ideas for amusement and knows such interesting people. Through her, I met the king and Mrs. Fitzherbert, her neighbor, and so many others."

"I am not surprised. I, too, find Agatha's company delightful. In the last few years, she has become something of an eccentric but it seems to suit her."

"I love how she dresses in bright colors," said Chastity. "I designed a pair of shoes for her with yellow sunflowers on the toes to go with one of her gowns. She quite liked them."

"You design shoes?" the countess inquired.

"'Tis a hobby I learned from my father. When we are not engaged in reading or some other pursuit, he and I design shoes, he most often men's boots. He only makes a prototype for the shoemakers to use whereas I design for my friends and family."

"What an industrious young woman you are, Miss Reynolds. I begin to see that your beauty is not the only thing about you that Sir Robert finds compelling."

Chastity felt her cheeks flame and dropped her gaze to the crimped cod in oyster sauce, just being served. Desperate to change the subject, she raised her head and asked, "Have you ever been to the fish market on the beach at Brighton?

"I have observed it from the Marine Parade on one of my morning walks with Agatha, but we did not participate."

"It was great fun. Sir Robert helped me select fish for Aunt Agatha's cook." She fought a laugh, remembering how much they had bought. When the countess furrowed her brow, Chastity said, "Between my friend, Rose Crockett, and Sir Robert's uncle, Monsieur Donet, we purchased a veritable feast of fish."

"You enjoyed yourself, then?"

"Oh, yes." She smiled recalling that morning. Perhaps that was the beginning of her softening to the man she had once called The Rogue. But why did he want to marry her? She wasn't beautiful like Rose or her sisters. She wasn't high-born like many of the ladies he could wed. His thought to marry her seemed impulsive, rash even. He might reconsider. And, if he did, perhaps, if they could be nothing more, they could be friends. But she knew that would never satisfy her, not after she had known his kisses, his arms around her.

As the footman refreshed their Claret wine, the countess said, "I kept the dinner simple tonight, knowing neither of us would have a large appetite. I do hope you find it adequate."

"More than adequate, my lady. In truth, this is a splendid repast."

"For dessert, there will be Italian ices from Negri's in Berkeley Square. A summer treat."

"Truly? I love ices, all flavors."

"Pistachio is my favorite," said the countess with a smile, "but we have pineapple and jasmine, too."

Chastity beamed her pleasure. It was easy to talk with the countess though she did wonder if she wasn't being interviewed. She half-expected the countess to raise her quizzing glass to consider her again more closely.

As they shared a glass of Madeira after dinner—a wine the countess told her she kept on hand at all times—the countess fixed her with a steady gaze. "What think you of Sir Robert's offer of marriage?"

Chastity let out a breath. She should have known the question would present itself at some point. "I hardly know what to think of it, my lady. 'Twas not even a proper offer. I recall no bended knee, no avowal of love. He merely kissed me—quite against my will, I might add—and informed me he would marry me."

"Oh, dear." The countess brought her palm to her chest. "I see he has gone about this all wrong. You are a romantic and must have a proposal that wins your heart."

"I never thought to wed," said Chastity. "On my twenty-first birthday, I will come into a family legacy, an estate of my own."

"And you foolishly believe that will be enough? No, my dear, it never shall. A life alone is not a life fully lived, not for a woman. You must wed for you will want children, a family. Oh, I daresay it will take an unusual man, but Agatha would be quite dismayed to think you had no desire for marriage. You must reconsider."

Chastity did not want to displease her hostess, the gracious woman who would see her back to Brighton. "At your urging, Countess, I will think on it."

Chapter 15

The next afternoon, after what seemed like a long journey, Lady Claremont's carriage came to a stop in front of Aunt Agatha's house. Now that they had arrived, Chastity was suddenly nervous. The bruises on her face had darkened, though the countess' maid had given her something to hide the worst of it.

She looked out the window to see her great-aunt and Rose standing in front of the gate, each wearing an anxious expression. Did they wonder what indecencies she had suffered? Did they worry the ruse of her having visited with Lady Claremont would not be convincing? That she would, indeed, be ruined?

Chastity accepted the footman's hand and stepped down from the carriage and into the arms of her great-aunt.

"Oh, thank God you are safe," cried Aunt Agatha, giving her a tight hug. "We were so worried but Sir Robert assured us he would find you and I see he did." Her great-aunt held her away, examining her like she might a broken doll. "Are you well?"

"She's fine, Agatha," said Lady Claremont, having descended from the carriage. "I trust you received my message?"

"Yes, thank you, Muriel."

"Good, but we could both do with some tea."

"Oh, yes, you are quite right. Cook has been baking all morning and we are prepared for tea in the parlor. It's so good to have you both here. Of course, I have told my friends that Chastity was visiting with you."

The two older women walked up the path to the front door, chatting like the old friends they were.

Chastity and Rose followed, Rose taking her arm. "You don't have to speak of it if you don't want to, Chas."

"I don't mind," said Chastity, "now that it's over."

"Was it very dreadful?"

Chastity remembered the man Augie pawing her and his brutal fist, the dank room in the East End of London, her fear of the man who led her captors and her dread of his intentions. "Parts of it, yes."

"We prayed for you every day."

"I expect that may be the reason I ended up where I did." At Rose's inquiring gaze, she said, "I'll tell you about it later."

Once they were seated in the parlor with their tea, Crispin came to sit at Chastity's feet. She set aside her teacup and lifted him into her lap. His warm body was comforting, his purr like a welcome home.

"He missed you," said Rose.

Aunt Agatha inquired, "What of Sir Robert and M'sieur Donet?"

Lady Claremont held her cup and saucer before her. "Sir Robert was the one who delivered Chastity to me, concerned for appearances once she was safe. I believe he and his uncle are pursuing the scoundrel who kidnapped Chastity. The dreadful man wasn't to surface for several days so Sir Robert had to remain in London."

"Two quid on the Spanish cock!" a man shouted from the rear of the tavern.

"Three on the black-breasted red!" came another cry. "He'll cut yer Spaniard to ribbons!"

Boisterous male voices rose to a crescendo as the cockfight, attended by sailors, merchants, and even some London fops, got underway.

Robbie grimaced. There was one form of gambling in which he refused to indulge—cockfighting. He could not enjoy seeing the roosters rip each other apart, the match ending only when one was badly hurt or dead. But since Ings had chosen to meet his men here on a Sunday, and that was the day The Prospect sponsored such entertainment, Robbie was unsurprised to hear the sounds of men eagerly anticipating the blood sport.

Not wishing to announce themselves before it was time, Robbie and Jack had disguised their appearances. Tiller had borrowed clothing from the crew of the *Tradewind*, Robbie's schooner that, by happenstance, was moored in the Pool of London waiting to be unloaded. To these clothes, they added wigs and sloppy hats and a few days' extra stubble to mask their normally clean jaws.

He had asked Tiller to inquire if any of the crew, who would otherwise be enjoying their shore leave, could be persuaded to join them at the tavern. Their fists might come in handy should the capture of Ings and his men turn into a brawl.

Over dinner the night before, Tiller had come to tell him all was in order.

Robbie asked, "How many volunteered?" He didn't expect even the four he'd requested. When in port, his crew always had family to visit and a list of entertainments to pursue.

"They were right happy to oblige, Cap'n. So many raised their hands, I had me pick of the crew. I chose the brawniest, like ye said."

He shot his valet an amused look. "Their response leaves me to wonder if it's for love of their captain whose face they've not seen for some time, or if it's because they love a good fight."

"Both, I 'spect." said Tiller, grinning. "The first mate's doin' a fine job as cap'n but they likes the one they had. And then there was the cockfight, it bein' Sunday."

225

"They may soon have their captain back," he said. He hoped Chastity Reynolds would delay his plans to return to sea. She might accompany him as some captain's wives did. As soon as he returned to Brighton, his first priority would be to convince her to accept his suit.

"Have you alerted the proprietor to our purpose?" he asked Tiller.

"Aye, Cap'n. He understands 'tis the Crown's business ye're about and that ye'll pay for any damage."

As they entered The Prospect, Robbie scanned the men at the tables between the windows and the bar, spotting his gunner and bosun. They briefly raised their chins telling him he had been recognized. He hoped Ings could not so easily find him among the crowd.

"Shall we venture toward the ring?" he said to Jack in a low whisper.

"I was hoping you'd ask. I can't say I've ever attended a cockfight. They have them in Calais but I've yet to witness one."

They headed toward the back of the long tavern to a large area cordoned off for the birds where the cocks were posturing before each other. Surrounding them a crowd of men stared intensely in anticipation.

"It's not very different than a fight among pirates," said Robbie. "Only instead of knives, the gamecocks use their spurs, sometimes enhanced with metal. Not to my taste."

Gathered around the ring, Robbie counted twenty-five men, all focused intently on the squawking birds, now furiously going at each other.

A few men glanced up at the newcomers, then back to the birds. Two were members of Robbie's crew, the sailmaker and the carpenter. The others might be dockworkers or sailors from other ships, save for one whose dark eyes reminded him of Chastity's description of Ings. The man briefly considered Robbie and Jack before returning his attention to the fighting cocks. His expression spoke of disinterest in the fight whereas every other man seemed fixated on the outcome. Both the man's hair and eyes were very dark. His face sported a mustache, a narrow goatee and chin whiskers framing his jaw, unusual for London gentry. Was the facial hair his own? His clothing was black, the cut of his coat speaking of fine tailoring. Robbie couldn't see his boots from where he stood but he suspected they, too, were black.

The short cockfight ended when one bird was pinned to the dirt, bleeding. Robbie wanted to leave. Instead, he fixed his steady gaze on the crowd.

"Well, what do you think of it?" he asked Jack.

"I see your point. *Répugnant*. Once was enough for me."

The man in black rose, as did one other man, passing Robbie and Jack on their way into the bar area. It was clear they were looking for someone and were disappointed not to find him. Robbie supposed his disguise worked better than he'd anticipated.

With a nod at his uncle, Robbie followed, all the while staring at the boots of the man in black. He and his companion claimed a small table, their backs to the paned glass windows lining the wall facing the Thames. As the man slid into his chair, Robbie caught sight of the stylized "R" on the shaft.

Robbie boldly confronted the man. "Waiting for someone, Ings?"

The man looked up, startled. "Why, yes, but you are not—" He peered closely at Robbie and a flicker of recognition appeared in his dark eyes.

"You are a thief, a despoiler of innocents and a dastardly reprobate, Ings." Withdrawing his pistol, Robbie aimed it at the man's heart. "On behalf of the king, I charge you with assault and kidnapping. You are under arrest." Robbie's speech, finer than his apparel, must have confirmed his identity.

"Powell!" Ings spit out as he got to his feet.

The crowd at the bar went silent.

"You are a traitor to all good Englishmen!"

"Not so the view of His Majesty."

Ings slipped his hand into the pocket of his overcoat.

"Take up that pistol at your peril," said Robbie. "If you don't hit me, you may hit one behind me, adding murder to the charges. Besides, half the men in the tavern are mine."

Ings looked around and snarled, "So be it! Striking them will strike at you!"

Just then, Ings' companion drew a knife from his waist and, reaching across the table, tried to stab Robbie. But Robbie was quick and knocked the blade from his hand with his pistol.

Jack grabbed the man by his jacket, holding a knife to his throat. "Give me a chance to draw blood and I will. My knife is thirsty." Jack thrust him into the chair. "Sit!"

"I, too, have men with me," said Ings. With a snake's smile, he drew his pistol. "You may have this one," he said, darting a glance at his companion, "but there are many others here."

Robbie sensed men at his back, but he couldn't turn to be certain if they were his. With dueling pistols ready to fire and Jack's blade at the neck of Ings' companion, his options were limited.

"Drop the pistol, Ings."

"And why would I do that? Now that I have seen to the ruination of your lady love, your death is all I seek."

Robbie laughed. "You err if you think you accomplished that. My lady has not been ruined. The place you took her is known to me and I to them. She remains untouched and safe."

Shock appeared on Ings' face. He froze, allowing Robbie time to strike the villain's hand that held the pistol. The gun went off before dropping to the floor, but the shot failed to hit its mark.

"Ye should have let me have the chit," said Ings' companion to his master.

"You must be Augie," snarled Robbie. When the man did not deny it, Robbie moved his pistol to his left hand and, motioning Jack aside, planted his fist in the man's face, content to hear his nose break. "That is for my lady you badly mistreated."

Jack resumed his hold on the man named Augie and pressed his knife deeper into his throat.

Ings shouted, "Take them!"

Robbie glanced over his shoulder to see a mêlée had broken out and his men throwing punches. "We got this, Cap'n!" his carpenter shouted as he slammed his fist into a man's gut, dropping him to the floor where he lay groaning.

The tavern erupted into a knockdown tussle, men shouting and fists flying.

"Robbie!" shouted Jack.

Robbie looked back to see Ings pulling a knife from his boot. Filled with disdain for the twisted miscreant, Robbie shot Ings in the shoulder.

Ings dropped his knife and staggered back, sinking into a chair.

"One down; one more to go."

"*Très bien*," said Jack as he smashed the hilt of the blade he'd been holding into the temple of Ings' companion causing him to fall to his knees and slide beneath the table. "That makes two, *mon ami*."

"I'll take that rope, now!" Robbie shouted to the barkeeper.

A coil of rope flew through the air. He grabbed it and handed one length to Jack. "Tie him up; I'll see to Ings." When both men were trussed up, Robbie said, "We'll hand them over to the Bow Street Runners. I imagine they will be pleased to arrest these who sympathized with the man who shot one of their own."

The fight in the bar was over. Robbie's men had prevailed with only minor scrapes and bruises. Robbie looked over the scene of bodies lying at various angles and groans emanating from those who weren't out cold. "A round of drinks for the crew!" he shouted.

"Aye," said his gunner, "and one for the Cap'n!"

"Hip! Hip! Hurrah!" shouted his men.

After dinner, Rose came into Chastity's bedchamber and perched on the bed, giving Chastity, who was sitting at her dressing table unpinning her hair, a curious look. "You seem different somehow."

"I imagine I am. One cannot experience something so traumatic without being affected. As well, I had much time to think." Mostly, she thought of Sir Robert, but Rose need not know that.

Rose leaned forward as if trying to close the distance between them. "I know you were kidnapped, Chas, and that the men took you because of Sir Robert's work for the Crown. He was unconscious on the ground when we found him but, when he awoke, he told us all."

"One of the villains told me they had hit him on the head. I was worried they might have killed him."

"Just a large bump. He and the vicomte went after you that same night. That's when they found the two left behind."

Concerned they might have gotten away, she asked, "Where are they now?"

"In the custody of the local magistrate."

Relieved, Chastity said, "Their leader took me to a dreadful part of London, the East End, I think. I feared I would never leave, that I'd be lost there forever."

"How awful!"

"It was. But I was not there long. The leader had plans for me. Plans designed to ruin me and hurt Sir Robert. He meant to give me to a brothel."

Rose's mouth dropped open.

"As it happened, he took me to a place called Willow House, an exclusive bordello, and threatened me, saying he would kill Sir Robert if I said anything. When I realized the madam was a kind woman who had discerned the truth of it, I told her my story. Before she could return me to Brighton, Sir Robert showed up, looking for me."

"How did he know you might be there?"

"He and M'sieur Donet were searching all the high-class brothels in

London and Sir Robert remembered Willow House, a place he has apparently patronized in the past."

"I see," said Rose, her forehead furrowed.

"Exactly. A rogue would know of such places, wouldn't he? Still, he was caring of my virtue, which, by the way, is still intact. It was his idea to have everyone believe I was visiting Aunt Agatha's good friend, Lady Claremont. When he explained to her what occurred, she offered to bring me back."

"He is thoughtful, Chas, no matter you think him a rogue." Rose got up from the bed and came over to embrace her. "You have been through a lot but, in time, this will pass."

"I hope so. Meanwhile, Rose, I have changed my mind about marriage. Lady Claremont insisted I reconsider my thought to live alone and I have. I should probably tell you that Sir Robert has mentioned marriage."

Rose, now sitting on the bed beside Chastity, took one of her hands in hers. "He has proposed?" she asked excitedly.

"No, not exactly. He has informed me that such is his intent. It was not at all romantic. We were arguing in the Pavilion gardens and I ran from him. Right into the clutches of the kidnappers, as it turned out."

"My goodness, Chas."

"Let's go find ourselves a glass of sherry. Or, maybe a full bottle."

Rose laughed. "Let's."

"There are two letters for Miss Reynolds and one for you, Lady Sanborn," announced Featherstone as he delivered the mail on a silver salver to the parlor where Chastity and Rose were having tea with Aunt Agatha and Lady Claremont.

Chastity's great-aunt took the letter addressed to her from the tray and indicated to Featherstone he should give the others to Chastity.

"I'll read this later," said Aunt Agatha, tucking it into her bosom.

Chastity tore open the first when she recognized the handwriting. "It's from my mother." Reading on, she said, "She wants me to return to Northampton for my sister's wedding. She says the preparations are proceeding and my presence is needed for a fitting."

"I would be sad to see you go," said Aunt Agatha.

"Indeed, yes," added Lady Claremont, "and Sir Robert has yet to return."

"If you must go home, so will I, Chas."

Chastity smiled at her loyal friend. "What about the vicomte?" Rose had not said much of her feelings for the Frenchman but her eyes, whenever he was near, had given her away.

Rose pressed her lips together. "I would miss him, but he has said nothing of his intentions and I could not bear to let you go alone."

Chastity reached out to pat her friend's hand. "It would mean a lot to have you with me."

"Then I shall remain with you," said Rose. "Who is the other letter from?"

Chastity studied the familiar writing. The letter was addressed to *Miss Chastity Reynolds, No. 54 Old Steyne Road, Brighton.* "I think it's from Sir Robert," she said, looking up. All three faces stared back at her with expectant expressions.

She skimmed the letter. "He assures me the villain, whose name is Aaron Ings, and his hired brigands are in the hands of the Bow Street Runners, but there will be some delay so that he won't be returning to Brighton for a week." She did not disclose the rest of the letter, the part that spoke of his love for her and his desire to be with her shortly. Were those his true feelings?

"Humph," uttered Lady Claremont. "That is disappointing, I must say. And with your having to leave, Chastity, we have little time to spend together."

Agatha, too, had recognized the handwriting on the letter addressed to her. She retreated to the small library, away from the others, to see what Sir Robert had to say. Breaking the red wax seal, she unfolded the note and read,

> *Dear Lady Sanborn,*
>
> *I don't know if Chastity has told you, but I have expressed a desire to marry her. I have come to love and admire your grand-niece and want nothing as much as to share my life with her. However, I think it would be prudent to seek her father's blessing before I formally ask for her hand. I am certain you would approve of my doing so, assuming you favor the match. I believe the Countess of Claremont had that in mind when she first asked me to call upon you. A clever matchmaker.*
>
> *With this in mind, I will go first to Northampton and then join you in Brighton. Please say nothing of this to Chastity as I want to be assured Mr. Reynolds approves of my suit before I proceed.*
>
> *Yours truly,*
> *Sir Robert Powell*

"Featherstone!" she called as she pulled the cord. The butler immediately appeared. "Please ask Lady Claremont to join me here for a glass of Madeira. You may tell her I have some very good news to impart."

Chastity went to her bedchamber after tea and sat before the fire, stroking Crispin's fur. She was oddly glad for her mother's request that she return home. While she hated to leave Aunt Agatha and Brighton and was finding Lady Claremont's company very pleasant, the summons home provided the excuse she needed. If she were still in Brighton when Sir Robert returned, she might be tempted to give in to him, his charm, his kisses and his awkward mention of marriage.

Her feelings for him had changed, so much so she feared she could no longer deny her attraction for the man she had once named "The Rogue". In truth, she had fallen in love with him but she could never marry a man who frequented brothels, engaged in assignations with married women and accepted the public fawning of tavern wenches. She could never be a wife who tolerated such behavior, particularly if she loved her husband.

A soft knock sounded and Rose opened her door to peek in. "Am I permitted to join you?"

"Of course, do come in. I've just been thinking..."

"Of going home or staying?" she asked as she took the chair opposite Chastity in front of the fire.

"Going home. I must, you know, for Pen's sake. Do you mind awfully?"

"I have loved being here in Brighton with you, but I always knew it would end and I cannot imagine staying without my dearest friend." Rose sighed deeply. "I would have liked to say farewell to the vicomte, but I can always leave him a letter."

Chastity studied the face of her friend. Cast in firelight, she was so lovely. "Do you like him very much?"

Rose gazed into the fire. "Yes, I think I like him more than I realized. The night of the ball told me much of his character. He was the stalwart one when you were taken. So calm, so able to cope while the rest of us were in a panic. He went with Sir Robert to search for anything of yours. That's when they found your slipper. And he insisted on going to London with Sir Robert. But he is of the aristocracy, Chas, and very wealthy as well. He could have any woman he wanted. I am only a country girl, who has not even had a Season."

"You are hardly only that, Rose. I think you a most wonderful woman and any man would thank his stars to have found you. Do write him a letter and see what comes of it."

"You are good to encourage me, Chas. When do we leave?"

"My mother gave me a week, but I think to leave in a few days, depending on the weather. I hope to avoid the mud-filled ruts we experienced on our travel to London."

"I will be ready."

Chapter 16

Robbie left Jack at The Swan Hotel in Northampton where they had secured lodgings and rode to the location not far from town where the hotel proprietor had told him he could find Dudley Hall. His uncle begged to remain behind to allow him inquiry after Miss Crockett's family in the hopes of gaining an introduction to her parents.

At first glance, the Reynolds' home appeared large and imposing, a two-winged brick edifice standing three stories high with six dual chimneys rising from a slanted slate roof. Four dormer windows were set into the third story roof.

He rode up the gravel path flanked by grass lawns. As he wasn't expected, he was unsurprised to encounter no stable boy. So, he tied his horse at the stone arch leading to the front door. A knock produced a butler dressed in a black suit. "Sir?"

Robbie handed the man his card. "Sir Robert Powell to see Mr. Reynolds."

"The master is in the library. I will see if he is accepting callers."

With that, the butler turned on his heels and disappeared down a corridor, leaving Robbie to look around. The floor beneath his boots was black and white tiles and above him a shining brass chandelier held a myriad of candles. A staircase at one side led to the floors above. He tried to picture a young, mischievous Chastity sliding down the banister and succeeded. Oh, yes, he was confident she had done that and likely been punished for it.

She had told him she had two sisters, one older and one younger. Were they at all like her? He doubted it. Chastity was unique and might have had difficulty fitting into an ordinary family. He recalled her words when she described them, "I have two sisters, one older and one younger. My father is a country squire and an eccentric designer of men's shoes and boots." She had made no mention of her mother.

The butler returned. "The master will see you. Please follow me."

The library was lined with bookshelves full of books. Behind the carved desk that was strewn with sheets of parchment was a fireplace and above it the painting of a beautiful dark-haired woman in an elegant blue silk gown. He could see a resemblance with Chastity but the coloring was different.

The silver-haired man behind the desk rose and came around to extend his hand. "Sir Robert, welcome."

Robbie shook his hand and looked into the same brilliant blue eyes that belonged to Chastity. "I come about your daughter, Chastity."

Mr. Reynolds gestured Robbie to a sofa set beneath a mullioned window that allowed light to stream into the library. "Would you care for a cup of coffee? 'Tis a bit early for brandy but we have that as well."

"Coffee would be welcome."

A footman was summoned and returned with two cups and a silver coffee pot. Mr. Reynolds waved him away. "I'll pour, Jackson."

Once they had their coffee, Mr. Reynolds took a seat beside Robbie. "Do you come from Brighton with news of my daughter?"

Robbie sampled the coffee, which was very good, before saying, "I come from London but I have been in Brighton, a guest of His Majesty at the Royal Pavilion."

"Is my daughter well?" Mr. Reynold's asked with a look of concern. "I've not had a letter recently."

"Your daughter is well and with her great-aunt, Lady Sanborn."

The man's posture relaxed and he took a drink of his coffee. "Then, may I ask your purpose in coming here?"

"I realize you don't know me at all, sir. I met your daughter this summer at the suggestion of the Countess of Claremont, a family friend, whom I greatly admire. Over the months, I have come to respect Chastity and enjoy her company. More than that, I love her. I come to ask your permission for her hand in marriage. I would ask her to be my wife."

"You are right, Sir Robert, I don't know you. But I do know of you. Does His Majesty the king know of your interest in my daughter?"

"Why, yes, but he did not know I was coming to see you. I have not spoken to him since I left Brighton for London."

"Then he must have anticipated your visit, for he wrote to me. His letter was quite clear. He said if you should ask for my daughter's hand, I should not deny you. He called you his friend, a noble servant of His Majesty and, as a part of Powell Shipping, a worthy man of means well able to provide for my daughter."

"I am taken aback, sir. I did not know that the king had attempted to pave my way. I would not be so complimentary of my attributes but, it is true, I am able to care for your daughter. I must tell you she thinks me a rogue of the worst sort though she is not indifferent to my suit. Her view is based on some impressions, perhaps of my life before I met her. But since that day, there has been no other woman for me. And there never shall be."

Mr. Reynolds' blue eyes twinkled. "It is not so bad to begin as a rogue, Son, as long as you end as a faithful husband."

"I have three brothers, sir. All are faithful husbands, as is my father."

"And what do you think of my daughter's interest in designing shoes?"

"I think she is very clever. You see, my brothers' wives all engage in unusual pursuits. Nick, the eldest, is married to an American who knows sailing ships as well as her husband. Kit, my brother Martin's wife, is an accomplished sketch artist. And, Ailie, my twin's wife, designs ships."

"My, my. That's quite a family. Yes, I begin to see," he said, nodding. "Chastity would fit in well, wouldn't she?"

"She would, indeed, sir."

The older man set down his cup and got to his feet. Robbie noticed his beautiful boots. "Are those boots one of your own designs?"

"Yes, would you like to see more?"

Robbie stood. "I would. There is nothing I like so much as a fine pair of boots."

"Well, then, young man, let us retire to my workshop." He began to stride toward the door, then turned. "Oh, and, yes, you have my permission to seek Chastity's hand in marriage."

Chastity stroked Crispin's fur and gazed out the window of the carriage that was taking her and Rose home. No matter the day was fair, the atmosphere in the carriage bespoke gloom. Neither of them seemed to be eager to return to Northampton. The same had been true of their one night in London. Grillon's Hotel had brought back so many memories that Chastity had been glad to leave it behind that morning.

"We don't seem to be very lighthearted today," observed Rose.

"No," said Chastity. "And I don't look forward to Pen's wedding either. Mother will parade all the eligible men in Northampton before me with unsubtle hints of my need to accept one of them."

"If it will help, I will stand by you, Chas."

"You must. I would die without your company. Too, Mother will not be so verbal of her desires to have me wed one of those men if you are there."

"Then we shall face the onslaught of your suitors together."

"I expect many of them would be happier to court you," said Chastity with a pointed look at her friend. "Or my younger sister, Lucy."

"After M'sieur Donet, I don't think I can find a man in Northampton to compare, much less appeal."

"You did not favor Mr. Cairo?"

"No, though he was very charming. Besides, Chas, it was you with whom he was smitten, not I."

Chastity recalled the watchmaker's effusive praise but attributed it to the kind of thing any man would say. And though she, too, found him charming, he never had her heart, not like Sir Robert. "Very well," said Chastity, "we shall face the music together."

"What do you mean *gone*?" asked Robbie stunned.

Lady Sanborn lifted a bejeweled hand into the air. "She returned to Northampton at her mother's request to prepare for her sister's wedding."

"And Miss Crockett?" asked Jack with a forlorn expression.

"Gone with my great-niece, I am sad to say. Even the cat. It's been very lonely since they left. Why, if Muriel hadn't decided to stay, I would be quite dispirited."

Robbie's brow furrowed. "Muriel is here still?"

"Oh, yes. She is upstairs just now having a lie down. Why don't the two of you join us for dinner and you can visit with her then?"

Without consulting Jack, Robbie inclined his head. "We accept." There was much he wanted to ask The Grand Countess.

"Good. In the meantime, you might enjoy a brandy in the library." She gestured toward a door a short way down the corridor.

"Most appreciated," said Robbie and signaled Jack to follow.

"Oh," said Lady Sanborn, "I nearly forgot. The young ladies left messages for each of you. I will have Featherstone bring them to you in the library."

Inside the library, Robbie shut the door and poured them each a glass of Lady Sanborn's brandy.

"I shall have to send the countess some of the Saintonge cognac," remarked Jack.

"She would appreciate that, I'm sure."

Featherstone knocked and entered with a small silver tray. "The countess wished you to have these."

"Thank you," said Robbie, lifting the messages from the tray and handing Jack's to him.

Robbie set aside his brandy and read the missive. "It seems she regretted having to leave and thanks me, once again, for delivering her to her great-aunt."

"The message from Miss Crockett is warm as well though it says little to encourage a man's suit."

"Given the two ladies, we could hardly expect that. Now," said Robbie, subsiding into an armchair, "we must discuss strategy."

"You have that look in your eyes, Nephew." Taking the other armchair, Jack asked, "What are you thinking?"

"You have met Miss Crockett's parents, yes?"

"I have."

"And secured their blessing?"

"It took every title I possess and proof of my residence in Guernsey as well as my bank holdings, but yes."

"Perfect. I'm thinking we are going to attend a wedding."

Muriel toyed with one of her long strands of pearls as she waited for Sir Robert to join her in the library. He had asked to see her after dinner, which aligned perfectly with her desire as she needed to speak with him as well. She had matched many couples over the years but Robbie might be her most challenging as rogues were difficult to place. But she loved them, one in particular. Like Sir Robert, the young Earl of Claremont had been very charming, and though she would confess it to only a few, he'd had a reputation as a rogue. She had laughed at his flattery, certain it was not to be trusted, but his decisive candor, intelligence and determination to forsake all others for her had won her heart. Sir Robert must proceed in the same manner if he wanted to win the hand of the headstrong and beautiful Chastity Reynolds.

Agatha had asked for her help and Muriel meant to give it. Really, one could not leave such important matters to young people.

The carriage ride from London to Brighton had told Muriel much about the young woman. Where she had expected overconfidence, even arrogance, she found an insecure beauty who used her intelligence and wit as a defense. Likely, they had gained her many an advantage and many suitors. She would have rejected any she considered weaklings she could dominate. Only a few men could handle the young hoyden without breaking her spirit. Sir Robert was one of those. He was, therefore, the perfect husband for Chastity. He just needed a bit of advice.

The door opened. "Lady Claremont?"

"Come in, dear boy, and pour yourself a brandy from the decanter and then join me by the fire." He followed her instructions and was soon ensconced in the armchair across from her.

"Now, Sir Robert, we must discuss your approach to Miss Reynolds."

"My approach?"

"Indeed, yes. She is not the type of young woman who can be dictated to or told whom she will marry, well, at least not at first, which you have done to your detriment. Moreover, she will be loath to trust a rogue."

"But—"

"Don't argue. I know you, Sir Robert. I married one much like you and ours was a love match that endured until the earl's death. Rogues do reform; I know it well. But Miss Reynolds does not. I doubt not she loves you—one can see it on her face when she speaks of you—but she is inclined to distrust you, for good reasons, I imagine. Worse, she has a notion she does not need to marry. So, listen carefully and I will tell you what you must do."

The handsome rogue leaned back in his chair, took a sip of his drink and met Muriel's steady gaze. "Go on."

"You must assure her of your fidelity as well as your love. She may put you off at first, in which case you must be persistent, as I know you can be. When the opportunity presents itself, and it will, you must strike quickly, giving her no chance to decline. Select a public place. By that time, you will have her heart and her respect."

"I can do that," he said.

Having accomplished her task, Muriel looked up with raised brows. "Was there something you wanted to discuss with me?"

"Ah...no." He shook his head. She thought he might be a bit dazed. "No, that quite does it, I believe. Thank you."

"I tell you, Jack, those calm gray eyes and silver hair are deceiving." Robbie gave the grays their heads on the short run back to the Pavilion. "I am convinced that woman could have given Napoleon a run for his money."

"That bad, eh?"

"Positively frightening. But I dare say, The Grand Countess is a wise one. Hence, I'm going to follow her advice."

"So we leave for Northampton tomorrow?"

"We do. Let's hope with all the wedding guests, The Swan Inn has a room."

Two days later, Chastity had just had her final fitting for the gown she was to wear to Pen's wedding the next day—a lavender confection with flounces she quite liked—when she decided to go in search of her father. Her mother had kept her so busy upon her return she'd scarce had any time to talk to him.

She found him in his workshop where he was bent over a new design. As she entered, he set it aside with a raft of other drawings. She liked the smell of leather and oil and the tools he used to make his creations. They were manly scents she associated with her father.

"Hello, Papa. Is that a new design?"

"A different boot for a man, yes. A half boot with laces."

"Fascinating," she said, tilting her head to the side to glimpse the drawing.

"You came to tell me something…"

She looked down, worrying her bottom lip between her teeth, wondering how to begin. "Yes…oh, Papa," she said, blurting it out, "I have fallen in love with a rogue!"

He seemed unconcerned, which surprised her. "A rogue? Are you sure?"

"I saw him flirt outrageously with a married woman who clearly had eyes for him, accept the kisses of a tavern wench on a very public street, and I know for a fact he has frequented a London bordello. Are those not the actions of a rogue?"

Her father's blue eyes looked deeply into hers. "They are the actions of a man, Chastity. A social flirtation at a dinner party? A grateful servant's kiss? A man's dalliance that must be paid for? Tsk, tsk, my pet. You are not a little girl any longer. You are a woman grown, old enough and wise enough to understand a grown man. I have always known you to have good sense.

"When this man of yours was a man with no future, of course, all he sought was amusement. But now—now he may seek something real, something that will last. Now he may seek love and contentment. Men do change for the right woman."

Chastity wanted to believe his words. She had planned not to marry or have children, thinking to leave that to her more beautiful sisters. But now she craved what she had once believed mattered little…a man to love her, a man to share her life. But not just any man. She wanted Sir Robert Powell.

"Perhaps if I'd had dark hair and eyes like my mother and my sisters. Their beauty is so dramatic," she said letting her thoughts wander. "I'm the only one in the family who is pale, the cuckoo in the nest."

"Chastity, come here my pet." She stepped closer to him and he took her hands between his. "Do you think my hair was always silver?"

"As long as I can remember, Papa."

"Well, before that, it was like yours. And my eyes, if you haven't noticed, are the same blue as yours."

"I did notice that," she said, blinking away tears.

"If you wonder why I indulge my middle daughter, it's not because I am weak, it is because you and I are much alike, not just in appearance but in what makes us happy."

"We are?" That one thought cheered her immensely.

"We are. Now, tell me, who is this man? And why do you love him?"

"His name is Sir Robert Powell. He was a guest of the king in Brighton. His family owns ships yet the men are also government spies." She wouldn't tell him about her kidnapping or her time in a London bordello or that Sir Robert was the cause of all that. "I…I don't know exactly why I love him, Papa. He is glib of speech and bold in his manner…and so very handsome and brave."

"I see."

"Do you? I was hoping you would understand."

"More than you know, my pet." He let go of her hands. "In fact, this same man arrived a short while ago and is waiting for you in the parlor."

"He is here? Truly?" At her father's smile and nod, she said, "Then I must hurry."

"Yes, do," he said, chuckling as she turned to go.

She stepped into the parlor to see him staring into the flames in the fireplace, one hand on the mantel and his other on his hip. He turned. "Chastity."

"Sir Robert, I did not expect you."

His gaze roved over her in bold assessment, his hazel eyes devouring her. "Didn't you? Did you think I would let you steal away to Northampton without even a goodbye?"

"Is that why you have come—to wish me goodbye?"

He crossed the room to stand in front of her, forcing her to lift her head to look into his handsome face. He took her hands and dropped onto one knee. "I came to tell you I love you, to promise my fidelity for all time and to ask you to be my wife."

"My father—"

"Has already given me his blessing."

His face shone like a saint's, his manner so penitent, so sincere. Still, something inside her hesitated. "He said nothing to me of that."

The rogue smiled. "There was no reason for him to do so." He got to his feet. "Chastity, you will marry me, you know. You love me and I you. Forget the past and think of our future, think of the children we will have."

"I shall do as you ask. I will think on it. Tomorrow is my sister's wedding. Will you be there?"

"At the wedding breakfast, most assuredly, as will my uncle, for he comes to see your friend, Rose."

With that, he kissed her lightly on the lips and bid her good day. "Tomorrow it shall be."

Chastity inclined her head to get a good look at her eldest sister standing next to her very acceptable groom in front of the good minister, who read their vows from the Book of Common Prayer. Pen looked lovely in a purple silk gown with white silk roses across the top of the bodice and adorning the scallops at the hem. In her hair were the strings of pearls Chastity had imagined would be among her wedding finery. She appeared happy with her groom and her life. Chastity would have been bored to think of it. She longed for excitement and travel and, yes, she admitted to herself, if God granted, even children.

Sir Robert was not at the service and she didn't expect him to be. It was a small affair for only family and their closest friends. Rose was among them. With all the last-minute errands she was assigned, Chastity had not been able to speak to her friend but there would be time at the wedding breakfast where the crowd would descend. She wanted to tell her about Sir Robert's proposal and her inclination to accept. The thought of it made her heart pound in her chest. With her father's blessing, whatever reservations she had were gone.

The rings were exchanged and the happy couple proceeded down the aisle to the applause of all.

"You look beautiful in lavender, Chastity," said Rose, coming alongside her. Rose's gown of jonquil silk was the perfect balance to her dark coloring. "Are those satin slippers new?"

"There wasn't time to design new ones but these are my latest creation. I merely embroidered lavender flowers on the toes."

"I have something to tell you," Rose said as they left the church together.

"What?" Chastity asked, wondering what had put that smile on her friend's face.

"I am to marry M'sieur Donet!"

Chastity stared at her friend, amazed. Tears blurred her vision. "When did this happen?"

"Oh, he has been ever so attentive. While we were still in Brighton, he came to Northampton to ask my parents for my hand. And when he proposed yesterday, he was very romantic, asking me in both English and French. Of course, I said yes. I never expected to have such a husband, Chas. I am so happy!"

"And I am happy for you. Of all your suitors, I like him the very best." They paused outside the church as the carriages came forward to receive the wedding party. "I also have had a proposal, Rose."

"Sir Robert?"

"Yes, he came yesterday to ask me. And he had my father's blessing." Then thinking on the timing, Chastity added, "It seems they were both secretive in gaining our fathers' approval."

"Well, they would, wouldn't they? After all, they wanted to be sure their proposals would be favored by our families."

"I assume my father has told my mother, but she has said nothing to me."

"So, Chas, what did you say to Sir Robert's proposal?"

"Nothing. That is, I have not given him my answer as yet. But he will be at the wedding breakfast with your fiancé so I will have a chance to speak to him then."

"And what will your answer be?"

Chastity's smile began slowly until it illuminated her entire presence. "Guess."

"Congratulations," Robbie said to his uncle. "You have won the hand of the fair Rose."

"I believe my parents will be pleased. An English Rose for a half-English Donet. My family will love her as will my tenants in Saintonge."

"Where will you be married?"

"In London, I hope, so both the families can attend. And then I might sweep her away to Guernsey and France for the honeymoon. She has never seen Paris."

"Will you one day live in the chateau?" Robbie was curious.

"Guernsey is home, but I might spend my summers in France to examine the grapes and walk among the vines. It is remarkably settling to do so. And what about you? Where will you wed?"

"Assuming I can persuade the virago to marry me, I, too, would want to be wed in London. St George's, I think. Chastity would like that but we'll need to pick a date when my family and hers can attend. Lady Sanborn and Lady Claremont will no doubt want to be there as well."

"Has she said yes, then?"

"Oh, no. It could never be that easy with Chastity. But I will have her heart and her hand in mine by the end of this day. Just watch me."

Jack laughed. "I can hardly wait to see it."

The day being a sunny one, it was decided that the wedding breakfast should be held on the lawn in front of Dudley Hall. Several old oak trees provided shade for the long tables set beneath them where food and champagne were served in great abundance.

When Robbie and Jack arrived, Robbie immediately spotted Chastity. By her side was Rose Crockett. "I'll join you, if you don't mind, Uncle."

"Not at all. I see your virago is with my intended."

"Snow White with Rose Red. The fairy tale has come to a successful end."

"Ah, but which of us is the enchanted bear, eh?"

"Why, it's me, of course!"

Jack laughed. "So you say."

"Come, let us greet them." Robbie didn't want to interfere with the celebration and so he bowed to Chastity, beautiful in her lavender gown, and sat dutifully at her side as the meal was served. He even waited patiently until the guests had risen from the table and began to wander about the lawn. He let Chastity drift away to speak with her friends, but she was never out of his sight.

A short time later, Robbie cast a glance in her direction to find her in the midst of a gaggle of what looked to be potential suitors. Among them was Henry Cairo, the watchmaker who lived nearby in Coventry. It was finally time to make his move.

He came up behind her and, placing his hands on her shoulders, whispered in her ear, "'Tis time, darling Chastity."

She whipped around. "Time for what, Sir Robert?"

"Excuse us, gentlemen," he said to the men, "but I need a word with my fiancée."

Startled glances appeared all around.

At Chastity's gasp, he lifted her into his arms and strode away with her to the other side of the estate. He was certain he heard a protest from her mother squelched by her father's "Now dear."

Finally, away from prying eyes, Robbie set her down.

She sputtered. "Whatever were you thinking?"

"I'm thinking that it's time you and I announced our engagement, formally, of course. And I wanted all those suitors of yours to know you belong to me. I love you, Chastity Reynolds. You will marry me, won't you?"

"Well, yes," she said, worrying her lower lip between her teeth. "I do love you."

"A good thing, too, as I have bought up all the land around the estate you will inherit." With a grin, he added, "Your father helped me. After all, our children will want the room for their many adventures."

"Presumptuous to the end."

And, with that, he gave her a kiss she would remember for always, and a story she would tell her grandchildren.

Author's Note

The Cato Street Conspiracy, as it was known, could have ended very badly had it not been for a certain spy, never named. Oh, there was a man named Edwards but he was not thought to be at the heart of the Crown's knowledge of the dastardly plot. I like to think that the scenario in my story could have well happened the way I have written it. A grateful monarch would have certainly rewarded the spy. Why not a baronetcy and a holiday at the Royal Pavilion? Even a matched pair of grays!

At the time of my story in 1820, construction was still proceeding on the grand Pavilion it was to become so that the king could not occupy his apartments. He stayed, instead, on Marlborough Row until 1821, when his apartments were complete and he moved into them on the Pavilion's ground floor. However, for my story, it seemed appropriate that he should be ensconced in the royal apartments.

I did much research on Brighton in the early 19th century to give you a feel for the resort town at that time, including the fish market, the shops and taverns, the racecourse and sea bathing. There was an abundance of entertainments to please those members of the *ton* who flocked to the seaside resort, including the occasional dinner and masked ball at the Royal Pavilion.

All the taverns, streets, hotels, inns and shops I have mentioned did exist at the time, as well as the small fly carriages, called "fly-by-nights". I know my readers expect authenticity and I do try to deliver. However, since some of you might be wondering, Willow House is not a real place but my creation. It was first seen in *Against the Wind* as the place where Sir Martin met Katherine, Lady Edgerton ("Kit"). That is my one story where I reversed the order of things: as strangers, they made love, then they married and then they fell in love. My friend, Shirlee Busbee, a *NY Times* bestselling author, described it as "A fabulous tale with exciting twists and turns reflecting a little-known event in England's history and, at its heart, a wonderful love story."

Henry Cairo, should you be wondering, is a real figure, but not as you might suppose. I was working on a trial this spring and one of our experts was a man named Henry Cairo. I told him I loved his name and asked if I could use it. He said he'd be pleased. I then did research and discovered the name has an Italian connection. From the 1820s to 1851 there were four thousand Italian immigrants in England, with 50% of them living in London. The regional origins of most were the valleys around Como and Lucca. The people from Como were skilled artisans, making barometers and other precision instruments. Hence my family of clockmakers, artisans in time.

Grillon's Hotel was a prominent place to stay in London and the coffee house, maintained by Grillon's as a part of the hotel, was the purview of gentlemen only.

The Prospect of Whitby tavern on the Thames featured cockfights at one point so I simply had to include that. And I should tell you that same tavern in the 18th century was named The Devil's Tavern and can be seen in *Echo in the Wind*, the love story of Jean Donet, comte de Saintonge, Jack's father and Robbie's grandfather.

I have described Prinny's yacht, the *Royal George*, in detail as my research provided. The great cabin really did have windows of plate glass, a skylight, gilded dark wood paneling, a Brussels carpet beneath a mahogany table and a pianoforte, among other accoutrements. As

Robbie said, King George IV liked to travel in style. And the yacht frequently anchored off the coast of Brighton when the king was in residence.

Maria Fitzherbert is presented as I came to know her…a virtuous woman who took her marriage to Prince George seriously even if he did not. It is also true that all of Brighton respected her. The king must have had her on his mind toward the end of his life. When he died in 1830, he was buried wearing a locket containing her miniature. Mrs. Fitzherbert survived him by seven years, dying at the age of eighty in Brighton. She was buried in the Catholic church of St. John the Baptist, where a mural to her memory may be seen today.

You might wonder why Chastity's sister wore a purple silk gown for her wedding. A bride in the Regency period would not generally wear white, unless it was her best dress. White gowns became the tradition in the Victorian era. In the Regency period, if the bride were from a moneyed family, she would have a new gown she would wear again.

Women of accomplishment have lived in all centuries. Chastity's antecedent, the Puritan Anne Bradstreet (née Dudley, which is where Dudley Hall came from), was born in Northampton, England in the 17th century. She was a well-read scholar who wrote poetry published in both England and America and she was the mother of eight children. I like to think that such women might have been the rebels who felt they didn't fit into the role society expected of them. Chastity Reynolds is just such a woman.

I hope you enjoyed this story. Unless my plans change, my next project will begin a new series, the Clan Donald Saga that I hope will extend through several centuries. So, at least for a time, I am back to the medieval era, which, I know, will please many of my readers.

See my research and the characters for *Rogue's Holiday* on the Pinterest Board.

www.pinterest.com/reganwalker123/rogues-holiday-by-regan-walker

Want to read the rest of the Agents of the Crown series? You can see it on Amazon.

Author's Bio

Regan Walker is an award-winning, Amazon bestselling author of Regency, Georgian and Medieval romances. A lawyer turned writer, she has six times been featured on USA TODAY's HEA blog and nominated six times for the Reward of Novel Excellence (RONE) award. Her novels *The Red Wolf's Prize* and *King's Knight* won Best Historical Novel in the medieval category. *The Refuge: An Inspirational Novel of Scotland* won the Gold Medal in the Illumination Awards. *To Tame the Wind* won the International Book Award for Romance Fiction and Best Historical Romance in the San Diego Book Awards. And *A Fierce Wind* won a medal in the President's Book Awards of The Florida Authors & Publishers Association and was an award-winning Finalist in the 2019 International Book Awards!

Years of serving clients in private practice and several stints in high levels of government have given Regan a feel for the demands of the "Crown". Hence her novels often feature a demanding sovereign who taps his subjects for special assignments. Each of her stories features real history and real historical figures. And, of course, adventure and love.

She lives in San Diego with her wonderful dog "Cody", a Wirehaired Pointing Griffon.

Follow Regan on Amazon and BookBub; and keep in touch on Facebook, and do join Regan Walker's Readers.
facebook.com/regan.walker.104
facebook.com/groups/ReganWalkersReaders

You can sign up for her newsletter on her website.

Books by Regan Walker

The Agents of the Crown series:

Racing with the Wind
Against the Wind
Wind Raven
A Secret Scottish Christmas
Rogue's Holiday

The Donet Trilogy:

To Tame the Wind
Echo in the Wind
A Fierce Wind

Holiday Novellas (related to the Agents of the Crown):

The Shamrock & The Rose
The Holly & The Thistle
The Twelfth Night Wager

The Medieval Warriors series:

The Red Wolf's Prize
Rogue Knight
Rebel Warrior
King's Knight

Inspirational

The Refuge: An Inspirational Novel of Scotland

www.ReganWalkerAuthor.com